Peter Black

The Trials

JAL Publications
www.johnalupton.com

Published by JAL Publications 2013

Printed in Ireland by Walsh Printers, Roscrea November 2013

Cover Image Copyright © Mary C. Lupton 2013

Text Copyright © John A. Lupton 2013

ISBN: 978-1-910113-00-4

This is a work of fiction. Names, characters, places, incidents and dialogues are
products of the author's imagination or are used fictitiously.

About the Author

John is from the beautiful
Emerald Isle, whose lush
greenery more than compensates
for the frequent rain. The
Second eldest of four, John is
often difficult, but constantly
original. Hard to pin down... but
always found floating somewhere
between loafer and dynamo, John
is currently working on his
second book.

To my family, with thanks for all their support

Those with imagination have no limits, those without need none. – John.

Sanctus Franciscus de Sales, ora pro nobis

Peter Black

The Trials

John A. Lupton

- Chapter One -

Peter Black's situation was a curious one, he lived in
a small cabin nestled at the edge of a wood with his
father, Tom, an unusually big man with a fiery red
beard, arms as broad and firm as tree trunks and
hands as course and weathered as those of a
seasoned fisherman. In contrast to first
appearances however, Tom was a truly warm loving
man; kind, selfless and dedicated. If anything, it
might be said that he was over protective of his
only son. Indeed, Tom saw his raison d'etre as being
intrinsically linked to Peter's welfare and happiness.
One of Tom's biggest desires for his son was that
he should receive a top class education from the
earliest of years and this despite the very secluded
nature of their daily lives. Now Peat's dad was
known in the local area as 'Big Tom,' due to his sheer
size. Tom, who had been born and raised in the
town of Lismore, was known to have been a nice,
mannerly youngster of average intelligence. In his
younger years Tom had excelled at sport, especially
football and wrestling. Tom's academic interests in
school were minimal though and his desire for
college didn't go beyond his dream of playing inter-
varsity ball, but a serious injury in his final year of

high-school meant his football dream was over before it really began. Instead of college, Tom, like many of his high school friends, joined the rank and file of the local coal miners. The following years were prosperous ones, the mining business grew and Tom worked his way up to a managerial post and soon had enough money to marry his high-school sweetheart, Megan. Unfortunately life is far from idyllic and the harsh drama of reality is never far from a person's door! A warm summer's eve would see the small slice of happiness that the Blacks had carved out for themselves crushed, but that is for later consideration. At present it suffices to know that for a very sensitive reason Tom had moved himself and his son far outside the town of Lismore while Peat was still a toddler, and for the same heartrending reason he choose to limit their contact with the townsfolk. Living in a type of semi self-imposed exile from the town Tom hoped to create a new bucolic life but he was equally adamant that the rural setting he had chosen would not be a barrier to securing a first class education for Peat. Tom had his own reasons for not sending Peat to school locally; tragically it was these very considerations that acted like shackles preventing the haunted father from leaving the area all together and making a new life for both himself and his son somewhere else. In spite of this liminal reality Tom actively took steps to ensure his child would have every opportunity in life, the foundation

2

of which he believed to be an education. Therefore Tom didn't hesitate in approaching the only person in the vicinity he knew who was likely to possess the necessary comprehension across a range of subjects to instruct a student in lieu of formal schooling. Providentially this person was himself a type of exile living relatively close to the Blacks' cabin.

A truly brilliant man with a thirst for knowledge which straggled the full gamut of inquiry; from the traditional classics like philosophy, history and oratory to the latest modern advancements in the empirical and social sciences. The question was often asked as to why such a genius mind, with an encyclopaedic grasp of so many things would be living in a seemingly self-imposed rural banishment rather than reclining on the green leathered seats found in the Harvard faculty rooms? Nowhere else was this question asked and answered with such crudeness and frequency than in Lismore's numerous taverns.

Paul Huttin, for instance, one of Lismore's native drunks, regularly postulated that the gifted Father Jim was, "crazier than a bag of wet cats!"

The eccentric cleric's trips to Lismore were so brief and infrequent that many in the locality simply counted him as an absentee priest, while the Pollyannas of the parish classed him as a hermit; living in isolation from others so as to deepen his spiritual connectedness with the Divine One. The latter contention was the official ecclesiastical story... but the truth of the matter was far more 'entertaining,' in the tabloid sense of the word. Father Jim, a member of the Society of Jesus, that is, the Jesuits, had something of a mental break-down while living in the Eternal City lecturing at the prestigious Gregorian College. Jim had become responsible for a litany of scandalous embarrassments which engulfed the College and the Society itself, among the many *faux pas* were; Jim's habit (no pun intended) of entering the lecture halls pants-less, and also his tendency to present Friday's eschatology lesson off campus in a nearby café much to the amusement of the patrons and frustration of the owners. Rumor among clerical circles has it that the final straw was reached when, late one evening, Jim apparently confusing his own domicile with that of a nearby nunnery, entered one of the bedrooms and began to undress for the night much to the distress of the Mother Superior who woke to find a stranger hopping around the room attempting to pull a cassock up over his head much in the same manner one might remove a football jersey. Sources say that after this the Superior General of the Jesuit order intervened directly and meeting with Jim and seeing his brilliant but overloaded mind, he thought it best to established a type of one man hermitage in the Doncanner forest, with very light pastoral duties in the nearby town of Lismore, should the fragile cleric feel up to it. This peculiar *ad hoc* arrangement was only made possible due to Jim's father, Frankie DeLouis, who assumed the role of primary carer and legal guardian. Mr. DeLouis provided for Jim's material welfare which, giving the fact that Frankie was a multi-millionaire, benefited Jim to no small extent.

Over the first few years Jim spent practically all of his considerable monthly parental stipend buying and reading books which could range in subject matter enormously, encompassing all manner of things. It would be fair to say that Jim was a pantologist in the truest sense of the word. It was not long before the ease and tranquility had a beneficial effect on Jim, eventually he began to order the materials and substances necessary to build two major multipurpose labs in which, and with scant regard for health and safety regulations, he stored the most diverse range of chemicals. Eventually Jim would convert many of the rooms in the large estate house that his father has secured for him, into labs with; metal and wood-work machines, surgical instruments, micro-scopes, and much more. After about a year Jim's ambitions and thirst for knowledge required more space for storage and practical experiments and so he had two large granary barns added close to the house. Now Jim had an all-round desire to study every aspect of the mystery of life he had a particular interest in astronomy. It's hardly surprising therefore that from among the cornucopia of apparatuses the cleric had accumulated, his most prized was a magnificent state-of-the-art telescope, whose modern appearance would capture a person's eye with comparative ease against the other scientific paraphernalia. As talented and gifted as Jim so obviously was, he soon realized that he needed help. It was to prove opportune that Tom should have sought out Jim just when the priest was coming to the realization that he would need to hire someone to help him with miscellaneous jobs and run errands as they arouse on a day to day basis. Now prior to contacting Jim, Tom wanted to make sure his son would be safe under this aberrant priest's tutelage and so in a prudent attempt to establish his trustworthiness he made dozens of phone calls to Jesuit religious houses and even the Jesuit Society's provincial offices, with all information he received pointing to the same assessment; Fr. Jim was a kind and good hearted soul even if a little "unconventional." When Tom first went up to meet Jim he found him both endearing and decisively bizarre. However, he also showed an intellectual brilliance that would more than meet his son's educational needs. Now the Jesuits have always been known for their teaching prowess so the opportunity to play a crucial part in this young person's development was something Jim looked upon with real interest but of course he did not reveal this to Tom. You see Jim also wanted to employ Tom, a strong and skilled tradesman, he would be perfect factotum to satisfy his current requirements. Therefore, instead of money, Jim agreed to instruct Peter if Tom would take up a full time employed position as his assistant. Tom was rather hesitant about the prospect of working for the cleric, but he'd saved enough money to get Peat through college and if new employment would guarantee his son the best possible start in life then... so be it. For Tom, his son's welfare was of paramount importance and so he resigned his managerial post at the coal mines to take up the novel position of Jim's 'Helper,' a position which, to Tom's delightful surprise, brought with it a sizable increase in wages compared to his former post. In truth Tom was happy in many ways to be leaving his job at the mines which had become very difficult over the preceding years almost to the point where his position was untenable. On top of this there was also a constant sense of guilt in Tom's heart for not having moved away from Lismore and given Peat a fresh start, for in creating this rural limbo Tom knew his son would miss out on some very important things.

As it turned out Peat had a very happy upbringing, he often went with his father on the monthly trip to town for shopping and essential supplies. Peat grew up understanding his living arrangement as being perfectly normal; his removed lifestyle, and daily trips to Jim's for hours of tuition were just taken for granted by the young lad. The only major oddity Peat noticed was in the monthly visits to Lismore town. They were always very brief and clinical in nature, Tom would enter one shop, produce a list and be served and leave without even the slightest amount of chit-chat. In fact, as Peat's social perception developed with age, he increasingly got the sense that store staff and others he met in the town were constantly seeking to avoid Tom and himself, it seemed to him as if they knew an open secret..., something about them. Tom seemed completely unconcerned which gave Peat a level of reassurance but unlike Tom however, it was Peat who found himself to be the focus of a constant barrage of concerned looks which were to be found chiseled on the faces of every adult that Peat would catch staring at him while he was walking around the town with his dad.

This proved most unsettling for Peat but anytime he sought to raise this matter with his father the explanation was always the same; "They're just a bit odd," after which Tom would quickly redirect the conversation. The creepy nature of these excursions meant that Peat often simply made his father promise to buy a few of his favorite things like for instance; cola, chocolate and potato crisps, and then he would just choose to skip the trip to town all-together and stay at home. This meant that on the first Saturday of the month instead of being cooked up in the jeep on the long journey into Lismore Peter could do what he loved best, that is, to continue working in the nearby forest on the tree-house that he and his father had started. As far a tree-houses go, it was really impressive with a rope ladder leading up along the trunk of a mature Ash towards a trap-door at the base of the house. Inside there was some furniture which consisted of two seats, there was also a large galvanized sheet of metal sensibly angled to act both as a roof and a slide which ran down to the forest floor. Peat loved working on his tree-house and designing new features, Tom had thought him many useful things about building but young Peat's technical abilities extended far beyond the mere elementary in any field. It was Jim who had made sure of this, having planned out a very detailed and comprehensive curriculum for his young protégé. Peat's instructions had started from a very young age and the five day week of lessons proved grueling, but children are very adaptable, and as it turned out Peter was naturally bright and, to the sheer delight of Jim, showed an impressive aptitude for nearly all the subjects Jim had introduced him to.

Peat particularly excelled at physical activities such as fencing and martial arts, two activities which Jim felt were an important part of, as he would often put it: "...establishing oneself in a capable but gentlemanly manner akin to the spirit encapsulated by Mr. Douglas' ethos of pugilism."

It's hard to convey the full intensity of Peter's routine, typically Tom would knock on Peter's creatively colored red and blue bedroom door at about 6 a.m. with an accompanying loud cry: "Are yah up lad?"

Thirty minutes later Peter would emerge from the bedroom his throat dry, his eye lids heavy with tiredness. Upon entering the kitchen he'd peer around the room hoping not to draw attention from his animated and chipper father, who was a big morning person. But like clockwork Tom would nearly always approach with a genuine smile across his face and, putting his giant arm around Peat's comparably minuscule shoulder, give him a big squeeze.

"What a morning Peat! We'd better get some food into yah, before we head," would be the general substance of most morning greeting by Peat's vivacious father.

Peat's replies consisted typically of a grunt of indifference and it was only in later years, on Fridays, when he could look forward to his rendezvous with his best friend Claire Smith, that Peat would feel inclined to utter a, "Morning Dad," or even perhaps, on very exceptional occasions, a conversation opener like; "How are things?"

The staple diet of Tom and Peat consisted mostly of natural produce, Jim was something of an ecologist; he kept bees for the honey they made, and a few cows for dairy goods. Of course once Jim's dream of self-sufficiency was replaced by a new project it was Tom who had to take charge of farming the animals and providing for their welfare, while his employer's attentions would move to fresh pursuits. Indeed, of the many roles that Tom found himself occupying while under Jim's employ it was that of 'farmer' that he enjoyed most. Tom's dad used to be Lismore's resident vet and had thought him everything about caring for, and farming, animals before his untimely death during Tom's early teenage years.

To digress somewhat, it's true to say that working for a man like Jim required a rather agreeable disposition and such was the personality of Tom, in fact the only request he would refuse outright would be to tend to the bees, as Tom would say emphatically; "I'd sooner walk barefoot across hot coal than go near those little winged pricks!"

In reality though Jim was extremely possessive when it came to his apiculturist pursuits and would never in fact allow anyone to substitute for him. This agricultural pastime was one of his few outdoor outlets for relaxation.

Notwithstanding that, the clergyman got a mischievous trill out of winding up poor Tom who had what Jim, at any rate, diagnosed as a phobia of bees, "Worst case of apiphobia I've ever seen Tom. You know, we could try a controlled experiment to test if you're allergic!" the playful priest would often gibe.

But to get back to my initial point, meals for Peat and Tom were mostly based around a non-processed diet but on occasion Tom would bring back a bottle of Coke, a few bars of Belgium chocolate and a couple of bags of chips, which were always left under Peats bed as I mentioned earlier, a tradition which had been going on for many years. Tom and Peat would arrive at Jim's estate before eight and after Jim had issued Tom with a list of duties Peat's instructions would commence, usually about half eight. It would be about seven in the evening when Peat's tutelage would cease; Jim usually finished each day with physical education or some practical based work. It would be fair to say that Jim's concept of a physical education lesson was very different than what one would find in an average school, but as with many students it was Peat's favorite subject on the cleric's curriculum.

Peat especially looked forward to racing against the clock in the obstacle courses that Jim would construct to test all aspects of the young lad's fitness, these wacky trials could consist of anything from climbing rope-ladders to swimming in the nearby lake and in every physical test there was an objective, or as Jim would playfully say, a "Mission," to be accomplished along the route.

It was indicative of Jim's holistic view on education that he would never simply test Tom's physical abilities but always incorporated a mental dimension to the trials; assessing Peat's abilities to problem solve, think creatively and be resourceful amidst high intensity physical endeavors. It's true to say that Jim became more and more committed to Peat's education as the years passed, relishing the chance at playing such a central role in the formation of this gifted youngster. So for instance, Jim would think nothing of having expensive scientific equipment delivered to his estate if he thought it might be of significant benefit to his pupil.

As for State examinations, Tom was adamant that Peat get all the qualifications necessary for him to get into a good college and while Jim made sure Peat was fully equipped to sit all the State issued examinations he openly ridiculed "the banal educational system with its industrialized mechanics of terminal assessment, systematically neutering the imaginative creativity of the youth in order to perpetuate a mass producing inequitable society…" and on and on the former academic professor would rant for a good ten minutes until eventually he would either tire, or forget what his original point was.

Incidentally one of Peat's most enjoyable capers was to subtly make reference to the mainstream system of education when the occasion allowed for it and in so doing intentionally set Jim off on a tangential rant while he engaged in some daydreaming, usually about his darling Claire.

By the time Peat had hit his mid-teens the lonely isolation from his peers began to weigh heavily on him. In his younger years Peat had tried to chat to other children when he was in town with his dad but all the boys and girls seemed to be frightened of him, or so he thought. Probably in part, it was because Peat had no other friends, that he became so attached to Claire. Peat would often dedicate his free time to either meeting up with her or in some way seeking to ameliorate Claire's situation which was far from easy. Now Jim had long encouraged Peter to carry out his own personal projects which would further his knowledge and skills in a given area. Jim provided the financial backing in terms of ordering the necessary supplies but everything else was left to Peter. The dexterous Peat often used these projects to help foster his friendship with Claire in one way or another, and if we jump forward a number of years, Peat's latest project saw him delving into the field of organology. Peat had borrowed from Jim's extensive library which practically encompassed every room in the old Victorian estate house, except for the turret tower which by that stage had been spectacularly converted into the cleric's own personal observatory and was strictly off-limits to all except the Reverend. Now while Peat had no particular interest in musicology or the science of instruments per se, he was, by his late teens, driven by a romantic zeal to make an ornate musical box with a revolving figurine. It needed to play the melody to Claire's favorite song, Kay Moore's 'Completeness.' Now for most 18 year olds

14

[remembering we have jumped ahead in our narrative] such a project would be extremely difficult even with technical support from a trained professional in this field but Peat had an aptitude and versatility which was complemented by access to all the material components necessary. Jim's father, Mr. DeLouis, had countless connections and as long as his son was maintaining his mental health the multi-millionaire was happy to secure whatever items were requested. It was not long before the young adult had all the central components for this special project; the ratchet lever, the multi-tuned cylinder with its intertwined studded pins , the lamellophone along with all the screws, springs and other essential bits. The cosmetic material was also on its way and soon assembly could begin. Peat's entire endeavor of course was set against a deadline, something which had always helped Peat keep motivated. In this case the deadline was Claire's birthday occurring on the third of July. After nearly five years of an increasingly affectionate friendship Peat had it all planned out; for the first time he was going to ask Claire out on a date after presenting her with his gift.

Now to a certain extent Claire's situation was almost antipodal to that of Peats, indeed if there's any truth to the euphemism, "opposites attract," then this pairing of friends would truly be a prime example.

Claire, like Peat, had only one parent, her father having being killed in a car accident when she was only three. But that's where the similarity of circumstances end, her mother, Stephanie, had suffered from multiple addictions throughout Claire's life and at the best of times she was a poor functioning alcoholic. Stephanie worked in the town's only estate agents, filing, and performing general secretarial work. Luckily for her the owner of the agent's was a close friend of her late husband and godfather to Claire, and for this reason he looked out for both of them, much to the annoyance of his pretentious wife whose own deceased mother, ironically enough, was also a chronic alcoholic. Stephanie had long since been labeled 'promiscuous' (and not without reason) although those who gossiped about such things didn't use such a technically discreet term. For Claire this all equated into an environment of instability and, as I'm sure you could imagine, the men Stephanie brought home were anything but chivalrous. Often Claire would appear in school with fresh bruises, and regional social workers were all too familiar with the Smith family file! Claire was terrified by the thought of being taken away from her family home and placed in care, she loved her dysfunctional mother despite everything and the young schoolgirl also found a sense of security in belonging to a perfidious high school clique, the workings of which seemed to make sense to her even if, paradoxically, she held in secret disdain the Machiavellian nature of its social dynamic. To safeguard her status quo therefore, Claire would often make up plausible excuses for new bruises and the occasional cuts which would come to her teacher's notice. She also had to ensure the house was well kept and fully stocked with goods in case of a surprise inspection from the social worker. Her attendance at school was very good and she even committed to doing her school work to a level which just about satisfied the relevant school figureheads and made it tolerable even if disgraceful that Stephanie failed to attend any parent-teacher meetings or open-school events. It was against this bleak social and tough economic backdrop that her friendship with Peat shun like a silver lining in her life. Now the location of Claire's residence meant she often had to cycle for a good 40 minutes to get to her bungalow from town, but the relative isolation from Lismore had its benefits, especially when it came to her mother's antics in the local bars. Claire could thus often escape much of the late night drama which all too commonly ended in a police car pulling up outside the house to drop off an inebriated and unruly Stephanie in the early hours. As chance would have it Claire and Peat had surprisingly first met when they were both only toddlers, both the Smith and Black families were actually very close years prior, although neither of the two youngsters had any memories or knowledge of this. In fact when it came to recollecting early childhood happenings neither Peat nor Claire were overly fond of the practice. For the latter, the death of her father was a painful event which tainted by association many of the earlier happenings in the young girl's life, while for Peat any attempt to garner thoughts of his earliest childhood caused him deep mental anguish. Peat didn't know why, but that something dark haunted his past he was in no doubt. Often while sleeping Peat would find himself involuntarily wondering deep into the recesses of his mind only to wake in a terrified state, drenched in a cold sweat.

But whenever he approached his dad about the matter Tom seemed unwilling to discuss the matter and simply attributed it to "bad dreams."

Peat knew it was something more than simply nightmares and regularly, throughout his years of learning under Jim, he would broach the topic of the unconscious with his teacher which always saw a lively academic treatment of the subject ensue but then when Peat would make reference to his own case his teacher would just look around, as if checking to see if Tom was in earshot, before employing some trademark evasive phraseology like. "Right now, down to work..." or "Time to refocus now."

Peat got the sense from both his father and Jim that he could not push the issue but this didn't stop him from formulating many creative and interlinking theories to explain firstly, the strange reaction of the town folk of Lismore to him and his father and, secondly, Tom and Jim's uncharacteristic aversion to queries about an innocent topic like his childhood years or some matters concerning his mother, whom he had been told died of pneumonia. At any rate, what Peat was certain of, was that these two anomalies were connected somehow. As for Claire, well she was like the rest of the townsfolk in that she knew more about the aforementioned peculiarities than Peat did, well, that is to say, she knew the conventional account of what happened. But as is so often the case the popular account failed to correspond with what the actually occurred on that Friday night in August many years earlier.

- Chapter Two -

Peat had just turned five the week before, it had been a beautifully clement August thus far. Indeed this particular week had been exceptionally warm and on that Friday night all the windows and doors in the Black household were open while Megan, Peat's Mom, was home cooking her weekly fish and homemade chips and setting the table for a late romantic dinner with her husband. Around ten o'clock she had put Peat to bed and the prepared dinners were being kept warn in the top oven at a low heat of about 100°. Tom called soon after from his office to explain that he would be late home, Megan insisted she'd wait up for him but after half an hour she'd grown very tired and nodded off on a comfortable old arm chair located in the corner of the front room, facing the front door which was still open. To his surprised Tom was actually relieved earlier than he had anticipated and hoped to make it back home before eleven, but about two miles out from the mines his tire blew out and in the pitch black he had to change it, a task which took a good twenty minutes. Close to eleven Megan woke up feeling rather cold so she proceeded to close all the doors and windows on the ground floor of the house before she made for her bedroom to retrieve her favorite cardigan, but just as she reached the staircase she remembered that she needed to turn off the oven before the dinners dried out.

Forgetting about the garment she went straight into the kitchen still awaiting the arrival of her husband when a triple knock came from the back-door which leads from the kitchen to a small porch at the rear of the house.

"He knew I'd be in the kitchen, cheeky." Megan said to herself referencing the playfully stereotypical 'housewife' banter which had been an on-going quip between the couple since they'd married.

Just as she opened the door to greet her returning husband with her characteristically warm and loving smile, suddenly a startling bang came from the front room as if someone had kicked it with great force, instinctively she turned to look. But no sooner had her head turned than the back door flew open violently smacking her hand which rested on the door handle, shocked, Megan took a step back as a medium height man wearing a blackened ice hockey mask and possessing the most striking blue colored eyes rushed in and grabbed her left arm. Almost immediately there was the sound of crying and a call for "Mammy" which came from the base of the stairs.

Megan shook off the assailant's grip and turning on her heel ran to the main corridor to witness Peter crying uncontrollably as he stood on the last step of the staircase in his blue colored onesie pajamas clasping his teddy bear in his left hand as it dangled down by his side. This was to be the last thing Megan would see as suddenly everything went dark. By the time Tom got home that night the whole neighborhood was lit up and police cars were cruising around the locality in large numbers. When Tom saw the ambulance at his house he sped to the front garden, pulled up in a haphazard manner and abandoning the car he sprinted to the front door where he was met by two equally burly police officers who asked him to wait where he was, but as if unaware of their presence, he simply pressed pass them shouting "Megan, Megan..." and burst into the front room to find his home full of people, mostly police and medical personnel, all of whom stared somberly at him.

Tom knew from their bleak faces his worst fears were surely about to be confirmed. He peered around the room at the living, hoping his eyes would meet with Megan and Peat among them and then he stopped abruptly as he caught sight of two legs protruding from the hall way over the doorstep that lead into the front room. He rushed across the room in a state of shock and distress feeling as though he were in a nightmare, he recognized the shoes but latched on to the hope that his darling wife was okay, until rounding the partitioning wall, he saw the face of his beloved. Falling to his knees he placed his hand on her shoulder-length, blood soaked hair and sobbed uncontrollably making heartfelt entreaties to heaven against an injustice which ravished this man's soul of much of the joy and happiness he'd experienced in life.

Unfortunately the popular account of these tragic happening was far more in line with the one touted by Megan's rancorous father, Ted, who always despised Tom and practically disowned his estranged daughter for having married him. In reality the police were satisfied with Tom's explanation that he was changing a tire, and they in no way suspected him of involvement. However, with no one ever caught for the murder, Ted saw an opportunity to vilify 'Big Tom' by relentlessly spreading the most defamatory stories implicating 'Big Tom' in his wife's death. The rumor mill churned ceaselessly in the small town while Tom became increasingly depressed and withdrawn from community life. He moved into temporary accommodation with his five year old son, who had been left so badly traumatized by what he had witnessed happen on that night that he actually refused to speak for nearly a year and when he did, he gave no indications of being able to remember the event. Tom came to realize that he'd have to leave the town for Peat's sake and sold the house to pay for the construction of his new dwellings. Yet Tom felt a strong attachment to the place where he'd grown up and fallen in love…, the potency of the good memories evoked in him whenever he visited Lismore far out weighted the bad, Tom felt that

this was a crutch, without which he could not cope.
Rightly or wrongly, Tom could not bring himself to
leave his home. Megan's father died about two
years after his only daughter but by that stage the
juicy gossip had taken on a life of its own regularly
changing and molding with a liberal license
depending on the source. In Claire's school the
latest edition held that the wife killer, Big Tom lives
outside town, about an hour... Fired from the mines,
he found work from a crazy old priest and keeps his
son like a prisoner in a small dank cabin near a
secluded forest. Of course this was the
popularized, sensationalist account and most people
took such innuendo with a grain of salt but there
was always palpable unease when Tom and his son
were in town. As a matter of fact it was actually
such back-fence talk among a group of students at
Lismore High one day that would set in motion a
series of events leading to that fateful meeting of
Claire and Peat.

At recess some of Claire's friends were
teasing her about being that particular person in
town who lived nearest to the crazed murderer Big
Tom. Claire was a plucky young girl, never one to
back-down, and she bet that she could get a photo
of the infamous cabin. And so, on a Friday
afternoon the fifteen year old went into the garage
at her house and dragged out a lively red colored
Motobecane Mobylette which had belonged to one
of her mother's male friends who stayed with them

for about two months the previous year, but who had since then, for all intents and purposes, disappeared; 'probably back to his wife and family,' Claire thought to herself. Whatever the reason, Claire had all she needed to accomplish her mission; a small rucksack, a Canon camera borrowed from her father's old stuff, the keys, a full tank of gas for the small motorized bike and a scant regard for road safety. Her first few attempts to ride this bike were comical and she picked up more bruises and scrapes in own in the front yard than she would at any time later in the day when she hit the road. But eventually after about an hour she was heading up the idle back road which experienced such an irregularity of traffic that weeds and grass had long since begun to pierce through and smother the tarmac. After twenty minutes journeying up the winding road Claire arrived at an old forestry entrance to a wooded area which trailed around the Black's homestead. She decided to conceal the bike in some growth near the gate and rather than follow the road which ran nearest the Black's cabin, Claire decided to cut through the forest on foot hoping to approach the house as inconspicuously as possible. The location of the cabin was common knowledge in the town of Lismore but navigating through the unfamiliar forest proved difficult for a disconcerted Claire. In addition to this an increasing feeling of fear welled up in Claire as she reflected on the potential danger she was exposing herself to, but when weighed against loosing face with her classmates she felt compelled to continue. Eventually she caught sight of the house's chimney and a trill entered her heart, Claire wanted to get a good photo to show her school friends while also keeping a reasonable distance away from the cabin. Climbing a tree seemed the best option but many of the Northern Hardwoods were impossible for her to scale so she moved ever closer looking for a suitable tree from which to perch.   Without knowing it Claire had got extremely close to the cabin and then looking to her left she saw the most beautiful mature Eastern White Pine which towered above the neighboring species and what's more it looked easy enough to climb for a seasoned pro like herself. Claire took off her sweater and tied it around her waist before ascending the big Pine with apparent ease and reaching a satisfactory height, allowing for a birds-eye view of the house she took her picture and began to descend with a feeling of accomplishment.

'Wait till they see this!' Claire thought to herself. She'd done it, faced her fears, got proof that would demonstrate her bravery to her peers and in doing so further her popularity, and perhaps most importantly she'd reassured herself that she was independent and capable of looking after herself no matter what the circumstances might throw at her. Claire had climbed dangerously high up the tree and so coming down was not going to be easy.

If anything Claire was descending the tree too fast but she had climbed many trees at home and felt more than capable, as she approached the last 20 feet or so she was startled to hear a soft trembling voice coming up from the ground saying, "aa... Hello, I'm..," but before an identity could be communicated Claire, had let a scream, in a state of alarm she lost her balance, falling.

Without hesitation Peat extended his arms as Claire came crashing down on top of him, both were flattened into the soft grassy-bedded floor of the forest.

"Aww crap...," Claire moaned as she lifted her head up off Peat's chest.

Peat, who was still just surprised to see a stranger so near his home, simply tried again at an introduction, "Hi, I'm..."

On hearing his voice once more Claire remembered why she'd lost her footing and springing to her feet, in a state of consternation, she asked, "Who the hell are you, Jesus... don't you realize where we are..., I mean you could have fucking...I mean don't you..aaa, Wait, who are you?"

Peat smiled and once again made an attempt at an introduction, "Hi, I'm Peat, ammm, I live here, that's our house," he said as he pointed towards Big Tom's dwellings.

Perplexed Claire stared directly at him for a moment and then, however unbelievable it sounded to her, she began to formulate a rough idea of what

this all might mean... but to be sure she'd have to
inquire further. In a manner which sought clarity
and also with a large amount of urgency (because
Claire had not forgotten where she was for one
second) she put it to Peat, "Okay, so let me get this
straight; you live in Big Tom's house, and your Peter
Black, Big Tom's son?"
Peat had not heard of his father being referred to
as "Big Tom" before but he responded in a
cheerfully affirming voice "Yeah."
What Peat was most curious about however was,
firstly, what was Claire doing here, and secondly,
why did she reference everything to "Big Tom?"
But posing these questions now struck Peat as
somewhat too direct, especially at this point. To
Peat this girl seemed clearly agitated and very
nervous on top of that. Peat didn't want to do
anything that might make her leave, she was the
first young person of his own age he could
remember meeting outside of his shopping trips and
without doubt this was the most intimate meeting
he'd ever had with a peer. Also, just standing there
looking at her Peat found himself attracted to her
jet black hair and pale skin which highlighted her
beautiful rosy red cheeks and lips. Then there was
that strong personality, full of attitude, which he
found so endearing. The instance Claire had
established Peats identity she knew something
definitely did not add up; he was happy, looked well-
nourished and was polite. In fact, his demeanor

reminded Claire of the boys and girls at school who came from the good families, whose parents took care of their children, unlike her own malnourished and deprived background. She decided to get out of there and just leave it alone, she'd got what she had came for and that would do.

Claire gave a typically confident smile, "Ok, thanks... Bye!" and she turned on her heels and started to walk away.

Peat didn't know who she was or why she was here, but, at that point the only thing he was interested in was getting her to stay.

She walked with pace back along the route she had taken and Peat followed her pleading with her to "hold on for a second."

About three minutes later she came to an abrupt halt and spinning around said, "Actually wait a minute, stand still for a second."

She proceeded to root through her rucksack and produced the borrowed Cannon camera and without any hint of a request she took a picture of Peat. Peat was more than a little dumfounded and simply stood there looking at her, she was truly the most curious person he'd ever met and that was saying a lot given some of the antics Jim would get up to. After she'd put the camera back in her bag and zipped it up she looked at a bemused Peat and commented "You know you're not half bad looking, I thought you'd be like...well you know."

Peat just stood there dazed with a blank expression on his face.

"I suppose I should be off," Clare said before turning slightly, gesturing to leave.

Picking up on this subtle social cue Peat hurried over to her and placed his hand on her left shoulder, "Wait, please stay for a bit, I mean, like... what's your name. I've never seen you around here before and like... do you come from Lismore?"

Suddenly he realized his hand is still on her shoulder and his proximity to Claire was somewhat familiar so he quickly removed his hand and shuffled back a step or two satisfied that she was going to stay for a bit.

"No I don't live around here, my house is on Turner Road close to the mines, I haven't seen you at school," Claire responds.

"No I'm kinda home schooled, ammm what's your name?"

Realizing she'd forgotten to give it she answers with a smile, "Oh yah, it's Claire, Claire Smith"

"Do you often come out to these woods, I mean I've never seen anyone else out here before...but it's really good to meet someone else... it gets kinda boring out here."

"I was just out taking a few pictures of nature and stuff and I saw your house, aaa... I mean like, I know what you mean it can get really boring living so far outside the town, I usually stay late after school and go to McSorley's for a Shake."

Peat knew she wasn't being honest about her reasons for being around his home but he wasn't over concerned about why she was here and chose not to press the matter, he just wanted an opportunity to chat and get to know her.

Picking up her mentioning of McSorley's, Peat noted, "Ah yah I was there about a year back, my Dad---" Claire interrupts: "You mean Big Tom?"

"Yah, well he brought me in on one of our trips as a treat and I had a mint flavored shake...It was heaven I'm telling you!"

Claire smiles at Peat's apparent innocence, "Yah mint is my favorite too."

An awkward silence ensues and to break it Peat asks, "How did yah get all the way from the mines, is there someone with you?"

With a sense of self-sufficient pride, "I have a bike."

"Wow, that must have took forever, I mean that's a long cycle"

"No no, don't be crazy I couldn't cycle that far, I use my motorbike!"

Getting excited Peat asks, "Really, cool can I see it?"

"Yah sure, amm... it's not like a real motorbike but you need gas," Claire qualifies.

"It's probably one of those French made Mobylette hybrids, they're really popular?"

"A what..?" Claire responds puzzled.

A little embarrassed and terrified of being considered a 'know all,' Peat explains lucidly, "Ahhh I just meant like a motorbike which has pedals, it's really cool I'd love to have a look at it if you'd let me."

Clare smiles and gestures with her right arm, "Come on Peat this way then,...I really love the color just wait till you see it."

On the way towards the forestry entrance where Clair had left the bike the pair continue to chit chat about everything and anything but Claire had made her mind up not to mention anything about the rumors concerning Big Tom, meeting Peat suggested to her that they were, at the very least severely exaggerated and possibly totally lies. And aside from this, Claire felt rather sorry for Peat and wouldn't want to upset him by broaching such a sensitive issue like his mother's death, she knew what it was like to have people gossiping about a suspect parent and felt a certain connection or parallel between her situation and that of Peats'. Equally, Peat was not willing to push for the truth even though, as I said earlier, he knew she was not being honest with him about why she was here and there was something suspect about the way she acted when mention of his father arose... it reminded him of the anxious and overly cautious manner in which people around Lismore seemed to act anytime Peat would accompany his dad on shopping trips! But Peat was content just to be with

32

someone of his own age, a potential friend to talk to, and such a pretty one at that! Eventually they reached the entrance but not before Claire had got a little lost, Peat knew the woods like the back of his hand but Claire was so intent on taking charge he didn't dare interrupt her intuitive navigation even when they were going in circles.

"There it is …isn't it great!" Claire says as she points to the bike.

Crouching down Peat knew at one glace the bike was in a bad way but as astute as ever he knew exactly what to say, "It's really cool you are so lucky to have this, you know I love mechanics and perhaps we could make a deal… I'll fix up your bike anytime there's a problem with it and in return you bring me some stuff from McSorley's every now and again, aammm…you know when you get a chance like?" Peat perceptively knew that this bike needed serious work to ensure that Claire could continue to use it because of course if she couldn't, there would be no way she could make the trip back to see him regularly, also from the subtle hints he had got from their earlier chit chat it seemed unlikely that she'd get any help at home. Peat also has a real protective streak, for example, he'd already had in mind an old motorbike helmet that Jim had gathering dust in one of his storage barns along with a number of bike parts which could come in really handy as replacements and upgrades for Claire's Mobylette.

Claire of course was equally shrewd and knew the bottom line was that Peat wanted her to call again but she decided to play it coy, although frankly she found Peat really nice and unassuming, she especially admired that fact that he was so capable, "Yah sure why not I suppose...but next time we have to paint it and name it, I think I'll call it the 'Kay'...ya, after my favorite singer," she said excitedly.

"Cool, yah know that old teacher I was telling you about?"

"The Priest," Claire asked, as she attempted to recall what Peat had told her about him?

"Yah, well he has like loads of stuff for painting and decorating, I'm sure he'd let me borrow some if I asked."

Claire looks a little amused and also curious, "Ha, that's a strange type of Priest!"

"You've no idea!"

As she lifts the bike off the ground she agrees saying, "Fine so it's a date, I'll raid McSorley's and you bring the paint. I'll see you here this time next week, ok?"

"Yah definitely, that's great," Peat adds.

Claire looks at the ground realizing the one big flaw in their plans and looking at Peat, in a very stern manner she tells him: "You can't tell anyone that I was here... ok? I mean no one, not your Dad, the Priest or anyone else! I'm serious, the deal is off if anyone knows!"

Peat's smile vanishes to be replaced with an expression of worry, he moves his hands up, opens out his palms as if receiving a blessing from above, "Of course, God yah. No one will know. I'll tell Jim I need the paint for my tree-house or something." Reassured Claire smiles and gives a little chuckle, "Aren't you a little old for tree-houses?"

Going as red as a berry Peat rattles on, "Oh well it's not really... I mean it is, but you know.., amm It's really advanced, like you should see it... I've an electrical cable running from the house and galvanized roofing and real comfortable couch and chairs and... aaaa..."

Then as if to throwing him a life line, Claire interrupts Peat's babbling, "Peat!"

Looking up from the ground where his eyes had been fixed out of embarrassment he mutters, "Uh?"

"I'm only messing with you; we need somewhere to hang out anyway! I better be off my Mom might get worried."

Just then she felt kind of bad for having mentioned her mother because of what had happened to Peats' but she also felt a little ashamed because in all likelihood she knew far from being worried about where her daughter was, Stephanie was probably passed out on her bed after polishing off a few bottles of Wild Irish Rose or some other cheap fortified wine, of course that's presuming she had come straight home after work.

With a couple of good peddles Claire had the engine
chugging and while bidding his farewell Peat thought
to himself, 'That engine needs serious attention!'
Claire sped off with an awkwardness similar to that
of a child trying for the first time to keep its
balance on a bike with no stabilizers.

Peat looked on with deep concern saying to himself,
"I need to get her a helmet!"

As she disappeared around the bend Peat was filled
with an exhilaration, for the first time he had a
friend his own age, someone he could talk to as a
peer. As it turned out this marked the beginning of
what bloomed into a beautiful friendship; Claire
would visit with more and more frequency over the
next four years and they both worked at various
little projects which served primarily to cement
their friendship, so for instance; the duo spent a lot
of their time over-hauling the 'tree house' to make
it more durable against the elements. Peat found
Jim more than willing to part with old materials
which had long being cluttering up his storage space.
Once the exterior of the elevated hang out was
taken care of, the interior became the new focus
and Claire in particular took the lead role in
furnishing and decorating, with Peat knowing exactly
how he could get suitable materials. Peat had
chosen to use his special bi-annual project that Jim
would sponsor, to acquire the materials necessary to
do the inside of the tree house, but when the old
cleric saw the list of items that Peat was ordering;

such as pink drapes, love heart cushions and a soft pink colored and Lilly flowed-shaped rug, alarm bells went off in the clergyman's mind. Jim had the stuff delivered and made no question on what he had always encouraged to be, Peat's own personal projects, but within a few days of seeing the order list the concerned cleric had introduced an intensive week long course entitled 'Christian Anthropology' a major aim of which was to establish clear gender lines for his young student. All of Jim's concerns went over Peat's head, the lad had far more pressing matters which were playing on his young conscientious mind; every so often, and despite her best attempts to conceal it with makeup, Claire would show up with fresh bruises on her arms or face. Peat would sometimes ask what had happened but Claire would just make up some lame excuse, like she fell, and then change the subject. Eventually Peat stopped asking but he remained concerned and part of his zeal for getting the tree house completed was attributable to his belief that it would serve as a type of haven for Claire, a home away from a troubled home. But of course comfort and at times necessity demanded Tom's house be used which meant a covert operation of sneaking in and out of the cabin to get supplies, use the toilet and so on. At times Claire's obvious phobia of Tom irritated Peat but it seemed to him to be a very real fear and so he thought it best not to force the matter. Indeed Claire's fear of Big Tom, was based upon years of being filled with vicious and disturbing innuendo and gossip which had only become more graphic and disturbing as she got older. Claire still had no idea what had transpired at 62 Stanford Road, Lismore (The Black family's old residence) but despite serious apprehensions she had become more and more comfortable about being in the same area as Big Tom during her visits. Also, the fact that Peat was always happy, cheerful and obviously so well cared for, made her feel at ease and she paid less and less attention to the vilifications of Big Tom at school.

As it turned out after nearly nine months of this evasive and secretive arrangement by which Peat would often distract Tom, for instance asking him to come outside and look at something while Claire went inside for whatever reason..., all this came to a dramatic end on Claire's Sixteenth birthday. Big Tom had gone away into Lismore on that Saturday in answer to an unprecedented request by Peat for a new pair of trainers... of course, the request for new shoes was merely pretense so as to allow the young pair to celebrate Claire's 16th birthday in the homely cabin. Peat had been practicing making cakes all week justifying the mountain of dirty pots and pans, and the numerous failed attempts to his dad by saying that Jim wanted a perfectly made birthday cake with decorative icing in order to satisfy the practical element of his domestic training.

Tom found this very curious, but as was his way, he simply surged his shoulders and muttered an off the cuff euphemism, "He's been watching too much Julia Child," before going about his business.

Peat had everything set up in the house and when Claire arrived in a beautiful blue dress with white and yellow polka dots, Peat showed her into the kitchen. Conscious that a girl's Sixteenth birthday was a big deal Peat was over the moon with joy that Claire had chosen to spend the day with him. Peat was in the Kitchen putting the final decorative finishes to an impressive three tier cake which, not knowing better, one would surely say came from a professional service. He carefully slid the cake from the kitchen counter onto a kitchen trolley which Tom had made earlier that year just after Christmas. It was a delicate procedure but Peat wanted the effect of wheeling the candle-lit cake into the living room. In fact, Peat was so intent and focused on doing everything right that he carelessly tossed an unquenched match into the nearly full dust bin which met with a rag covered in cooking oil, which had been used earlier to clean up a spill of the very flammable liquid. Peat was totally unaware of the almost instant burst of flames which came from the bin behind him as he gently wheeled the large cake out into the hallway with a wrapped present tucked into a compartment under the trolley's primary surface.

"Close your eyes!" Peat shouted as he pushed the trolley towards the living room.

Peat had already pulled the curtains shut and turned off all the lights so Claire was expecting a cake, but nothing homemade and definitely not to the scale and quality Peat had attained, in fact the aesthetical quality the young baker had attained actually surpassed anything one could find at Misses Butler's Bakery and therein lay, Peat hoped, the big surprise.

"Okay," Claire responded playfully.

"Are they shut...?"

"Yah they're shut, you know it's so dark in here I couldn't see anything even if----"

Peat interrupts with a, "Surprise," Claire opens her eyes to see this giant cake with countless amounts of candles lighting up the room.

"O my God" she gasped in disbelief, a stunned silence followed for a few seconds as she examined the cake before asking, "Where did you get this, wow..."

"I watched a few cooking shows and it's really not that hard, I mean..."

Shocked, Claire interjects, "...You're telling me you baked this,"

Hoping to downplay it Peat replies, "Yah but like..."

"...Jesus Peat you've got some amount of talent!" Claire says, feeling really stirred by this gesture and then, without thinking, she continues: "You're one hell of a cook that's all I can say, it's no wonder

I suppose..., I mean everyone says your mum was really good at cooking too."

She realized immediately that she had broached a topic she had not intended to and Peat's smile lessened as a more bewildered one takes shape.

"My Mum?" Peat stated in a manner which expressed both wonder and curiousness.

Before Claire could even attempt to redirect the conversation she noticed an ominous glow coming from the hallway as she peered just over Peat's left shoulder.

"What's that?" she asked in some alarm.

Peat turned to see what had caught her attention and when he saw the amber glow he rushed quickly towards the living room door and looking out onto the darkened hallway he was horrified to see flames emerging from the kitchen.

"Oh shit," he exclaimed to himself before turning to Claire in a panic and pointing to the living room window he said, "Quick, get out the window."

Peat moved up the hallway to get a closer look.

"Wait, Peter come back." Claire shouted as she went after him.

"I just need to close the door... it might smother it! I'll be fine, just get outside," Peat pleaded with Claire as he moved towards the kitchen door.

"Ok, get the door shut," Claire says as she presses close to Peat in a clear sign that she is not going anywhere.

"Stay here," Peat says to Claire.

He then quickly removes his jumper and wraps it around his right hand before dashing across the face of the kitchen door so as to take up the best position so as to be able to reach in a grab the door handle. The smoke is beginning to fill the hallway and causing both Claire and Peat to cough with alarming regularity, breathing is becoming more difficult and the heat emanating from the Kitchen makes it almost impossible for Peat to turn his face towards the doorway let alone reach into the Kitchen and grab the door's handle. After summoning some courage he pivots through the doorframe and leans in till he feels the door handle, his face is still turned away from the flames, and grabbing it firmly he pulls the door closed with as much strength as he can muster. The door slams shut and Peat, losing his footing, stumbles backwards falling against the wall. Claire helps him to his feet and they both make their way towards the front door. Now Jim was a fan of epigrams and one of his favorite was; 'It never rains, but it pours,' well this saying epitomized how Peat felt when, as he and Claire lay outside the house on the grass attempting to catch their breaths, he saw Jim's little green Austin Morris appear in the distance about three minutes out from the house.

"Oh dear," Peat sighed as he looked at the approaching vehicle.

"Is it your Dad, that's not his car though... Is it?"

"I wish...", Peat responded as if musing to himself. Then as if he had just remembered that the fire was still burning he jumped to his feet, "There's a hose around the back we can try douse the flames." Claire nods as she gets to her feet and sprints around the back of the house with Peat following her. As they are running around the side of the house Peat notices that pitch dark smoke is bellowing into the clear blue sky and he remembers that he left the kitchen window open "Ah no" he says to himself.

They reach the back of the house and Peat is relieved to see no sign of flames coming out the window but there's a steady stream of smoke and Peats makes a dart for the head of the hose which is lying about five yards from the window close to the tool shed. Meanwhile Peat directed Claire to the tap, thankfully the hose was already attached to the faucet and without even waiting for the 'go-ahead,' Claire turns the tap on fully. Peat meantime had crouched down underneath the kitchen window-still with his right hand raised overhead pointing the hose into kitchen intending to spray in an indiscriminate manner.

"Ok, turn on...," before he could finish the sentence his hand jerked with the pressure from the water now flowing from the end of the tubing.

Peat used his finger to increase the pressure with which the water issued from the tip of the hose in the hope of reaching as much of the kitchen area as possible. Claire had taken up position beside Peat and looked for some sign of amelioration, after a few minutes she noticed that the volume of smoke was thinning out.

"It's dying down a bit and definitely the smoke isn't as black," she said reassuringly.

Peat, while still spraying the kitchen with water, took a peek over the window-still but the smoke was still too thick to get a clear look inside and crouching back down he looked at Claire with a cheerful grin.

"At least I saved the cake," Peat jokes!

Claire bursts into laughter and sitting down beside Peat, relaxing against the house's frame, she exhales deeply and murmurs "O Peat."

Peat's face suddenly drops and he exclaims in a panic "Jim" and bundling to his feet he races around the house, Claire following.

"What? What is it...?" she queries with deep concern as she struggles to keep up with Peat.

They just reach view of the front door when they hear Jim shouting "Anyone in there?"

They then see the worried cleric moving closer to the front door about to enter and Peat shouts, "Jim, Fr. Jim, it's okay!"

"The startled priest looks around at the two figures approaching, "Ah Peat my lad what in God's name, all the smoke! Where's Tom?"

"There was a fire but it's ok now... I think we've put it out. The Kitchen is destroyed I'd imagine though!"

" 'We've..?' " Jim says aloud looking at a rather nervous girl standing almost directly behind Peat as if embarrassed or ashamed.

Peat takes a step to the side and introduces Claire to Jim, "This is Claire, ammm she lives near the mines and well..."

"She's from the town...!" Jim says with an uncharacteristic level of surprise?

Claire seeks to interject with honorable intent, "It's my fault really you see Peat..."

Peat talks over her "...No it's my fault I was baking a cake and I must have left the oven on or something after I took out the cake because, well..."

"A cake?" Jim remarks with curiosity.

"Yes, you see it's my birthday today and Peat just thought that, well it was a surprise you see and... I mean it really is an incredible cake and amm..., it was just a horrible accident Father I swear!" Claire attested.

Looking at the two worried faces, Jim, in a calm and reassuring voice, offers some comforting words, "I see... well I'll tell you what, let's go around the back and survey the damage from the kitchen window. Then perhaps we can find that cake which, as I understand it...Peter managed to save, am I right?" Peat nodded with a smile.

"Excellent, I've a full flask of tea in my car along with a picnic set in the boot and do you know there might even be a few biscuits. But first things first let's make sure it's safe to go back inside."

"But what about Big Tom," Claire said with a genuine concern?

Peat and Jim looked at each other and while only the latter understood the origin of this deep fear both knew it to be unfounded. In fact, Peat had been far more concerned about Jim's likely reaction than his fathers.

With a comforting tone Jim sought to allay Claire's fears, "Don't fret my dear you'll find 'Big Tom' is far smaller than you thought."

Then, aware he had digressed he continued "...now let's go check out this kitchen, actually..., if I recall correctly Tom had mentioned to me that he was hoping to redecorate. You know Peat, Claire, you both may have acted as unwitting catalysts..."

Jim continued along this reassuring and encouraging line of talk and after they'd determined the fire was out they went inside and inspected the kitchen which had been almost totally consumed by the flames. The two youths were in awe at how much damage had been done and yet relieved that it was confined to one room.

Jim looked around and inspected what was left of the food cabinets before saying, "I think it's safe to go and have a look at this cake you baked Peat and perhaps I'll join you two love birds in treating myself to a slice or two."

Peat and Claire looked at each other before blushing.

Peat felt compelled to retort, "Ah no Jim we're just---"

But already Jim was half way out the Kitchen door and, seemingly oblivious to what Peat is trying to communicate, he asks, "Now, which way is that cake my young pyromaniac?"

With a smile, Claire instructs, "It's right Father."

Claire looks at Peat as if to say 'What kind of Priest is this?' and Peat offers a nod in concurrence.

After about an hour of sitting outside on the lovely sun kissed grass of a July afternoon with the Kitchen trolley on the edge of the gravel path carrying a now two tiered cake the trio are suddenly startled by a loud bang coming from the town direction.

Peat looks around asking, "What was that?"

As astute as ever Jim answers, "Sounds like your dad needs to check the spark plugs in his Jeep, that's probably what's causing that ungodly sound."

Claire has become rather uneasy and obviously a little distressed. Noticing this Jim decides to alleviate the tension, "Peat, I'm presuming that present, sitting in the cavity of what can only be your father's poorly constructed kitchen trolley, is not for me, would I be right?"

A little embarrassed, Peat mutters, "aah... yes, it actually, amm..."

As if to conceal Peat's stammering, Jim directs him, "Exactly. So why don't you take Claire inside and let me have a word with Tom, I need to be off then."

Turning to Claire, Jim continues speaking, "...Claire, it was a pleasure, and again happy Sixteenth." Comforted by the Jim's frank but soothing manner she responded with a confident familiarity, "Thanks Jim."

Interestingly, Jim had actually known exactly who Claire was from the moment Peat introduced her, although most people considered Fr. Jim's pastoral involvement in Lismore to consist of one Mass per week and an hour of confession. In actual fact, Fr. Jim was extremely clued into the happenings of his parish community through his close tie with the local good hearted busy-body Mrs. Thompson who happened also to be the mother of the Principal of the town's high school. Through this connection Fr. Jim was able to keep tabs on those who were on the margins of the Lismore community, and drawing on a charitable fund he convinced his father to set up, he secretly funded local groups who offered home support, counseling services, rehab, addiction therapy, and much more..., to people like Claire's mother.

Peat brought Claire inside to the living room and handed her the disc shaped parcel.

"Ok so I don't think I need my three guesses…, it's a record right?"

"Yap, wait till you see it!"

Unwrapping the present slowly Claire got more and more excited as a feeling of suspense rose "O my God" she shouted, almost reaching a minor scream. The record was that of Kay Moore's new album '*But to Dream.*'

"I didn't think this was out yet…, O thank you, thank you, thank you, this is the best present ever, I mean… ."

At a loss for words and deeply touched by the thoughtfulness of the gift her eyes begin to tear up and spontaneously she hugs Peat and kisses him on the lips much to the happy surprise of the teenager who could hardly have had envisaged, two hours ago, that this would be anything but the worst day of his life having set the kitchen on fire. And now, as things stood, it was surely the best.

A little embarrassed at the impromptus of her kiss, Claire quickly looked around the room and in an attempt to lighten the atmosphere she asked, "So where can we find a record player around here?"

"Peat," a loud call came from the hallway.

"Is that your Dad," asked a worried Claire?

"Yah." He replied.

"How angry do you think he'll be about the kitchen," Claire inquired in a hushed voice.

"We're in here dad," Peat yells out as he moves towards the living room door while also continuing to

reassure Claire, "...No it's fine, don't worry, my Dad
is totally relaxed."

"Will he mind that I'm here," Claire rambles on.

"No, not at all, come on I'll introduce you," he says
as he opens the living room door.

Tom walks into the living room and Claire is visibly
tense; the man's massive size, his fiery red hair are
terrifying to her especially when set against the
years of negative conditioning all young people of
Lismore are exposed to in the forms of baneful
speculation and innuendo. Tom though, having
spoken with Jim, is fully informed of the situation
regarding the kitchen and Claire, and is ready to do
his best to assuage the young girl's fears. In truth
Tom was thrilled at the idea that Peat had met a
friend and indeed the moment he heard it was little
Claire Smith a flood of fond memories came gushing
back. Tom had actually known Claire's father,
Harry, as a young man; the two were good friends
and played on the local football team. In fact, it
was Harry who first introduced Tom to Megan at a
school dance many years ago. Tom and Megan had
watched painfully as Stephanie began her steady
decline after Harry's untimely death. The Black's
had offered a lot of support to Stephanie up to the
time Megan was murdered.

"Ah this must be the birthday girl Jim told me
about. Hello, I'm Tom," putting out his hand. Claire
reciprocates with her comparatively minuscule

extremity, and Big Tom gently shakes her hand before Claire responds.

"Hi, I'm Claire, aaa sorry about your kitchen Sir," she says in a cautious voice anxiously waiting to see how he'll respond. Tom glances at Peat and burst into laughter.

"Hah hahahha... No need to say sorry Claire I'm just happy no one was hurt, and in fact, I'd been thinking that I needed to redecorate that room and upgrade some of the kitchen units, and now I've an excuse to get Peat to help with the work ha ha,..." He says winking at Peat in jest before continuing, "...anyway enough about all that, what age are you today?"

"16 Sir." Claire replies.

"Well I heard you both already had some cake but really; a 16th needs a bit more. I've a few treats in the car, I'll bring them in and Jim left us his picnic kit so we'll have cups and all..., so sure... I'll set up in the kitchen and when you're ready... "

Peat pips up, "Dad, where's the record player?"

"I think it's on the top shelf in the closet. Will I get it for-"

Peat interrupts, "...No, we can get it."

With a smile signifying that he understands, Tom makes to leave the room saying in an empathic tone, "Awee say no more, take your time, I'll see ye in the dining room in a while."

Once gone Peat looks at Claire as if awaiting feedback, Claire smiles and, as if she had been cool with Tom from day one, says, "He's nice. Now where's this record player?"

A little taken aback by the seemingly sedate nature of her reaction to this figure which had so evidently struck fear into her heart, a confused Peat struggled with his reply, "amm, aaa... well, it's in the closet, aaa.. Ok so let's go get it."

They left the living room but for the rest of the evening Peat was slightly captured in thought, trying to figure our Claire's almost anticlimactic reaction to meeting his father. Interestingly, this unsettled Peat far more than the months of accommodating Claire's seemingly irrational fear without ever the slightest notion as to its cause.

- Chapter Three -

Things went from good to great for both Peat and Claire now that they could freely move around the house even when Tom was there and this saw Claire spending far more time at the Black's. Claire was always bringing Peat stuff from town and on a few occasions they would take the bike and sneak into Lismore to catch a movie. Not that Tom would mind them going into town, in fact he would have had insisted on giving them a lift, but the pair didn't want anyone else to identify Peat. Peat had made some serious upgrades to Claire's modest moped so that it could easily carry them both and reach a decent speed. Of course any time Peat went into the town he would always take steps to hide his identity; a base-ball hat would be pulled down over his face with a high rising jacket collar concealing his lower face. And whenever Claire got her way, Peat would reluctantly agree to wear a pair of sunglasses which he maintained made him look even more stupid, but Claire disagreed remarking that the shades were "stylish". Claire was always hyper protective of Peat when he was around town with her and pretended he was her cousin. As regularly happened, when the pair were hanging out with other kids talk of Big Tom would arise, but the instance it did Claire would either change the subject abruptly or, failing this, make up an excuse and leave pulling Peat away with her. Peat found this bizarre and tried to explain to Claire that he wanted to hear what was being said about his father but Claire simply dismissed it as gossip that she personally couldn't stand to listen to. Peat didn't fight her on this point because she seemed so adamant, just like his father would get when he broached the same subject. But also, in part, Peat just liked Claire's take-charge style when they were around the town, she would always be holding his arm which he loved. The secretive excursions into town were few and far between but of all the things the pair did, Peat's favorite activity was attending the cinema, something he had not done before. It was not all fun and games however, Peat helped Claire with her school work and even persuaded Jim to give her revision classes on subjects she found particularly difficult in preparation for her exams. Peat had hoped she might get into college and Jim had discreetly mentioned to her that there were a number of local college grants offered for students who reached a certain mark but whose economic situation didn't afford them an opportunity for college. Both Peat and Claire developed personally and academically over the next two happy years and their contentment was also a great source of joy for Tom who always felt a deep guilt, and a certain shame for raising Peat in a kind of self-inflicted purgatory rather than leaving the area all together after Megan's tragic death. The quartet of Peat, Claire, Tom and Jim became rather close, akin to a family in many respects and as such there was deep concern among three of the group as Jim, almost overnight, had become very detached and more than a little paranoid.

Jim had written to the local Bishop to have a replacement priest minister Lismore on the grounds of ill health. He also had his father's office handle all matters relating to his philanthropic initiatives in the town. The only real connections to the world that he maintained were with Tom, Peat and Claire. Out of the blue Jim had begun spending an inordinate amount of time in the tower of his old Victorian estate house. Earlier that year Tom had finally given in and agreed to help Peat attach the most remarkable ringed platform which extended out around the roof's vertex. It was accessible through a hatch in the ceiling, which itself was reached by a ladder running along Jim's bedroom wall. Tom thought the whole project was 'un-natural' but after a number of years working for Jim, his notion of what was 'normal' had, by that stage, been stretched considerably. Jim was delighted with his new observatory deck and used it almost every night, bringing up his telescope and a folding chair. In the winter months when Peat and Jim would head home after it had got dark they would sometimes see Jim out on the deck observing the heavens. But of late, Jim had become very reclusive, on a typical day he would come out to meet the arriving father and son smelling of cigars and with numerous coffee stains on his shirts, his eyes red from lack of sleep.

"Something's not quite right...," he would sometimes be heard to mumble before giving Tom his list of jobs and disappearing back to his room, there was little if any conversation or banter as the duo had long since become accustomed to. Peat would get started on a mountain of pre-prepared exercises Jim had left for him to do but there was no one-to-one tutelage anymore, Jim only emerged once or twice from his cloister to check on Peat's progress and as for the outdoor activates which Peat always looked forward to, they completely ceased. At the end of the day Peat would leave his work on a tray atop Jim's desk and take home the corrected worksheets from the previous day, there would be no goodbye. Something was wrong, Jim was working right through the night and sleeping very little, it seemed the only time Peat would leave his room during the day was to check on Jim or, far more commonly, to retrieve another astrology book from his stacks. It struck Peat that his teacher was allowing a once hobby, to turn into an obsession that was consuming his life at the expense of his own mental wellbeing. Jim no longer even tended to his beloved bees, a job which fell to Peat, as Tom could not bring himself to go near them. The concerned trio of Peat, Tom and Claire often chatted about the peculiar behaviour Jim had begun to exhibit. Tom postulated that he was having another breakdown, like the one he had when he was in Rome. Tom and Peat often sought to discreetly air their concerns with Jim when, on the rare occasions, they would catch him out of his room and usually this was before 8 a.m. when the boss would give Tom his list of jobs or, for Peat, it was when he came down to check on his progress. But any attempts they made to voice their concerns whether it came in the form of an invitation to join themselves and Claire for dinner at the weekend or more direct questions as to why he was spending so much time in his room, all were either dismissed out of hand or deflected with an imperious remark. And to be fair, questioning Jim's actions had always been taboo and Tom had known this when he took on the position as his factotum. The arrangement, as Jim had made clear from day one, was that he would pay a salary to Tom and provide free master level tuition for Peat and, as Tom had requested, "...get him into College." Indeed, anytime Tom had previously expressed concern about one of Jim's more audacious tasks, the cleric would often simply walk away and while paraphrasing a selective snippet from Lord Tennyson which was intended to mildly reprove the insubordination, "Theirs not to make reply, Theirs not to reason why, Theirs but to do!"

Things went on like this for about six months before the night of the great storm.

It was a Friday in early August, a severe storm had been forecast and Jim seemed to have reached a new height of anxiety, close to erratic. He insisted that both Tom and Peat go home early because of the inclement weather. As they both loaded up the car with a few extra supplies that Jim had kindly put aside in case the storm made travel into town impossible for a day or more.
"That's it, the last of it," Peat said.

Placing his hand on his lower back and stretching, Tom said with a moan, "My poor back."

"You know he was worse than ever today," Peat said with a cautious look directed at his father.

With a profound sigh, "I know, I know... but you know yourself!"

"Yah, it's just sad to see him like this," Peat laments.

Shutting the boot with the large thump Tom looks to the sky and says, "Come on, I don't like the look of that sky, they're expecting serious winds and flooding too."

Things got pretty bad that night and Tom had the shutters fixed across the windows which he also boarded, all the garden equipment and the jeep were stored away in a garage that Tom had built adjacent to the cabin with the help of a small number of his old friends from the mines. Peat, unlike Tom, had a cetin sentimental liking for the tempestuous weather conditions and loved listening to the rain as it pelt off the roof, and the wind as rattling against the house. However, what Peat didn't like was the dreaded duo of thunder and lightning which unfortunately were out in force on this night. Claire was trapped in her house alone; Stephanie had imprudently gone to the bar after work and left it too late to make it back home before they closed the floodgates across the only bridge which led out towards the mines. In all likelihood Stephanie would probably shack up with one of the local hobos or rely on the good graces of one of the publicans to accommodate her for the night in the bar. In fact, one of the only people in the area to be outside as it approached midnight, when the storm was reaching its zenith, was Jim, and of course true to form, he was out on his observatory platform. Luckily Tom had insisted on installing a number of heavy duty ground anchors and the purchasing of a body harness to ensure Jim, and whatever equipment he had up there, did not fall off. In addition to a harness which tied down the telescope, Jim had attached a rope running across the platform so that he could move around in the high winds which, by that time, had reached gale force. Jim had always prided himself on been prepared for every foreseeable eventuality, however, there's no doubt but that this was a precarious situation in which he had placed himself.

59

He was dressed in a long cassock, covered with a full length rain coat. Standing on the observatory platform with one hand firmly gripping the balancing rope and the other placed on the edge of the telescope's eyepiece, every few minutes he would look down at his watch to check the time as if waiting for something to happen.

At about 12.30 a.m., after staring intently through the scope for about 10 minutes without a brake he jerked his head upright looking into the sky and said in an astonished voice, "There it is!"

Having been overcome with excitement he forgot about the current inclement conditions around him and letting go of the balancing rope in a state of sheer jubilation he immediately was blown backwards and catching his foot on the taut rope which lay on the ground behind his heels. He fell backwards onto the platform's base and rolled towards the edge.

Jim managed to make it to his knees just before he reached the edge but before he could even breath a sigh of relief a gush of wind jostled him face first over the ambit and with an "aaugh," from the terrified clergyman, suddenly he found himself suspended as he faced out over the slated roof of the turret, his arms flailing in the open air.

"Oh Christ," he exclaimed peering around to see what act of God had kept him up and then he remembered the body harness he was wearing. Slowly stepping each knee back just a few inches he brought his hands down towards the deck and wobbled the rest of his body back onto the surface like a seal moving in reverse. Flipping over and grabbing the harness line Jim got to his feet and pulled himself towards the balancing rope and used this to get to the platform ladder which he then promptly descended down into his bedroom. His bedroom was covered in mappings posted to the walls; there were tea cups all over the room and fag butts heaped up in plies over what were once overflowing ash trays.

"Where is it, where is it?" an agitated Jim questions aloud as he frantically lifts up bundles of papers and astronomy maps.

Stopping almost in a state of defeat and frustration, "St. Anthony PLEASE," the priest invokes before pausing for a moment of silent prayer, and then, looking across the room at a stack of books he muses to himself, "hum."

He pushes the stack to one side and opens a small storage cabinet and looking inside says, "aweha, there you are," and with a nod to a picture of St. Anthony in the corner of the room he pulls out a small hardware case and hurries out of the house. Jim seemed as if he were completely ignorant of the storm, whatever had him outside on this night surely superseded, at least in his mind, the inclement meteorological conditions. Jim, with flash light in hand, quickly ran to his car throwing the case on the front passenger's seat as he set into the car and immediately turned on the ignition. The man seemed almost unaware of the fact that just five minutes before he was literally hanging off a precipice. This was a mind preoccupied and whatever he had seen in the night's sky lit a fire under him, which was burning strong. Reaching over to the case Jim pulled out a sheet and unfolding it against the steering wheel he shun the torch on it to illuminate what was a map of the local area with a red circle drawn around a densely wooded zone about a twenty minute drive from Jim's house. "Right," he said with missionary forthrightness before placing the map in the glove compartment and driving off, at some speed.

He drove erratically up towards his destination veering around sharp bends, as if he were driving for his life, this was a journey made all the more treacherous by the pelting rain which impaired visibility. Eventually, he reached a large mound of gravel at the edge of the forest where the road ended. From there Jim went on foot through the trees with the flash light in this right hand and the case in his left. He'd stuffed the map into his overcoat pocket and placed an old biretta which he found under his car seat on his head. There was no real discernible path through the woodlands yet Jim seemed to know where he was going as if he was familiar with the area, steadily he moved with purpose further into the dark forest where the growth became denser. Soon there was little rain falling on him as the shelter provided by the leafy trees was so complete, only a constant trickle of droplets could be felt falling from on high.

Then he suddenly stopped and shun his flash light around, "It should be…, somewhere here," he said pensively before all of a sudden stopping his light on a tree which had a large blob of yellow paint coving the surface of the trunk.

"There you are," the adventurer said as if he'd being playing a game of hide-and-go-seek.

He moved closer to this apparent marker and placing the case on the ground took out a compass which he then placed in his right jacket pocket before reaching in again and producing a pair of high quality binoculars. Binoculars in hand he looked upwards and wondered around searching for a clearing among the branches so as to get an eastern view of the sky. After meandering about twenty yards around the area with his eyes fixed upwards he finally found the perfect vantage point for whatever aerial phenomenon he seemed to be expecting.

Looking through his binoculars Jim stood gazing, motionless he watched, "won't be long now," he said, expectantly.

Seconds later there was an unmerciful rumble of thunder followed by two bolts of lightning which lit up the sky in a wonderful display. No sooner had

63

the sky quietened again than a small single celestial light appeared. It moved in a gradual manner. Travelling across the night's sky it's trajectory seemed to suggest that it would pass right over the woods and come down miles away but suddenly the object, which most would surely think a comet, took a nose dive towards the region Jim currently occupied. As it did so it began to reduce in speed the lower it got. Eventually, it went out of the observing cleric's sight as it approached ground level and Jim dashed back to his marked tree. When he was at the designated tree he took out his compass and placed the map on the ground to work out where he was in relation to the circled spot on the map. After getting his bearings he gathered his things, rushed off in a south-easterly direction towards a creek which led into a small lake close to what would be the center of the forest. As Jim ran through the forest the conditions seemed to have calmed; the rain had stopped falling, the wind was hushed and the dreaded duo could neither be heard nor seen.

But unlike the comparative metrological calm Jim was even more panicky than before as he hastened through the wood; "I should be near it, where on earth is...," before he could fret any further a powerful pulsating light caught his eye in the distance.

Jim adjusted himself and dashed towards the light which emitted the most powerful deep red glow. On reaching the source of this ostensible beacon Jim saw the most peculiar oval shaped object, smaller than a man's hand at about five inches in length and four in diameter. It had a single pole projecting from its base which held it erect off the ground no more than half an inch. But despite its tiny size it radiated the most powerful light which seemed to come from a blob of gel of some kind which itself flowed across the surface of the device stopping every split second at a different point before radiating its ruby colored beacon. Jim could not look directly at this pulsating light because of its brightness. Kneeling down in front of the object in a very reverential manner he took out a pair of tongs from his case and clasped the ovoid firmly, then almost instantaneously the miniature stilt withdrew into the base of the object and the emitting light stopped with the gel-like substance disappearing into the object's core. The light having ceased, Jim turned his face around to get a proper look at the gadget and raising it up close to his face he shun the flash light on it.

With an expression of sheer astonishment on his face the priest said to himself in a hushed manner, "How very curious!"

There came a rustle in the bushes to his front and looking up for a moment, Jim quickly took hold of the object in his hand and placed it carefully in his pocket before putting the thongs back in the case and closing it up. Getting to his feet he used the compass to get his bearings and then, with haste, he made his way back to the car and drove away. When he reached the house he went straight upstairs to his room and locked the door.

– Chapter Four –

"Peat, you up yet," was the first thing Peat heard
Monday morning as he rolled over on his bed?
The storm had passed and another week had begun.
Tom was in his usual chipper self and sat in his new,
year and a half old kitchen, gulping down a big bowl
of runny porridge sweetened by multiple spoonful's
of Jim's honey.

"How can something so sweet come from such pesty
little insects," Tom mused aloud as Peat drudged
across the room with his typical morning blues?
As the pair approached Jim's estate Peat raised a
concern which had weighed heavily on both Tom and
himself all weekend, "I hope Jim got through the
weekend ok!"

Tom nodded his head concurring and unconsciously
drove a little faster towards his employer's
premises. As they drove up the laneway to Jim's old
Victorian estate house they caught sight of the
most peculiar happenings occurring near the storage
barns.

"What the fu..,"

"PETER!" Tom said sternly, both checking Peat's
unfinished imprecation and also reprimanding him at
the same time.

"Oh, sorry Dad! But what's going on," Peat inquired?
Tom was equally perplexed and simply shuck his
head as he gazed ahead.

Far from the typical isolationist scene they had
become accustomed to over the years, and
particularly of late, there was now to be found six
massive delivery trucks with dozens of work men all
over the grounds. The storage barns were being
emptied and most of the material being put in two
large trucks. Those men who were not working at
removal were unloading various items and
apparatuses which both terrified and baffled Tom
and Peat in equal measure. As they drove up to the
house to park the jeep they passed Jim who waved
at them with an enthusiasm and gregariousness
they'd never seen before.

Tom glanced at Peat who stared back at his father
who in turn said, "He's finally flipped!"

What it was that had stunned and terrified the pair
was the various; swords, defensive objects, suits of
armor, helmets, shields, etc…, which were being
unloaded from the trucks.

Running up from the storage barns Jim shouted,
"Peter, Peter my lad."

Tom and Peat were thrown by the jovial approach of
Jim but still they were primarily captivated by what
they had seen coming out of the trucks.

"Father," Peat acknowledged in an almost frightful
voice as Tom stood there perplexed.

They both initially presumed that Jim had finally lost his mind but waited to hear what he had to say, "Good man Tom, on time as always, now here's a list of jobs I want you to get cracking at. Go talk to the foreman Al down there, he'll give you the heads up on what you're to do."

"Foreman...?" Tom responds bewildered.

"Fret not Tom my mam, you're in charge I've explained that to them but I had to get started immediately, couldn't wait for you to arrive, sure you understand. Now don't take any slack from them down there, you're the boss! Off you go then I have to talk to Peat about his new curriculum, we've serious work to get done and time is against us!"

Feeling like a new kid who's just arrived late for school orientation on the first day Tom simply takes the list and looking at it as he walks befuddled down towards the barns, he simply utters "Ok."

"Good man Tom." Jim says waiting for him to get out of earshot before turning to Peat with a clandestine expression far removed from that on show just five minutes earlier.

"Peat, something big has happened. Now I can't go into as of yet but you'll have to trust me. I've being a little standoffish of late.."

Peat looks at Jim as if he has just made a serious understatement, Jim reads this and continues, "...oh ok fine; I've being bordering the misanthropic, but that's not important now. What's important is finishing your education, Peat you've developed into a brilliant young man, a credit to your father and yourself but we still have one last thing to do. I can't explain my reasons yet but I need you to go with me on this, can you do that?"

"Yes, I suppose aaa…"

"Peter I need your complete assent if we're to do what needs to be done, no matter how bizarre it may seem I need for you to go with me on this. Just give me six months, that's all I ask. What do you say?"

Peat was astonished at the collegial manner in which Jim had appealed to him, also he had grown very fond of the old cleric who had always taken care of Tom, himself and even Claire (at the behest of Peat) and therefore, despite the suspicion that Jim might have lost his marbles over the weekend, he acquiesced to the request.

"Okay Father, sure, six months…" the young man stated!

Suspending his serious look for a moment Jim returned to a more carefree spirit, "Great, now on inside, I've a busy day of lessons planned."

Jim noticed Peat was looking intently at the equipment being unloaded from the trucks and remarks, "Don't concern yourself with that yet Peter, first things first, we have to feed your mind."

Jim brought Peat into a room he had cleared out next to his parlour and equipped for study with a

beautiful desk and ornate lamps strategically placed, a lovely green leathered chair and the most wonderful slide show projector which Jim had also called one of his greatest "pedagogical aids."
At the other end of the room there was a plain work station consisting of a desk and a wooden chair. Peat instinctively went to the quotidian desk and put down the books that Jim had handed him but to his great surprise the teacher directed him to the ostentatious work station set up at the other end of the room.

"Peat it's time you took full responsibly for your own learning, my role from here on is less the teacher and more the facilitator; I'll direct and guide you but you've got to make the decision as to whether or not you want what's on offer.... We need to train you; body and soul, every part of you must be attuned to goodness and right, with the capability to defend yourself and others with fortitude and adroitness. As I've explained I cannot yet tell you what's the particular purpose of this all this yet, but trust me when I say there is one. What I can say is that this is much bigger than just you or me... Okay so let's begin... In the often neglected *Eudemian Ethics*, Aristotle ..."

Over the next six months Jim facilitated Peat's learning across an unusual range of subjects from ethics and astronomy to military studies and combat training. Peat actually began to like the lessons and although he was more and more convinced that Jim had a mental breakdown of sorts he found the subject matter being covered fascinating, and when he wasn't working on creating the music box for Claire's Eighteenth birthday, he was reading all the assigned material Jim gave and indeed to the facilitator's surprise the dexterous Peat would often take the initiative to read ahead of the syllabus. However, as much as Peat loved the theoretical side of this *ad hoc* course he was captivated with the practical aspect which, on the other hand, caused Tom a great deal of consternation. The barns had been transformed into the most spectacular training centers. One of the barns had been effectively converted into a gymnasium, with every manner of fitness apparatus and generous supplies of equipment. The other barn was far more controversial possessing as it did an array of weapons and defensive objects. When Tom heard Jim intended Peat to train with these he was more than angry and not shy about expressing his outright opposition to the idea. He unequivocally told both Jim and Peat in no uncertain terms that there was no way he'd allow his son to train using such deadly weapons and openly questioned the mental stability of any mind that would think up such 'craziness!' It's hard to express the amount of cajoling and concessions that Jim undertook to training with such instruments. For example, Tom insisted on sitting in on Peat's combat training for the first week or so and the cleric had to ensure that all the weapons had been fitted with a thick padding at all times, on top of this Peat would always have to wear protective coverings, sometimes even armor. And there were many other safety features Tom insisted on before his begrudgingly permitted Jim to train Peat using weapons. Tom of course, like Peat, believed that Jim had lost leave of his senses to an extent, yet the priest seemed back to his normal eccentric self in many ways. Every night Tom, Peat, and Claire when she was there, would try to make sense of this new enterprise but at best all they could agree upon was that, overall, Jim was acting much more sociably than he had been in the preceding months. Peat however, did not share, to the same degree, Tom or Claire's belief as to Jim's supposed 'breakdown.' He mentioned nothing about the tête-à-tête he had with Jim prior to his training. The young trainee eventually decided to reserve his assessment of Jim's mental health until the six months had elapsed. In the intervening time Peat pondered almost every hour as to the reasons why he should be the kernel of Jim's latest endeavors, 'Why me?', 'What happened over the weekend to spark this whole new project...?', 'Why was it so important I learn about combat?', 'Why does Jim not spend any real time in his make shift observatory anymore...?' These were just some of the questions that would run through Peat's mind on a daily basis but having had a rather sheltered upbringing, and being so familiar with Jim's strange ways from such an early age, Peat eventually became use to the intense physical and mental regime that Jim had put in place. The transition to such a demanding routine was no doubt made easier by the fact that Jim had always kept a very structured daily plan for Peat from a young age and then there was also the fact that an end point to this grueling formation had been set, with six months being the agreed timeframe. Peat did of course have his own guesses as to Jim's motives besides those of mild insanity, which were mostly postulated by his dad; his main one was that Jim saw this as the last stage of Peat's tutelage after so many years and the cleric was simply adopting a core element of the classical style education which placed a strong emphasis on courage, discipline and physical skills like wrestling etc. God knows, Jim had always made enough references to classical Greek and Roman practices, and so to suggest that this was his inspiration seemed highly plausible to Peat. Form Peat's perspective the toughest part of the whole thing was that his Saturday's were now totally filled with training and every second week Jim would usually employ experts in; martial arts, fencing, pugilism etc... who would visit the estate for a few days and give Peat an intensive introduction in their respective fields. This often meant staying full time at Jim's house which, as tough an experience as that would be in itself, also meant that time with

Claire was at a premium and this was at a point where the two had become very close friends indeed. Claire and Peat had grown very fond of each other. Claire had reached young womanhood and things at the local high school had become more complex, many young men were seeking her attention and the desire to fit in was intense. Understandably, Claire found her lot in life a lonely one, with Stephanie's serious drinking problem, her own commitment to studies, and the all too infrequent meetings with Peat. Claire often wanted to make plans at the weekend with her friends and accept some of the many requests she received for dates but she felt a strong affection for Peat and didn't want to pull back from their friendship although its maintenance required sacrifice. Perhaps the most difficult thing of all was that she had no one with whom she could talk to about her relationship with Peat, definitely not her mother and if any of her friends from Lismore knew she spent time at the Blacks' she knew it would cause trouble for both Peat and Tom . Claire was truly a person of great depth, conscience and emotionally very mature in many ways. Peat was more unworldly and idealistic than Claire, but given his sheltered upbringing that was hardly surprising. That said, Peat's affection for his friend ran deep... Peat placed his relationship with Claire as of paramount importance and his commitment to her had grown from their first encounter. Peat, like any young man of his age found it difficult to articulate what he was feeling, yet he knew that if he didn't make some attempt to move his relationship with Claire on from friendship he'd lose out to someone else. This was why he put so much effort into making Claire's 18th birthday extra special, presenting her with a tailor made musical box struck Peat as the ideal prelude to asking her on a formal date. Peat's plan was perhaps a little quixotic but his affection for Claire was genuine; like any man he was course was driven by a level of eros, Claire's physical beauty had only increased as she got older and Peat often found himself daydreaming about her jet black hair, ruby red lips and pale white skin. But his desire encompassed much more than the physical, Peat's love was truly that of agape. Agape being the unconditional form of love, which enables someone to look upon another with perpetual hope and affection, wanting selflessly always what is best for them.

Since Peat began his training he'd lost many Saturdays with Claire, and the phone bill grew even higher with the two spending countless hours on the phone, just chatting. Now strangely Jim had become somewhat standoffish towards Claire on those rare occasions when she visited Peat at his estate. He would never be rude per se but rather distant and cold towards her. Peat didn't notice this but Claire picked up on it straight away and couldn't figure it out, she got the sense that Jim did not look favorably on her close friendship with Peat anymore. But to be honest her visits to the estate were so rare that when she was there, this social awkwardness did not become a major issue. In fact, on the few occasions she did visit, Claire's interests were far more taken by the marvels to be found in the externally deceptive mundane barns which inside had been transformed from storage facilities. On Claire's first visit after Peat's new training had commenced, and against Jim's strict instructions, Peat brought her to one of the barns, inside she was impressed to see the entire structure had been reinforced with a steel frame, from the roof ran climbing ropes which Peat hated having to use, there was also a cylindrical pole which ran around the barn close to the roof, it was affixed roughly one hundred and thirty feet off the floor. Peat would often have to maneuver along this elevated pole at speed after having ascended climbing pegs which littered all the walls of the barn, Jim of course had a harness installed for safety. At ground level the barn was a *de facto* gymnasium with all the typical apparatuses; weights, punching bags, a ring, climbing frames, a pole vault, mats, numerous pieces of gymnastic equipment and much more. Claire wanted to see the other barn but Peat told her that it had remained just a storage facility for Jim's old stuff. Peat didn't want to deceive Claire but he was worried that she would be unsettled by what she'd find in the other barn. The problem with Peat's attempted deception was that Claire could always tell when he was being less than honest with her. Peat went about locking the pad lock on the barn door after Claire and himself had finished but the moment he'd bolted it shut Claire, without warning, threw her arms around him and planted a big wet kiss on his lips. Peat was taken by surprise and dropped the keys as he instinctively went about putting his arms around Claire. But abruptly she broke away, quickly picked up the keys from the ground and darted across to the other barn, calling back to Peat, "Are you coming?"

Peat savored the experience for a few seconds before the ambidextrous nature of Claire's actions became apparent to him.

Peat called after her, "Claire wait, aaa...,"

But she proceeded to unlock the second barn and by the time Peat reached the door she had already entered.

Claire was shocked upon entering and after a few minutes walking around she found her voice, "Jesus... this is crazy, I mean like look at this place. It's a horror house...", an incredulous Claire remarked after which a long pause ensued, as she gazed at some of frightful training apparatuses. Then she continued as she shook her head, "...I know you said Jim had you doing weird training but this is...., he's lost it! There's no doubt about it Peat!"

Taking a few steps forward Claire turned her head to Peat while pointing to a particularly frightful

bladed apparatus, "I mean do you see th-"
Interrupting, Peat says as he points to a large
storage press in the corner, "I know, I do know how
it looks but we keep all the blades covered with tick
padding and I always have to wear full body armor,
all the time when I'm training. And I only ever come
in here when Jim has experts who want to train me,
and aaa... , well I knew you'd be upset."
"Look Peat; you look great and you know I totally
love Jim, but there's something off about this, I
mean he's being acting strange for months, not
coming out of his room then over one weekend he
completely flips and buys all this stuff just to train
you...? Come on, something's not right!" Claire says
as she looks at Peat appealing to his reason.
Peat looks away towards the ground feeling a little
deflated, Claire had always being the one pushing
the boundaries; heading into Lismore, playing pranks
on some of the not so nice locals, even on one
occasion sneaking Peat into Mr. Monsel's chemistry
classroom and setting up a few pranks, but on this
occasion her concern for Peat far out weight any
jovial sentiment and Peat knew she'd made valid
points.
"You're right, you are, but I gave my word to go with
him on this for six months and then that's that, it's
over! ...Anyhow next year we'll be in college and I
just thought... well, I was wondering if you'd made
up your mind which one you're going attend?"

Claire lets a big sigh, "Well if Tom and yourself thinks it's okay then I suppose I shouldn't be too concerned I just don't wanna see anything bad happen to you, you know…"

Peat smiles and stares unwittingly at Claire for a moment before directing his eyes to the ground saying, "Yah, I know."

Claire then picks up on the matter of college, "…I'm not sure where I'm going to college but it would be nice if we ended up close to each other maybe…"

Looking up from the ground, Peat responds a little awkwardly, "Yah definitely, it would. And your grades are really good, if you got into the nursing college you were talking about, it would be really close to the place I was thin---, Aaamm but whatever you want… oh, did I show you the study Jim prepared for me in his old parlor? Wait till you see it."

Over the next few months things were relatively normal for the quartet; Claire was doing very well in school and was on course to get the scholarship grant which would enable her to attend the nursing college near to where Peat had planned to study. Jim was receiving full cooperation from Peat. And Tom was content that his son was both happy and safe, and therefore could go about his own work without constantly fretting for his son's welfare. As for Peat, well he was enjoying the things that he was learning and the incredible skills

80

and personal tutelage he was receiving from masters across various disciplines, each with his own ethos. Peat was also really happy about the manner in which his relationship was progressing with Claire. Although Peat didn't pick up on it, Jim was not favorably disposed to Peat's growing attachment to Claire which he had taken a sudden interest in after the happenings of that watershed weekend. Indeed, Jim would often use his lessons to stress the need for self-sacrifice and detachment in serving others and would regularly rant at length about the nobility of a celibate lifestyle. Peat soaked all this up but that it was directed at him personally, never dawned on him. The entire orientation of Peat's combat training was based on self-defense not aggression and this was stressed at both a theoretical and practical level. The months rolled on and the training became more intense as the final month approached, Jim became noticeably agitated and a little jumpy which was, for those who were used to his controlled and self-assured manner, very unnerving.

But Peat had truly excelled at every aspect of his formation, his agility and strength reached an incredible level and even Tom could not get over how much "his little boy had filled in," as he would put it. But perhaps Peat's greatest advancement was in his combat abilities, something which was only seen by Jim, Peat and the select trainers that were brought in to instruct the novice. One bright day in late June, just as the six months were about to run their course, Jim requested Peat spend the day with him next Friday.

He informed him that this would mark the last day of his formal training and, as Jim put it; "I'll explain all."

Tom would be away on an errand for the entire day and Jim was to drop Peat home that evening. Peat agree without hesitation, he was excited at the thought of Jim finally coming clean about why he had bought all the stuff, brought in so many experts and dedicated half a year of his time and energy to this most unorthodox of courses.

But while on his way home that evening he realized next Friday was Claire's birthday, "Shit," he blurted out without thinking and immediately Tom looked at him sternly saying, "Peter!" Peat responded apologetically, "Oh sorry Dad!"

Thinking on it he figured that if he could be finished by three o'clock and back to his house by 4.30pm at the latest, then he'd have time to set up the house for Claire's birthday before she arrived. Peat had already finished the musical box which worked like a charm, he's also added a personalized engraving at the base which read; *'Happy 18th Claire! Love, Peat.'* The final week of the course proved the most arduous, there was no longer any study with Jim, Peat's daily activities consisted more or less entirely of practical testing designed to evaluate his proficiency in every area. Aside from the hours of academic study Peat had done under the guidance of Jim, his practical lessons came from experts in a whole range of disciplines including; martial arts, fencing, wrestling and pugilism to name but a few. Now Jim had arranged for most of them to return at the end of the course to assess the young trainee. Over four days, Monday to Thursday of the last week Peat was visited by nearly all his old instructors who administered frightfully demanding physical challenges to test the lad. Each expert had their own means of testing Peat's abilities but incredibly the young man was not only able to keep pace but actually excel. Peat had truly become a person of extreme combat capabilities and yet all Peat's training was geared towards preventing violence and using force for defense only, indeed Jim had dedicated many hours seeking to lay a noble bed on which Peat's newly acquired skills could take root. Jim was always on the lookout for opportunities to cultivate positive and lofty ideals in his young student and on the surface at any rate the young trainee's demeanor remained its typical reserved and self-deprecating self.

The structure of Jim's course was far from haphazard, and there were clearly certain areas that received a good deal of attention. One area in particular received more focus than any other and that was that of swordsmanship. Now most experts came for a few days and left after some intensive training but Jim had manage to get one of Japan's most famous swordsman, Master Miyamoto Takeshi, to come and tutor Pear for three straight weeks. This happened about four months into the course and proved to be a turning point for Peat personally; Takeshi's influence on him was immense. During Miyamoto's stay Peat lived in Jim's house and every hour was accounted for; rest periods, meal times and training. Peat found himself continually surprised during the three weeks he spent under Master Takeshi's instruction; the quiet and unassuming manner of the elderly man seemed to contrast the reputation Jim spoke of. Unlike the others, who seemed to focus primarily on their respective field's Master Takeshi, speaking only elementary English, began his time with Peat by seeking to foster in him a sense of stewardship towards living things while also placing an emphasis on detachment. Peat found a deep connection to much of what Miyamoto said, it resonated at a most profound level with him. Peat also admired the serenity of this old sage. Now, although Peat simply presumed that Jim had hired Master Takeshi as he did the others, to come and train him, this was not the case. The link between Jim and Master Miyamoto was a far more substantive than that of monetary enticement. As a young priest Jim had been sent on the missions to Japan and was there during the 1940s, he'd experienced first-hand much of the suffering endured by the locals living in Kagoshima. Jim had developed a good reputation in the Kagoshima Prefecture and was well regarded among all the locals, not just the small Christian community. The enterprising cleric was responsible for; the founding of two schools, the development of the fishing industry and the establishment of a community bank which provided loans to local indigenous businesses. One of the families to benefit from the industrious priest's initiatives was Master Miyamoto's brother's family. It was through these connections and using his father's networks that Jim was able to request help from Master Miyamoto who, as a matter of honor, ceded to leave his picturesque alpine hermitage in Kamikōchi at the bequest of his brother and travel, under the auspices of Jim's father, to the rural countryside of America. When he had first arrived Master Miyamoto spent almost three hours speaking to Jim (who was competent in Japanese) and then for the following three weeks the clergyman effectively disappeared to his room, entrusting his oriental guest with his young novice. The thought of having to spend three weeks cut off from contact with Claire was upsetting for Peat but these were the conditions Jim laid down, and in fact even Tom was asked to keep contact to a minimum. The first day proved to be a real eye opener for Peat, he had expected to follow on his earlier sword training at which he'd become rather adapt. Early that morning Peat came into the study to meet his new teacher for the first time only to find Mater Miyanmoto on

the ground meditating. At first Peat gave a small
cough to announce his presence but as there was no
reaction he simply presumed that he too was meant
to join in. Now while Peat was used to prayerful
mediation at intervals throughout the day, this
prolonged silence eventually saw him become
restless, but Mater Miyamoto seemed completely
phlegmatic on the floor in the lotus position his eyes
closed. Peat had attempted to emulate his teacher
for the first hour or so but after this he had given
up and became increasingly frustrated by the
unresponsive Mater Miyamoto, who's only apparent
movement consisted in rhythmic breathing and an
occasional display of eloquent hand signals.
Finally Peat decided to break the silence and he said
"Hello, I'm Peat." but no reply came.
After a few more minutes Peat spoke again, "Hello
Sir I'm Peter Black." but again there came no
response.
Peat felt as though his teacher's lack of a response
was itself a type of chiding and so he kept silent.
Over two hours passed and Peat had become
restless to the point of frustration, it was
approaching midday and having exhausted all his
customary self-control and courtesy Peat decided
to break the silence once again before he totally
lost his cool, "Hi, I'm Peat," he stated with a firm
introductory tone.
Following a short pause, which to Peat felt like an
eternity, the sensei moved his hands and holding the
86

right hand with the palm turned outwards in front of the chest and joining the thumb and forefinger he opened his eyes and smiled at Peat and bowing his head slightly he said, "Dharma." Peat smiled back and made a mental note to look up the meaning of the word 'Dharma,' but in all honesty at this point he was just terrified that his teachers would close his eyes again and go back into a trance like state. But to his relief Master Miyamoto rose to his feet and with the exhort, "Time," he made his way out of the house towards Jim's gymnasium with Peat following closely behind.

After entering the barn Master Miyamoto turned to Peat and summarized the morning plan, "Every morning center self, harmony. Then only can advance!"

This routine was very different to the rushed urgency which all the other trainers had employed, even Peat's study assignments set by Jim would be accompanied with tightest of deadlines. Peat, while dutifully accepting what was being said, inwardly felt frustrated that every morning would be 'wasted' sitting in silence. The next few hours were the most physically and mentally grueling that Peat had ever endured. There were no breaks except to take on some water and go to the toilet, all the exercises were designed to strengthen Peat's equilibrium but all the energetic youth wanted to do was show off what he'd learnt in combat training over the previous four months. Peat feared that

Master Takeshi might have underestimated his
abilities and desired to prove to him that he could
handle more advance things than balancing
exercises. Master Miyamoto seemed solely
concerned at this point with Peat's ability to
balance. So, for instance, in one of the exercises
Miyamoto had Peat stand uniped on one end of an
elevated narrow plank of wood for prolonged
periods of time occasional throwing objects for him
to catch while keeping his balance. Once Peat had
perfected one task Miyamoto would usually make
some slight alternation and retest Peat. For
instance, after Peat had managed to perfectly cross
an elevated narrow plank of wood without falling he
would have to do likewise with a jar of water on his
head. And this was to be the routine for the first
four days of Peat's training under Master Miyamoto;
close to five hours of silent meditation in the
morning and equipoising activities from the
afternoon till late at night. And through it all, Peat
bottled up mounting frustrations which included;
being cut off from contact with Claire, the thought
of doing hours of balancing exercises for over two
more weeks, the fact that he was being taught by
allegedly the "greatest swordsman of the century"
(as Jim had claimed) and yet he'd seen nothing from
this timid little man that would justify such an
accolade. These and other little things like the
short rest periods during the day and the bland
vegetarian dishes prepared by Master Miyamoto

that he had to eat, were all pent-up inside Peat. The frustrated youth reached boiling point on the fifth day of training, it had already been an arduous few hours, Peat was feeling rather weak from the low sugar intake over preceding days and the long hours of difficult exercises and on top of this Peat had a poor night's sleep staying in the room next to that of Master Takeshi who snored loud enough to alarm any otolaryngologist or resting neighbor. Peat had just managed to again successfully walk across a narrow plank of wood suspended six foot off the barn floor with a jar of water on his head while holding a long pole which had two buckets of water on each end, and all without spilling a drop.

The sweat was flowing down his forehead as he reached the end of the narrow plank and tossing off the pole he was carrying and putting the jar on the ground, Peat jumped down in frustration, "There, done", Peat said as he clasped his hands to his legs, leaning over and breathing heavily. "Good, good, again," Miyamoto said.

Peat raised up his face remaining hunched over and out of breath, looking at his instructor's emotionless face he lost his self-control and snapped back at him...

"No, not again... I've done it! My balance is perfect, I have total 'equilibrium'. You're meant to be training me to fight and all we do is this nonsense day in, day out, non-stop and for what, you're meant to be like, like the best swordsman alive and, like aaaa...I don't know..."

After the outburst Peat feels drained emotionally and simply sighs as his temper dissipates. The teacher simply stands there poker faced, a picture of calmness, staring at Peat. Peat feels really awkward and a little ashamed.

Then joining his fingers together making a pyramid with his hands Master Takeshi gives a subtle grin as if he'd been expecting this all along he responds saying, " 'perfect balance', hum.. Show me!" as he points with his right hand towards a long black blanket in the corner.

Peat makes his way over to the blanket, a little nervous because of the uncharacteristic insubordination he just exhibited and also worried about what might be going to follow - did he just make a bad situation worst he wondered? Peat unwrapped the blanket to find about a dozen bokkens, of various types.

"Bring over," Master Takeshi summoned waving his hand.

Peat laid them at his sensei's feet. Leaning down the Master picked two ligneous long-swords from the pile and handed one to Peat along with a scabbard to tie around his waist. Now Peat was really nervous and regretting his outburst, as he strapped the sheath around his waist he stood wishing that he was still walking over the plank carrying water instead of preparing to face this apparent legend. Master Takeshi directed Peat to copy him in taking a water filled jar and stand on one end of the elevated wooden plank. Peat did as he was told and stood on the opposite end of the long plank placing the water filled jar atop his head just as Master Takeshi had done.

In a calm soft voice Miyamoto explained, "Cross other side, spill not one drop!"

Peat's nervousness grew as he stood looking down at the hay covered ground, then in an attempt at self-motivation Peat recalled his grievances and convinced himself this was his opportunity to show this master swordsman that he could more than hold his own. This self-affirmation help Peat subdue his fears and focus his determination on proving himself. Peat had been in training just over four months by the time Master Takeshi arrived and already he had been visited by many experts in swordplay and under each he had excelled. Reflecting on this, the young trainee was able to rouse his confidence speaking numerous reassuring affirmations to himself: "This is just a wooden stick you've trained with steel swords,' and so on... After about a minute of quite meditation Master Takeshi suddenly opened his eyes and let a loud, forceful bellow, "Hajimari" which was followed by a graceful bow.

Peat attempted to replicate the obeisance only to have the jar fall to the ground spilling all the water. Red faced, Peat jumped down and refilled the jar and again formalities were followed but this time Peat survived the courtesy bow and manage to make his way out about three foot along the narrow plank carefully balancing the jar on his head, while keeping his eyes fixed on the approaching Master Takeshi. As his sensei approached in a surprisingly relaxed and temperate manner Peat drew his sword and carefully postured his body ready to strike, hoping his teacher would over-commit and it would be simply a matter of knocking the bucket off his head but Master Takeshi did not flinch as he continued to approached. Peat panicked lunging forward with his bokkan, the moment he'd reach full expanse he knew he connected with nothing but air! The realization that he'd missed his target had just come to him when he felt a forceful dart to the outside of his left knee cap and then before he even had cognition of what exactly had happened Peat was lying on the hay below the plank and Master Takeshi was standing the far end of the plank.

Then in an assertive voice Miyamoto said, "Again!" By the time the surprise of how quickly he had been dispatched wore off, Peat finds himself standing once again at the opposite end of the board waiting for his sensei to give the signal. Then Peat suddenly felt a surge of energy, months of training and he didn't even pose a challenge... this enraged Peat and he resolved at that moment to keep going no matter how long it took until he made it across to the other side.

After over three hours of back to back attempts Master Takeshi still stood atop the plank of wood calling down to Peat, "Again!"

Tom had long since gone home and it was approaching midnight but Peat was nothing if not determined and after each attempt he sought to modify his strategy somewhat and learn from his mistakes and indeed there was signs of improvement. He eventually managed to stand toe to toe with his renowned teacher forcing two to three sword sequences before being sent plummeting to the ground. Hours had passed and Peat felt that he'd exhausted all the sporting strategies; he thought to himself that perhaps charging at Miyamoto might be enough to unsettle the pro and cause him to drop the water vessel which sat atop his head. They both bowed carefully and as always Master Takeshi treaded steadily towards Peat's end of the plank, hands by his side, and his bokken resting in its sheath. Suddenly Peat charged shouting at his antagonist and swinging his sword violently. The master swordsman let out a forceful shout and hurled his bokken towards the oncoming novice shattering the tick glassed water jar which had previously survived many falls onto the hay below. Stunned by the sudden spatter of water and the sound of the shattering glass Peat lost his footing and once more found himself prostrated on the hay below.

Master Takeshi, totally unfazed by the incident, stood once more at his targeted end calling down to Peat, "Clean up glass, then, again!"

A dejected Peat cleaned up the broken glass, took another water jar and filling it to the brim as he made his way to his end of the plank.

By this stage it was now nearly three in the morning and Peat, feeling both miserable and dishonorable knowing he'd allowed desperation to make him act in a boorish manner, uttered a heartfelt submission; "I can't do it, I can't beat you. I'm just... I'm too tired; I just give up, ok!" There was a prolonged silence, Peat felt his eyes creeping shut out of tiredness when suddenly the wise old man asked, "What is aim? We will think on what is aim."

Miyamoto then closed his eyes seemingly going into a trance like state, as if meditating. Peat stood there pensively, he knew he'd just being given a clue but he was so tired and disheartened that he found it hard to recall what the objective actually was. "Getting to the other side is the aim," Peat murmurs to himself repeatedly like a mantra for nearly three minutes until all of a sudden he is filled with an uncontrollable rush of joy and loudly exclaims, "I got it!"

Peat then opens his heavy eyes and immediately Master Takeshi shouts, "Hajimari" and follows with a slight graceful bow and commences to walk steadily towards Peat along the very narrow board.

94

Peat takes two steps forward and stops, standing motionless his bokken undrawn.

Finally the two come face to face at which point Master Takeshi slowly raises his right hand up away from the handle of his undrawn sword and very gently takes hold of the front of Peat's shirt. Peat does exactly the same firmly gripping his Master garment in front of the chest, then with a grunt from the teacher both commence to agilely maneuver their bodies around each other, using one another as counter weights until both parties stand on the opposite side, slowly both withdrew their hands and proceeded to the two ends of the plank without spilling a drop! For Peat this incident became the focal point of deep reflection for a number of weeks and sparked a process of introspection for him which gradually led to a fundamental shift in the way Peat understood and approached his training, seeing it now anew within a larger process of personal formation. Peat never felt that his new combat abilities had impacted upon his peaceful manner and yet when pushed he found that mentally he harbored presuppositions of confrontation and strife. After that enlightening fifth day of training, Peat began to treasure the quite time Master Takeshi set aside each morning and he used this as an opportunity for some honest introspection. Peat learned many profoundly holistic life lessons under the tutelage of Master Takeshi and from the end of week one onwards the sensei dedicated countless hours teaching Peat mastery of the sword and countless defensive and offensive combat skills. While he would never say so, Miyamoto was thoroughly surprised at how acquiescent and prehensile a student Peat was.

- Chapter Five -

On Friday morning, the final day of Jim's
extraordinary course, after dropping Peat off at
the estate, Tom departed on his errand to the
Windy City not due to return till Saturday night.
Peat felt so excited he found it hard to contain
himself; today was the day when Jim would finally
explain what sparked this whole unconventional
program of study and training, and more to the
point, why all his efforts revolved around him (i.e.
Peat).   Ignorance of Jim's motives aside, Peat was
very grateful for all he had gained during the last
six months in terms of his own personal, intellectual
and physical development. There was also another
reason for Peat's excitement on this beautifully
sunny July day, and that was: Claire's birthday.
He'd left the musical box parceled on the sitting
room table and planned, at long last, to ask her out
after she'd opened it.
Around eight that morning, seeing Peat approach
the house on foot and Tom driving out the estate
laneways, Jim shouted from the veranda where he
had been lounging with a cigar and glass of his
favourite Irish whiskey, "Peat my lad, today is the
day!"

The animated cleric made his way from the porch towards Peat, looking around him as if he was guarding an important secret, then as he approached closer he said, in a much softer voice, "Come on inside you'll need a good breakfast before you see what I have to show you, a revelation of galactic proportions... huumm; quite literally in fact!" Peat, a little caught unaware, answers, "aaa... I've already had breakfast."

Jim puts his arm around him and leads him inside briskly. Now there was a certain smell of cigar smoke which constantly came from Jim's house but this odor was particularly potent today as Peat entered. Peat glanced across the corridor into Jim's own private study and he could see a mountain of books piled up on and around his solid mahogany brown leather Georgian desk. From this, the pre breakfast cigar and aperitif; Peat could only assume that Jim had pulled another 'all-nighter.'

The preparation of breakfast by the cleric was a comical spectacle, "I know I have..." the absentminded clergyman mused to himself as he pulled back a clump of papers lying in a pile at one end of the Kitchen.

"Here we are...,"he said opening a fridge which was tucked in under what was once a kitchen counter but now in effect served as one long book shelf. He took out some cheese and smelling it stuffed it quickly back into the refrigerator and grabbed a bottle of milk and closed the fridge.

He then went to the overhead cabinets opening three presses before finding the compartment in which the bowls were kept, "Are you sure you're not hungry now Peat , you'll need a strong stomach for what I have to tell you?"

Still disgusted at the sight of the moldy cheese, Peat smiled politely responding, "Oh no thanks Jim I amm…, had a good feed at home, thanks."

As he looked for a spoon in the drawers Jim remarked light-heartedly, "Ahh yes, Tom is big on breakfast isn't he, yes. You know I've never seen a man with such an appetite."

Jim then plunges the cereal bowl into an industrial size bag of muesli before sitting at a small circular table in the middle of the room and pointing to a cabinet above Peat's head he requests, "Oh Peat, reach up there and get me a jar of honey, good man."

Peat places the jar on the table as Jim gestures for him to sit down and then speaks, "Peat they think I'm half cracked you know..," Jim says looking intently at Peat across the table as the sense of blitheness leaves the atmosphere. Peat is surprised at this sudden change in tempo and responds hastily, "Oh no Jim, I mean who thinks that…, I mean like…"

Jim leans in towards Peat and in a firm and sober voice say's "Peat!" Jim might as well have said 'cut the shit' because Peat felt totally exposed.

"Ok, but I mean in fairness you can't blame us, you spent months in your room, only coming out to look up at the stars. Then you set up a whole training camp just for me and like..., I mean I really appreciate it, I really got a lot out of it but... you haven't left the estate in months and you must have spent a fortune on all the stuff in the barns and...I mean the experts you brought in.

And the hours I had to spend studying and then the training, 'training...' but training for what?" Peat begins to feel a little angry as he continues, "...And I mean like I went along with everything, I made a promise and I kept my side of the bargain.

Tom and Claire are convinced you've flipped and I...well I...I kept my promise, I worked like a dog for the last six months, day and night..., I mean I loved it don't get me wrong and I am grateful, but what was it all for...what happened that weekend of the storm?"

Peat looks at Jim in anticipation of an answer which would satisfy his long held curiosity. Jim leans back on his chair and sighs before responding, "We did have an agreement and you were true to your word. Over the last six months you went with me despite the intense nature of..., I'll admit it,...of this *bizarre* arrangement. Believe me when I say I didn't see any other way. You know me Peat..., I've always honored the autonomy of all disciplines, in particular the hard sciences. Tirelessly I've always sought to empirically verify my hypothesizes..., well one night nearly a year ago now I was on my observatory deck when I caught sight of a small light, something falling from the sky. At first I thought it was a comet or some manner of debris but as I followed its descent using my telescope I could see that this phenomenon was omitting a flashing light. A little surprised I wondered if I wasn't seeing things after eating that God awful tuna sandwich your father left for my tea and... I suppose... I may have had one or two many digestifs. At any rate, I gave the lenses a good clean and looked again to see the same tiny celestial light flying across the sky but getting ever closer to the ground, in fact it got so close it seemed as though it were going to crash down somewhere in the vicinity, perhaps a few miles away from the estate. Then the most peculiar thing happened, it changed direction! It was as if it were being controlled, operated I mean... and even more excitingly, its new trajectory saw it coming towards the estate. It picked up speed... I gazed through the telescope as it got closer and closer until I could actually see better with my naked eyes. I was amazed; it crashed onto the estate near the ground by that old stone wall...you know where I'm talking about. Well I can tell you I got out into the yard as quickly as possible... As I got closer to where it had come down I saw this most beautiful red light pulsating from behind the far side of the wall... oh it was so strong I couldn't get over it... When I reached it I found a little silver ball. At first I poked at it with a stick but nothing happened so I decided to move in for a closer look although the light it gave off made it difficult to observe closely. Crouching down I could see these wonderful markings on it, they were like nothing I'd seen before, symbols of some sort. But anyway, I went to pick it up, well, I had no sooner touched it than the flashing stopped. Oh Peter... it was so exciting! I brought it straight into the lab. I must have spent hours running tests simply seeking to establish what the object was made of but I couldn't, it was something other than metal, but before I could run more intrusive tests the ball suddenly transmogrified in front of my very eyes, all by itself it took the shape of a cube. Then from an opening which appeared on the top of the cube out came periodic flashes of white light. I was stunned. It took me a few seconds but eventually I came to my senses, there was something about those flashes, the sequence struck me as familiar. I got a torch and turned off the lab lights and bingo I knew it immediately, the machine was using light signals to communicate, you know; optical communication and all that... anyway the reason I recognized the flashes was because it was using Morse code, imagine, Morse code! Ahem, anyway, I obviously presumed at that stage that this must be some type of covert military devise but after I transcribed the message...amm...well..."

Jim looks at Peat who is totally engrossed in what he's being told and pauses for a moment. Peat meanwhile comes to the realization that for the first time his garrulous teacher is stuck for words. "What did it say?" Peat asks inquisitively.

Jim sighs profoundly and then looks at Peat with a steely determination before standing up and moving to one end of the kitchen.

Keeping his back to the confused lad and gazing up at the corner ceiling Jim continues, "Peat I've…., I've always been frank with you and there's no point in me stopping now. The message basically warned of a pending battle for this planet's future and, it also referred to civilizations beyond this world."

Peat is mesmerized by what he has heard coming from Jim's mouth and is unaware that his face is conveying an expression of complete incredulity.

Reading Peat's expression of disbelief Jim exclaimed with mild indignation, "Well of course it sounds deranged, I suspected it to be some sort of ruse but technology like this just doesn't exist…anyway that's not the whole thing, the message concluded with a plea for help and response instructions followed by contingent coordinates and a time for the next message. Well you know me I couldn't resist; I had to know…., so as per the instructions I flashed the special code into the sky the following night at the allotted time, actually I parked the car on the hill slope behind the house and flashed the high beams… I felt rather foolish I don't mind telling you. But anyway, that done I still had to wait for over three months before the next message was due to arrive..., I mean I still didn't believe it I..., I spent the next few months trying to work out what had happened considering all possibilities and explanations until finally the night arrived... I was still didn't really believe anything would happen but I suppose by that stage I'd become *a little*..., oh well alright, I'd become *totally* obsessed with the matter, I just couldn't figure it out. But I felt that once designated date passed and nothing happened my doubts would be confirmed and I could finally get back to normal. I mean in the first month I thought something might happen... I even went so far as to check out the location of where the next message was to arrive, it was in a dense wood just past the old cavalry fort. Well... on the fateful night there was a really bad storm, you remember?"

Peat gives a stuttering, ""Ye..ye..yes, yes I do."

Jim turns and moves close to Peat, "Well what can I say, it landed exactly where it was meant to, Peter I tested both messaging devices whatever they comprised of I couldn't find it on the Periodic table, I've no doubt but that there origins lie outside Earth! But that's not the bombshell, Peter wait till I show you the second message!"

Standing upright Jim puts his hand on Peat's shoulder, "Remember now Peter, everything we've done over the last six months, our whole

104

arrangement was built on you trusting me and for
my part I want you to know, before I show you this,
that I only ever wanted to help you to get to a
stage where you'd be ready to make your own
choice. Whatever you choose, I'll support you in
that!"

Peat simply sits there looking blankly at Jim
thinking to himself that Tom and Claire were right
all along, the poor old man has taken complete leave
of his senses.

Then with an air of defiance Jim makes his way
towards the door, leaving an untouched bowl of
honey covered muesli on the table and says loudly,
"Right then, let's go and have a look, shall we!"

Peat follows but in a state of shock and
bewilderment, trying desperately to come to terms
with the apparently inescapable fact that Jim has
indeed gone totally insane.

By the time they'd reached the room at the top of
the stairs Peat had finally managed to formulate a
question, "What did you mean by 'choice' Jim, what
choice...?"

Jim turned his head as he entered the room, "You
wouldn't believe me if I told you, hell I still don't
know if I fully believe it. I'll have to show you!"

Like most rooms in this grand old house there were
books everywhere, what was distinct about this
room was the number of used cups sitting around
and the numerous little piles of ash which were
mainly concentrated on and around a desk which

105

itself was submerged in stacks of papers. On the walls were star maps of constellations and astronomical surveys. In fact, the only indication that this was a bed room was a dressing table upon which there were some framed photos of Jim's family and friends, and a bed which lay inconspicuously in the corner of this large attic-like room. Jim went to the end of his bed and bending down pulled out a small black case, "Here we are then," he said to himself aloud.

"You keep the devices under your bed?" Peat asked with a hint of derision.

"As good a place as any... Now here we are." Jim states as he picks out two small objects from the case and places them on a desk in the center of the room.

Peat looks intently at both and after a moment or two he reaches out to take hold of the ovoid device but Jim anxiously says, "Stop! If I were you I'd try this one first."

And picking up the sphere he tosses the device to Peat who is more than a little taken aback by Jim's insouciant attitude in handling one of the devices, compared to his seeming wariness of the later.

"See the symbols?" Jim asked Peat who is examining the gadget closely.

"Yah," Peat responds holding the sphere up to his face for a closer inspection.

"Well, they actually form a code which allowed me to activate the second device," Jim reveals.

Approaching the table and leaning in over the device Jim pressed in on some of the slight protrusions at the base of the ovoid and looking up at Peat before taking a few steps back from the table he says, "I hope you're ready for this."

Peat then moved closer to the table and glared in at the ovoid as it began to transfigure on the table, as it reached its final imaginal stage the device looked like a four legged spider with an antenna-like pole sticking out from the upper tip. Peat was fascinated by this and as he leaned in even closer he noticed a coloration had become manifest at the tips of the antenna and without warning an explosion of light burst out. Taken by surprise Peat recoiled and as he staggered backwards, blinded by the light's brightness, he slipped and fell rearwards onto his back while releasing the sphere into the air. Jim moved to helped Peat to his feet and with a devilish grin on his face whispered into Peat's ear, "Would you believe the same thing happened to me!"

Both stood there staring at the wondrous display unfolding before their eyes then after about thirty seconds Jim, showing his experience, said, "Right, here it is...," and placing his arm across Peat's shoulder he led him backwards a few steps and then the long cylindrical column of light dissolved out, covering most of the room in a thin sheet of light. This was followed by the emergence of a three dimensional figure from the center of this disc-like sheet of light; it was of a tall man with a long robe covering his body, his face was chiseled and looked worn and aged. Both Peat and Jim stood silent, the former in a state of amazement, the latter, more in a state of anticipation at what was to come.

The dyad listened carefully as the mysterious figure began to speak, "Greetings to you Peter Black. I am Patriarch Donamis Ron, protector of the planet Tryloss and fellow guardian of the planetary union of Koinonia. The selflessness you have demonstrated in answering our call is truly worthy of the highest acclaim. I now implore you to listen to my words carefully, this account of events was passed down to me by my late father, Teea Ron, and as fate would have it, is now of the gravest concern to you! Far beyond your home Galaxy lies the planet of Tryloss, our richness in natural resources and gifted scientists saw our race become the first to master interstellar travel, as our technological advancement continued, the limits of our space exploration continually lessened. Soon we had established commerce and trade with many of our neighboring planets and in mutual exchange we learnt much from each other. We flourished as a people and soon other planetary civilizations learnt from our technology and over many lifetimes the process of galacticization occurred; trade routes opened and inter-planetary travel became common place with new ideas, languages and customs being learnt throughout the galaxy. However many societies feared invasion from foreign forces and so the era of military proliferation began. Soon skirmishes arose between small planets on the galaxy's periphery but there was neither precedent nor any political will for the wealthier planet's to intervene. But the plight of the planets on the galaxy's edge spread as more and more societies became embroiled in strife. As the violence spread many planets, ravaged by war, sued for peace but their enemies did not want an accord and refused to relent. In desperation they turned to us for help, Tryloss reluctantly answered the entreaties and a coalition called Koinonia was formed to restore the peace. Demanding a cessation of hostility my forefathers led the small coalition of planets but the warmongering continued. Going to war Tryloss' superior weapons ensured a quick, all be it brutal, defeat for many of the belligerent forces. After much loss of life on both sides the peace was restored once again. While Tryloss' military superiority was unquestioned at that time all knew that this would not always be the case and so at the behest of the then Patriarch, the inter-planetary union of Koinonia was permanently established. As time passed the peace and prosperity enjoyed by planets in the Koinonia union became a model of peaceful co-existence throughout the galaxy. For an age many of my ancestors enjoyed living under this blanket of peace and prosperity but unfortunately this would not last. During my grandfather's early rule one of the greatest and at the same time, one of the most ill-fate things happened; our planetary explorers were operating well beyond the established frontiers and came across a small unrecognized ship floating in open space. After they secured this craft, the Tar Limatu as it became known, they found it to be crewless. It was brought back to Tryloss and became the subject of extensive examination by our engineers and scientists. The technology was like nothing we had ever seen before, the whole ship operated by a type of bio-neuro mechanics. But whatever the promise of advancement that lay in the ship's technology it would pale against the discovery of what was being stored within the craft's hull. Close to the back was discovered a concealed room in which there were hundreds of glass tubes. Inside each glass capsule there was a single tiny creature, a new species had been discovered. They would become known as Sumboi. Our biologists were fascinated with the creatures; their oval shaped heads and multiple miniscule tentacles, with single organic needle which could be protracted from the core. The creatures were sustained in a type of primordial fluid but when our experts sought to remove them from this then unknown substance they decayed almost instantaneously. While kept within the liquid, examination of the Sumboi did lead to a greater understanding of these life-forms, but it was the ship itself which initially yielded the most promising

110

findings and the resulting advancement in our own bio-mechanical technology was truly staggering. The ruler of Tryloss however, my grandfather Patriarch Feelexus Ron, grew impatient with the examination of the Sumboi..., you see both his sons had become obsessed with learning more about these creatures. The Patriarch had only two children both of whom he cherished dearly, and each, in his own way, had a brilliant mind. Teea Ron, my father, was the younger of the two siblings, a mild mannered child he spent most his time in study. Greeto Ron, the elder, was far more confident in himself and held a deep attachment for Tryloss' traditions and grandeur. From their earliest years both brothers had been close to one another, they collaborated on everything and their synergy had served them well in all their endeavours, they were truly a credit to their father. But obsessed by the Sumboi they had become reclusive seeking night and day to garner more information about these mysterious creatures. Fearing this pursuit was taking ruinous hold of his sons Feelexus reassigned both of them to the more promising study of the Tar Limatu itself which was constantly revealing new secrets. However word reached the Patriarch that his sons were disregarding his new commission and, in defiance of him, still pursuing their study of the Sumboi. In a fit of rage Feelexus ordered that all the remaining Sumboi be destroyed. When the brothers heard word of this they were distressed,

111

for you see they were convinced that the Sumboi were the Tar Limatu's most precious cargo and not, as their father had decreed; some 'parasitic creature.' The night before the extermination was purportedly scheduled to be carried out the two brothers secretly made their way into the Sumboi chamber with the intention of preserving a few of the creatures by removing them to their own private labs. Misfortune struck though as Greeto dropped one of the incubating capsules which shattered on the ground leaving the small creature struggling for life on the floor. Then, ignoring the protestations of his brother, Greeto reached down to pick up the decaying creature making, for the first time, direct physical contact with the organism. The instance Greeto gripped the creature he felt a sudden sting but when he released the Sumboi it used its powerful gripping tentacles to attach itself firmly to Greetos's skin after which, as if by intuition, it crawled with great speed up his arm and reaching the nape of his neck the Sumboi injected its needle-like rod. The creature then dissolved in through the needle. This apparently all happened so quickly as to make my father's efforts to help his brother futile. He witnessed as Greeto experienced the most tremendous pain, falling to the ground in state of violent convulsions. Ironically, it was in the hope of helping his son, who lay suffering excruciating pain for two days, that the Patriarch ordered all the

112

creatures to be preserved. To the astonishment of Tryloss' best physicians Greeto failed to respond to any form of treatment. After two days the affliction seemed to simply stop, it was if nothing had happened, but such was not the case! Despite the most persistent and forceful requests, Greeto refused any examinations and while alone with his brother they discovered the full extent of what had happened to him. As eventually became apparent to us all, the creatures are symbionts; joining with a sufficiently advanced organism for mutual benefit. The effects on Greeto was both wondrous and terrifying, his strength, agility, senses…, in fact every aspect of his physiology was advanced phenomenally. But this was not all…, at will Greeto found he was able to generate an almost impenetrable bio-suit, a high functioning epidermis which secreted from the pores of his skin. This suit had other impressive capabilities also and when Greeto demonstrated the full extent of these to his kin, Feelexus and Teea shared in the initial awe and excitement. It all too soon however became apparent that Greeto's mind was unable to handle the new state in which he found himself. His outstanding physical and combact abilities fed a growing appetite for power and prestige. He now looked with contempt at the coequal and congenial relations Tryloss had built up with other planets. Over time Greeto began to espouse discriminatory and elitist doctrines which argued for raising

Tryloss and its native peoples above other civilizations. Greeto found no shortage of followers, especially from among the ranks of military officers. At the same time his fraternal bonds with his brother were almost shattered and he had become estranged to his father who by now was critically ill. Teea Ron knew his brother was unable to cope with being in union with the Sumboi and pleaded with him to allow the royal surgeons to attempt an extraction, but all to no avail... The ailing Feelexus along with Tryloss' Governing Council feared the instability Greeto's antics were causing across the galaxy and, although it broke his heart, the Patriarch publically issued a proclamation declaring that Teea Ron would succeed him, not Greeto as had been expected according to our established tradition of primogeniture. Unsurprisingly, Greeto Ron and his supporters attempted a coup which was suppressed with brutal efficiency, however the power of Greeto's suit was seriously underestimated and he daringly escaped from Tryloss' capital Ros Crae only to rally more supporters to his cause. This blow to the government of Tryloss was compounded soon after by the death of the Patriarch and the ascension of the young and inexperienced Teea Ron. A civil war ensued which engulfed our world and indirectly resulted in numerous interplanetary wars across the galaxy. The ranks of rebels swelled, due in no small part to the fame of their supposedly indestructible

114

leader Greeto, and despite inferior resources they gained the upper-hand in the conflict until, after nearly a year of ferocious fighting, the overthrow of the Patriarch Teea Ron seemed all but assured. In desperation, the Patriarch, chose three of his most trusted generals to take the burden of the Sumboi onto themselves. This proved very effective; many who followed Greeto revered the uniqueness of his mysterious abilities but this illusion was shattered by the appearance of others with similar extraordinary abilities. The fall-off in support after the dilution of Greeto's grandeur increased morale among the government forces knowing they too had the famed power of the Sumboi on their side. It took another year of bloody fighting but eventually a victory by government forces was in reach, yet the cost in life had already been so great both on Tryloss and among other planets in the galaxy that Teea offered his brother favorable terms to end this costly war. Under the accord Greeto and his forces were permitted to leave the planet unhindered and, with generous supplies, they were to be given safe passage to Crastus, a remote and sparsely populated planet upon which they could settle. This treaty had many faults but prolonging the war was not an option for Teea who had already received numerous pleas for assistance from planets within the Koinonia union whose sovereignty was being threatened. After the civil war ended, Tryloss was free to restore peace to Konionia and stability gradually returned to most places within the galaxy. Everything changed however when in an act of the most treacherous malversation General Ty Uites, a trusted friend of my father, stole all the Sumboi that were placed in his charge and fled with them to Crastus which by that stage was completely under Greeto's rule. My father would live out the rest of his days regretting not having destroyed all the Sumboi when he had the chance but prudently he had divided the remaining Sumboi soon after the civil war ended and stored half of these precious creatures in a secret location unknown to General Ty Uites. Still haunted by the violence of the last civil war the Patriarch chose not to pursue the stolen Sumboi. For his part, Greeto knew well his brother still possessed many of the Sumboi along with formidable military alliances with a host of other planets in Koinonia, therefore he was careful not to put himself in a position whereby he could be openly found guilty of breaking the terms of the treaty. Meanwhile the reputation and reverence afforded to those who joined with a Sumboi grew dramatically and spread from planet to planet, they became known as Xtarons. Using this revered status Greeto managed to foster substantial influence in planets neighboring Crastus and as time passed Greeto, exploiting the fears and greed of the leaders from strategically significant planets and using grandiose displays of his power as an

Xtaron, he managed to forge significant alliances of his own. The most worrying of these was with Tryloss' old rival Piallatar, a planet of equally rich natural resources and mass wealth. Pillatarian society had long cultivated a deep festering resentment for its old enemy after Tryloss had decisively defeated it many generations prior. The promise of many Sumboi for leading figures in Pillitar's society proved irresistible to the leadership and with masterful duplicity Greeto worked his way into a position of some influence in Piallatarian society. By the time the leadership became suspicious of Greeto's intentions it was too late, a native Piallatarian, General Ilex was gifted a Sumboi and using his influence as an Xtaron, he led a coup and took control of the planet's governing body. He executed all of the council leaders along with the planet's King and proclaimed himself, the first Xtaron Pillatarian King, ruler of Pillatar. He was welcomed popularly by the masses but off course in the shadows lurked Greeto, the real mastermind behind the council's overthrow. Tactfully Greeto married into the Piallatarian elite and by the time of his death his own son, Defas, had managed to utilize all the Sumboi that his father had smuggled into the capital in carefully orchestrated push to remove Lord Ilex from power. With over a hundred Xtarons, Defas seized control of the royal palace and murdered King Ilex in the most brutal of manners. Defas then spent a considerable amount of time consolidating his grip on Pillatar before seeking to extend his authority far beyond the planet's traditional sphere of influence. Becoming an ever increasing threat, Defas began to openly use force in coercing and exploiting planets. It must be understood though that my father and Tryloss' Council leaders were of a generation still haunted by the savagery of the civil war and so refused to support the other planetary leaders of Koinonia in calling for action against the ever increasing risk posed by Defas. Without Tryloss' support other planets within the union would not act. As is now clear, failure in acting early proved costly; Pillatar grew in strength and eventually formed a formidable military alliance of planets called, Apoleia. It soon became clear that Defas would not be satisfied with small territorial gains, but by the time Teea and the Council accepted this, Apoleia had grown too strong. Confronting Defas would mean war on an unimaginable scale and so the Apoleia- Koinonia Peace Accord was signed. My father died soon after the Treaty came into effect however, since then an uneasy stalemate has existed between the planets of Koinonia and Apoleia. As Patriarch I have worked tirelessly for peace however, Defas has inherited his father's jealously and hatred. I fear a galactic war is but a matter of time.

Soon after becoming Patriarch I received reports from one of our inter-galactic probes; for the first time, a life sustaining planet was located beyond our galaxy. I thought it best to keep this planet's discovery a secret for the time being, even Tryloss' councilor were unaware of its existence. I selected a small number of leading planetary experts and commissioned them to study the planet from afar, the planet of course was Earth. Since then we have learnt much about your civilization and the planet itself. Regrettably though, word of the existence of a life sustaining extra-galactic planet leaked and spread throughout the galaxy, although as of yet Earth's exact location is still not commonly known, this is unlikely to remain so for long. You see...Earth's particular location makes it strategically very desirable for Defas' allies in the eastern quadrant, they I fear would not respect any claim of neutrality and therefore Tryloss was obliged to act on Earth's behalf. Under article 62.5 of the Apoleia-Koinonia treaty newly discovered inhabitable planets are subject to unilateral claims of affiliation from both parties. Apoleia cannot be trusted to respect Earth's independence therefore affiliation with Koinonia is the only way to safeguard your autonomy and security. But it is not simply a matter of Tryloss affiliating itself with Earth and placing it under the protection of Koinonia, Pillatarian tradition heavily influenced many aspects of the treaties' clauses and this was very much the case in matters relating to 'disputed territories lying outside the agreed domain, as indeed Earth

119

does. Accordingly, two Representatives, each one chosen by the two claimants, and of equal age, must complete the Trails, these consist of a set of challenges designed to test the Representative's body and mind in the most extreme of settings. The Trials must be carried out on the planet of Creaton. Thankfully, because Tryloss will be first to declare the discovery of Earth, we shall have first choice of Representative, although it is also because of this that we must act urgently while Earth's exact whereabouts is still unknown to Apoleia. The council and I thought it in Earth's own long term interests that the Representative be a native of the planet. Once the discovery of Earth has been officially proclaimed by Tryloss the Trials must take place within one year, by your calendar. By the time you will be listening to this message Earth's discovery along with Tryloss' claim of affiliation will have been made official. After this Earth will be monitored closely by both Koinonia and Apoleia but fear not, Defas will not act to openly breach the treaty and so Earth's fate will decide by means of the Trials."

Donamis' tone changes from proclamatory to collegial as he continues, "...What I've told you Peter Black is profound. It is unfortunate that circumstances have forced me to hasten this monumental contact between our two great planets but nonetheless, the promise of the future is bright. Along with seventy other candidates you

have selflessly put yourself at the service of all...
After seven months we will contact all the
candidates and assess each before choosing five to
travel to Tryloss in preparation for the declaration
of Earth's Representative. A warning however, you
must remember that Earth is now under observation
by not just the Koinonia but also Apoleia... therefore
do nothing that would draw attention to yourselves
as a potential representative. I advise that you
spend the next six months rigorously training,
preparing yourself both body and mind for what will
no doubt prove to be a grueling experience for the
selected candidate. I commend you for your
sacrifice and bravery."

Then the holographic display which had given such
life to Donamis' narration suddenly vanishes and the
small contraption retakes its original egg-shaped
form lying on the table as a stupefied Peat and
pensive Jim stand silently at the edge of the room.
Jim glanced over his shoulder at Peat who remains
dumbstruck in a state of shock, with a look of
disbelief plastered across his face. Raising his
eyebrows and wetting his lips Jim gently breaks the
silence, "Peter..., Peter," he whispers.

Peat turns his head slightly as if to acknowledge and
yet it's clear that his attention is far from Jim's
murmurs.

Either not picking up on this or, more likely, simply
disregarding its importance Jim continues, "...I hope
you understand that--"

Jim had no sooner started than Peat comes to life, as it were, and with righteous indignation directed at his teacher, he rages, " 'Understand!' ...I understand you've tricked me into preparing for some sort of war, I mean..., what am I even saying, that can't be real...," he points to the device on the table, "...this whole thing; it's just...," he then trails off putting his hands on top of his head and meandering aimlessly around the room in a disorientated fashion.

Jim waits a few moments and responds in a consoling tone, "Yes Peter, quite true... mea culpa. truly I'm sorry. When I responded to the original message I had suspected this was a scam and I had absolutely no inclination that it had anything to do with you..., after all the first message landed on my property! They must have confused where you lived amm..., but I venture they know quite a bit about us. But what I mean is..., look, I just wanted you to be in a position to make your own choice either way." Peat stops and moving towards the cleric in a forceful manner, "You can't be serious Father, this *is* a scam! Look, I'm sorry but the bottom line is you're being fooled...," again he points to the device on the table and raising his voice he asserts, "...that's not real!"

Reassuringly Jim raises his hands and opening out his palms, appeals to Peat, "Peter I'm sorry to have burdened you with this, it really is too much for young shoulders to carry and that's why I wanted to begin your training first, I knew you'd be skeptical and rightly so but Peat you know me... To paraphrase the great Scot's man, Sir Doyle: 'When one has eliminated all that which is impossible, then whatever remains, however improbable, must be the truth.' I examined the evidence...," pointing to the messaging device on the table, "...this technology should not exist..., this very substance should not exist, but there you have it!"

Moving towards the door with his head bowed and eyes staring at the floor, "I have to get out of here for a while, I need to think," Peat states.

As peat exits Jim calls out, "If you need me, you know where I'll be."

– Chapter Six –

Peat wondered around the estate for hours grappling with the countless implications of what he had heard. Constantly he moved back and forth between credulity and disbelief, at one moment flirting with the possibility and tapping into all the things he'd learned from Jim about astronomy, then in a flash, repudiation would rush into his mind accompanied by stern self-admonition for even considering the mere possibility. This dialectical battle raged in Peat's mind right through the morning and well into the afternoon. He visited all those places which evoked strong memories of both good and not so good times. More than anything he found himself searching for the peace of mind and relative carefreeness that he'd had upon first awakening that morning. But what he'd seen, what he'd heard could not be ignored and Peat was far too bright to accept any simple explanation which whitewashed over inconvenient realities. Jim, for his part, remained where he had indicated he would be, that is, in his room. Jim wanted to give Peat space and time to work things out on his own uninterrupted and for that reason he remained in his room. Eventually, just after five, Peat wondered into the house, in the kitchen he managed to find all the necessary things to make two cups of tea and located a pack of dark chocolate biscuits which lay in a glass press above a stack of medical journals heaped opposite the small refrigerator in the corner of the room. He then proceeded up the stairs towards the tower carrying a serving tray. As he ascended the steps he could hear music growing louder, classical music, a piece Peat recognized as familiar but unlike Jim he was not a high cultured melomaniac. Jim had often sought to impart his love of classical music to Peat but, in so far as Peat enjoyed music, his tastes were far more akin to those of his peers and he enjoyed contemporary disco and rock. As he approached the door Peat picked up the unmistakable sound of a radio which accounted for the symphonic music he was hearing, yet somehow the song was amplified. Pressing his shoulder against the door which was slightly ajar Peat quietly entered to see Jim sitting on the far side facing out the elongated glass window which gave such a beautiful, even if not full, view of the garden at the side of the house. The priest had a glass of whiskey and his car keys placed by his foot and resting on his left shoulder was the lower bout of a violin across which his jaw reclined. Peat was impressed to see the grace and speed with which the cleric drew the hair of the bow across the strings while keeping in harmony with the piece blaring from a small radio which sat on a bench next

125

to Jim's bed. Jim always kept the dials on his radio-set tuned to region's only classical station. Peat stood for a few moments absorbing the wonderful ambience stirring in the room before putting down the tray on Jim's work desk. The slight clatter of the cutlery was enough to distract Jim and he turned.

"Awee Peter, I'm first violin but..., I think the Vienna Philharmonic can handle Beethoven's Fifth without me," he said with a smile as he got to his feet.

"Aaa, tea and biscuits," Jim says with a profound sigh.

Peat knows that Jim will wait for him to broach the subject that is on both their minds but he is, for now at least, happy to let the simple chat continue.

"I didn't know you played the violin Jim."

Jim responds as he moves over to the table and takes a cup of tea in hand along with a biscuit, "Oh yes, not to toot my own horn, if you'll pardon the pun, but I'm something of a multi-instrumentalist. I once played with my college orchestra in Rome however nowadays I must content myself with a remote substitute, as you've seen... but it's enough to keep me 'sharp,' haha another paronomasia, ooo... dearie me, I am really on cue today!"

Peat reacts with his typical indulging grin while shaking his head slightly and then takes up his cup and two biscuits which he eats at some pace.

126

Noticing the speed at which Peat scoffed down the biscuits Jim asks, "Did you get the Tuna sandwiches your father left on your study desk in the old parlor?"

"No"

"Humm... well going on past experience I'd be inclined to say that's fortunate but...we can't see you go hungry. I'll be back in a minute," Jim says as he picks up the tray and moves to the door. Just as the cleric is leaving Peat tries to catch his attention, "Aaa Father, I..."

"Yes," Jim says attentively as he turns back around.

"I just hoped that we might..., aaa, well you know earlier and ammm..."

"Yes of course... I'll be two seconds and then we'll continue our tête-à-tête... but if Tom found that out that you went all day without food my fate would already be sealed!"

While on his own, Peat explored around the room and there on the table in the middle of the room laid the ovoid device, seemingly unmoved since last he'd seen it. It evoked in him feelings of trepidation and uncertainty. But he nonetheless approached the table and carefully picked up the messaging device and examined the groves on the side. It was clear that despite his apprehension Peat had become curious about this morning's revelations and hoped to get his head around it. As he stood pondering in the center of the room all of a sudden the device came alive again, flashing a bright green light. Peat looked at it and then it began to change in his hand, stunned, he tossed it on the table at which point this shape shifting gismo had fully morphed into its earlier transmitting form as if it were going to relay the same message again. But this time the holographic image displayed the frontal view of a figure wearing what appeared to be a type of mask; he also seemed to be operating a vehicle of some sort.

Almost instantaneously a loud thundering voice came from the virtual figure, however the message was broken and only bits could be discerned by Peat; "Peter Black, I am Lynextius, Satrap of Oleald and Spe--- Adviser to the Co----- and Patriarch of Tri---. Please ----en carefully. All -------- ------ ------ compromised. I repeat, all Representatives ---- ----- compromised. ----- ----- where you are! I'm enro---. ----- ---- ---- should you --- ---m, I re----t do not ---- ----m."

Then it just ceased transmitting. The obvious impromptu nature of message and sudden activation of the device made Peat think the transmission must have been live or at least recently received by the device, at any rate, the alarmed tone of the messenger and the general substance of the message fragments which had been describable was unsettling for Peat and after a brief reflection on the content of the message Peat beckoned Jim with a few loud shouts of his name. Jim came rushing up

128

the stairs and getting to the door he looked at Peat while trying to catch his breath, inquiring, "What's wrong?"

Pointing to the device which had now retaken its ovoid shape as it lay still on the table, Peat said, "Another message."

Jim hurried over to the table and examined the device but could not activate any new message, only the one that he had initially found. "I can't find it," an agitated Jim lamented, "...Can you remember what it said?"

Peat took a sec to recall what he was able to get from the incomplete message, "It was broken up but some man with a mask, he was talking about the Representatives having been compromised and said something about being 'advisor to the Patriarch...?' It sounded like a warning but...".

Jim interjects in a state of panic, "Dear God, they know where you are!"

"Who, who knows?"

"Apoleia! Remember what Donamis warned.., and now we've been compromised. Ooo we need to get out of here post-haste," the animated Priest said as he gathered bits and pieces from around his room and put them in a large suitcase he had pulled from the closet.

The radio was still playing in the background and yet Peat thought he heard something originating from outside of the room, coming from the hole which opened out onto the house's turret.

"Do you hear something Jim?" Peat asked.

"It's just the radio, now come on, help me find my... ahhh there they are," Jim responded as he picked his car keys off the floor along with the glass of whiskey which lay next to them.

A loud noise then begins to compete with the radio which catches Jim's attention. Grabbing a pair of binoculars from the case Jim runs to the ladder and making his way up to the observatory deck he shimmies out onto the surface. Peat followed him but Jim seemed unaware of anything else other than identifying the source of this celestial noise. When on the observatory deck, Jim looks to see a distant speck making the most unholy of shrieking sounds. Peering through his binoculars Jim gets a close look at this unidentified object, the speck is actually a craft of some kind and far from being a small speck it was of significant size.

"What is it?" asked Peat.

Jim turns and as if he'd totally forgotten that Peat was still in the house he implored, "Dear God Peter, get out of here hide in the woods I'll be right behind you, GO!"

Jim watches Peat descend the ladder but when he turns to check on the incoming object he is terrified to see that it's now clearly visible to his unaided eyes, about a mile out and obviously travelling at a considerable speed given the ground it had gained in such a short period.

Jim, stands and stars at this incredible sight, wide-eyed and pale faced he whispers to himself, "O my God," before hurdling down the ladder and grabbing the case which contained everything from the two extra-terrestrial gadgets he had collected to a very worn breviary and set of rosary beads. As he made his way down the stairs he heard a hissing sound as if gallons of water was being poured on a red hot surface. He rushed out the backdoor which provided the most concealed pathway towards the woods but as he made his way across the lawn he could not help looking back over his shoulder at the incredible sight of a spacecraft; it stood about twenty foot tall and fifteen across, its body consisted of the most glossy platinum colored material. Without realizing it Jim found himself standing in the middle of the lawn captivated by this sight and then a figure jumped from a hatch located close to the base of the craft. It appeared to Jim to be a tall man but his face was covered by what appeared to be a type of mask, black in color with two dark yellow strips forming a V-shape joining at his lower jaw. He wore a plain black over cloak which reached down to his shins and was fastened across his body by two purpled clips located on his right shoulder.

Seeing Jim frozen on the grass this mysterious stranger moved with purpose towards him and then stopped, after making a slight bow of the head he spoke, "Greetings, I am Lynextius special adviser to

the Patriarch and Council of Tryloss. Where is
Peter Black we must leave now, it is no longer--- ."
"Haaay," a shout is heard from the wooded area,
both Jim and Lynextius turn their heads to inspect
this disturbance.
They see Peat standing at the edge of the
hinterland, "Hay, haay over here, you want me?
Come and get me."
Having got their attention Jim shouts "Peter run!"
Peat stands his ground admirably trying to draw off
the perceived threat, "Here I am, come and get
me!"
Noticing the bag next to Jim, Lynextius quickly
reaches for it and opening its contents onto the
ground he picks up a the ovoid device while also
producing two small star shaped metallic objects
from a pocket in his cloak, he attaches them to the
ovoid as if they were magnets then throws the
device on the ground. After a split second the two
tiny objects rise from the ground and morphed into
ring shaped objects after which three beeps come
from a control on Lynextius' arm.
Raising up his right forearm and using his left hand
to operate some sort of attached electric device he
seeks to assure Jim, "You and Peter Black have no
need to fear me, but it's imperative that we leave
Earth as quickly as possible."
Then a loud ding came from the device on Lynextius'
lower arm and off hovered these two small devices

at a frightening speed towards Peat who held up a stick defiantly.

Lynextius continues to explain to Jim, "...I appreciate you don't trust me, this is understandable for I have come early... but I had no choice. Apoleia have learned the home location of all of Earth's candidates scattered throughout the globe, many are already dead but..."

Before he can finish Peat lets a shout as the devices latch onto his wrist and forcefully dragged him out from the boscage towards Lynextius and Jim.

Bound by two brightly colored metallic rings Peat is brought to Lynextius whom he then recognizes, "You're the person who sent the last message Lynex---"

Before he could finish his sentence the manacles have released him and he falls to the ground. Lynextius leans down and reaching out his hand helps the perplexed lad to his feet.

"Peter Black, we must leave this place immediately, there is a good chance my arrival was spotted." Recoiling at this Peat looks towards Jim and says, "Wait, 'leave...' I thought, I don't understand."

With a heavy sigh Lynextius expounds, "There was not meant to be any contact for another month this is true, but somehow Apoleia came into possession of a list detailing the locations of all Earth's candidates, we only just became aware of the leak. It appears that hours earlier a coordinated purge took place against nearly all of Earth's candidates. So far we have been unable to make contact with any of them. Fortunately, the leaked list detailed your primary residence and not that used for correspondence. I knew I would find you here at this time, but it's very likely that you will track you here soon, we must ge--"

In a perturbed state Peat retorts, " '*My primary residence*,' " before rushing to Jim, "quick Jim the car keys, YOUR KEYS."

Befuddled by the unexplained panic that has engulfed Peat, Jim reaches into his shirt pocket pulls out the keys at which point Peat snatches them from his hand and runs towards the font of the house where the car is parked. Both Lynextius and Jim look on as Peat races around the house making for the vehicle. Jim shouts out, "But Peat, Tom won't be back for--"

Even louder Peat shouts back over him, "It's Claire..., she'll be at the house!"

Racing across the lawn after Peat Jim gesticulates to Lynextius with a frantic wave adding, "Come Lynextius, hurry!"

Unsure about what's happening Lynextius follows at pace and Jim shouts at Peat who had just started the car's ignition, "Wait for us Peter."

Both hop into the back of the car and Jim rapidly speeds down the front lawn over the rose beds towards the estate's exit while the two backseat passengers struggle to keep steady.

"Who is Claire?" asks a confused Lynextius.

With an ardent and steely determination on his face Peat responds, "She's my friend and now, because of your stupid war her life might be in danger."

There was an anxious silence as the gravity of Peat's words sunk into the consciousness of both Lynextius and Jim. In record time Peat made his way towards his house and as he rounded the final bend Lynextius pointed to the sky saying, "look." Black smoke was streaming across the sky, coming from the area where Peat's house was situated. Peat increased speed, almost losing control as his eyes found it hard not to look up from the road towards the smoke in the sky.

"Peter keep your eyes on the road, keep calm!" Jim said as if to both scold and at the same time console him.

Lynextius looked to be operating on a different level of thought and warned that there may be danger waiting, he suggested approaching Peat's house on foot through the tick woods.

Jim concurred and persuaded Peat by pointing out that; "We'd be no good to Claire dead." Discarding the car on the side of the road they moved into the woods, Lynextius then paused for a moment before producing a handful of metallic pellets and tossed them to the ground. Then using the device on his lower arm to activate them, they dispersed out across the vicinity.

"They will create a perimeter around us and issue an alert if someone approaches."

Jim found it hard to keep up with the other two and by the time they'd reached the edge of the woods next to Peat's house, Jim found himself a few yards back wheezing uncontrollably. Upon reaching the cabin Peat looked on in horror at the remains of his family home, almost totally consumed by fire. Peat could think of only one place Claire would instinctively go to hide and unaccompanied he took off across the lawn towards the old tree house. Meantime Lynextius had been directing the scouting devices to survey the wreckage for life, hostile or otherwise, and had not noticed that Peat was running across the open lawn. Jim had just reached the wood's edge after Peat departed, the cleric leaned over trying to catch his breath and called out to Lynextius, "Where's Peter?"

Both looked at each other before Jim saw Peat in the distance across the grassy lawn. Lynextius had also spotted him and took off in pursuit darting across the field. At the far side of the yard Peat slipped back into the woods and by the time Lynextius reached that point there was no sign of Peat, Jim came hobbling along, drenched in sweat and out of breath.

"Any, any, any sign o--" Jim panted but Lynextius shushed him.

"Do you hear that?" the Satrap asked.

Jim perked up his ears but could hear nothing except the internal pulsating of a throbbing headache, "No I can't hear a thing." the cleric responded.

"This way." the agile alien said before briskly taking off again into the woods followed at a distance by a physically tormented Jim.

Soon they were both met by Peat carrying Claire in his arms, frantically he exclaimed, "We need to get her to a hospital."

Claire's clothing was singed and her face and hand had serious burns on them, Jim moved forward and checked her pulse and looking her over he said, "She should be ok but we need to get her to a hospital quickly."

Lynextius put out his arms and approached Peat as if to insist that he would carry her, Peat gave her to him and they hurried back to the car. Lynextius ran so fast that Peat could not keep up. Just as they reached the road on which the car was parked a loud ominous sounding noise came from Lynextius' forearm. He passed Claire to Jim and checking the device on his arm he spoke solemnly, "They're coming, we don't have much time. Peter Black we must get to my ship."

"I'm not leaving her, I'm not leaving my home..., This is my life."

"You don't understand, the assassins will only be recalled from Earth when it is known that all of Earth's candidates are either dead or no longer on

this planet. As long as you remain you are
endangering the lives of those close to you. Come
with me, and once word of your escape reaches
Apoleia the assassins will no longer seek you among
your family and friends. But we must hurry!"
Peat looks at Jim as if seeking guidance but then
glancing down at Claire he responds, "Ok fine let's
go!"
Peat places Claire in the car and straps her in
hurriedly, "Okay Jim, get her to the hospital!"
"But how will you get back to the estate, you surely
can't go on foot?" Jim inquires.
"Don't worry I've got an idea." Peat glances at
Claire for one last time and leaning in gives her a
kiss on the forehead and as he leans back out he
notices something clutched in her right hand, gently
taking out a piece of crumpled paper, Peat is about
to inspect it when suddenly Jim speaks, "I'm so
sorry about this Peat, had I but known... Well, I'll
find Tom and explain everything, as best I can and
I'll take care of Claire also, don't worry I'll make
sure everybody is safe."
"Just get her to the hospital," a teary eyed Peat
states as he instinctively shoves the crumpled piece
of paper into his pocket and slams the passenger
door shut.
Jim slips into the car and in a flash is tearing down
the road en route to the hospital.
"Peter, we must go now!" Lynexious stresses to a
melancholy Peat.

Vivified by Lynexious' exhortation, Peat leads the pair in running down the road about 500 meters where they find Claire's modified vélomoteur.

"I hadn't counted on someone of your amm stature, but it's definitely quicker than jogging to the estate"

"Are you sure?" Lynextius asks.

"Look, you're the one who said there's no time, so come-on hop on," Peats gibes as he pulls the bike from the ground and takes the driver's seat. Lynextius sits on the tiny pillion seat that Peat had added, and off they go speeding back towards the estate. Nearing the estate Lynextius directs Peat to pull over.

"What's wrong?" asks a concerned Peat as he dismounts from the bike.

"One of the security ambit motion sensors around my ship has been tripped."

"Maybe it was just a fox or a squirrel?" Peat says reassuringly.

"I suspect it may be a trap. Follow me?"

Peat is confused on how Lynextius can know where he is going as he ascends up the road side slope into the adjacent forest but docilely he follows. At the top of the ridge Lynextius once again throws down some pellets which float off ahead of them. After about thirty minutes of hard pressing through some thick forestry they reached a brook, Peat takes a drink from the water as Lynextius hops over the stream and crouches up against a mound. He peers out over the embankment across the estate; everything seems just as it was when they had left it less than an hour earlier. Lynextius turns around and rests against the embankment while rubbing his hand across the base of his jaw as if in deep contemplation.

After a about a minute Peat breaks the silence and feeling a little frustrated at not knowing what was going to happen next he inquires, "So what's the plan?"

Rising to his feet and hopping back across the water Lynextius stood beside a tree and drew from his waist a long narrow object which he then proceeded, in full sight of a curious Peat, to open out 360° forming a disk, similar in many respects to a large toy flying disk. Peat looked on in wonder as Lynextius pressed one side of the disk against the bark of the tree and upon removing his hand the device remained fixed to the bark.

Walking away from the tree, about 15 yards, Lynextius singled with his hand for Peat to join him, both now stood facing this device and Lynextius, after he'd issued some type of command through his arm console, told Peat, "When you see the flash we'll move towards the tree as if we were approaching the ship."

When a small but powerful blue flash went off the two walked towards the discoid, no sooner had they commenced their promenade than a light blue laser was projected from the hub of the device and ran up and down both Peat and Lynextius at some speed, as if scanning them. When they were about two yards from the tree the device gave off another flash, this time red, and Lynextius stopped his circumspective walk and approaching the device pulled it from the bark of the tree. Then taking up position once again against the mound on the far side of the stream he placed the disk atop and turned to Peat saying, "We need to get closer, but I must be able to have a clear sight of the ship." Peat thinks for a moment, "Got it, there's a narrow spillway my father dug out which runs close to the house, it's only about 30 yards downstream."

"Excellent," he replied.

Before leaving though, Lynextius placed the disk on the top of the mound.

After wading through the mud and marshy plant life they reached the edge of the spillway and very slowly Lynextius cropped up his head above the bank to get a view of the ship. Then using his left hand he began to operate the device on his forearm with the most skillful of claviature. Peat raised his head also but remained perplexed as to what was going on, but Lynextius had warned him not to interrupt. At any rate, it soon became clear to Peat what was happening as he noticed perfect life-like holographic replicas of both himself and Lynexiuos walking across the lawn. Peat could only look on in amazement at the reality of these projections and although the grass prevented a clear sight, he presumed the hologram was being generated by the quick moving disk which itself was somehow being remotely controlled by Lynextius. Soon the phantom figures were very close to the ship and the main hatchway opened out as if to greet this phantasm, and just as the mirage reached the base of the hatch the ship exploded with a stunning flash of light. In a state of shock Peat didn't know what had happened but he felt something pressing over him. Lynextius withdrew his arm and Peat glanced aimless around in that surreal dream-like state one experiences immediately after a sudden and unexpected traumatic event.

Initially Peat could only hear a ringing in his ears but gradually there were breaks in this resonating sound and through it Peat could hear bits of words, "Are --- ---," "--at ---- --- ok," "--- ------ hear --- --- you ----", "--ter, can you ----, ar-- you ok...?"

Regaining his hearing Peat was able to understand what was being asked by Lynextius and answered, "Yes, yes I'm fine, I think." Peat looked down at his body examining for injuries.

Lynextius instructed Peat, "Stay down and keep quite."

After about three minutes had elapsed with Lynextius peering out over the mound and Peat lying low against the muddy embankment, two tall figures emerged from the woods close to the back of the house. Peat could obviously see nothing of this but

Lynextius caught a glimpse of them through the smoking wreckage.

He then slid down to Peat, "Stay here and keep your head down no matter what, ok. I'll be back in a minute.".

"Where are you going," Peat whispered?

"To get a new ship," Lynextius responded.

By this stage the two malignant characters stood inspecting the wreckage with their backs towards Lynextius who was approaching them with increasing speed. Peat knew he should listen to Lynextius but his curiosity got the better of him and he scurried up the mucky bank and peeked out towards the wreckage where he saw two darkly dressed creatures holding what appeared to be guns in their hands. To Peat's dread one of the creatures turned around just as Lynextius was about half way across the lawn. In a split second they'd both opened fire but to Peat's astonishment Lynextius produced a shield as if by magic and continued to advance undeterred. By this stage it was dusk and for a closer view Peat leans over the bank's edge onto the lawn as Lynextius made his final advance, the young onlooker could not believe his eyes when Lynextius raised his right hand in the air and, although it was getting dark, it seemed he generated a type of plasma gel. The mass then extended outwards and took shape, forming what appeared to be a solid sword with a glowing yellow strip running along its edge. Peat now crawled even closer to see his protector, undemonstratively and with extraordinary skill, dismember his enemies with only minimal effort. In the blink of an eye the whole affair was over and Lynextius, showing no sign of possessing sword or shield, was waving Peat over. Peat ran over, his eyes fixated on the dismembered corpses which lay on the bloodied grass, "What were they?" the overwhelmed earthling asked.

"Trilots, mercenaries and assassins hired by Apoleia."

"How did you--"

Lynextius interrupts, "We have little time Peter Black, we must find their craft as soon as possible. Is there somewhere to land a small craft in those woods," he asked as he points in the direction of where the Trilots had emerged from.

Taking a moment to consider this Peat's face lights up as he answers, "Yes, yes there is actually! There's a big clearing about a ten minute jog into the woods."

"We must hurry," states Lynextius.

Less than eight minutes later a gasping Peat reaches the glade to find Lynextius is already halfway up the hatchway yelling, "Hurry, I'll start the engines." It is dark now and everything has happened so fast that Peat feels all he can do is try to keep up but as he takes the first step onto the walkway he turns around for a moment of quiet reflection. The surreal nature of the occurrences which have taken place over the last twelve hours; the heartbreak he feels at being separated from his father, Claire and Jim, the anxiety and uncertainness about Claire's welfare, his own future, all these things are stirring in his mind and heart like one big tumultuous hotchpotch eroding his peace of mind. Then as he gazes pensively up at the beautiful stars he puts his hand in his pocket and sighs profoundly, his fingers brush against something and taking it from his pocket Peat sees that it was an old photo, the thing Claire had clutched in her hand. Finally getting the chance, Peat straightens out the crumpled old photo to take a look; he smiles warmly and is filled with a deep sense of affection... for it was the picture of him which Claire had taken the very first day they'd met. With barely time to savor this beautiful moment the roar of the engines intruded, Peat turned making his way up the gangway confident that his departure secured the safety of his loved ones. The walkway retracted and the hatch door had just sealed when the craft rose off the verdant carpet, and angling itself it shot into the twilight sky.

- Chapter Seven -

Peat spent the first hour of this intergalactic voyage in quiet contemplation, trying to make sense of all that had transpired. He felt a strange comfort in knowing he'd done the right thing and after the constant barrage of thoughts and emotions subsided somewhat, Peat made his way to the flight deck, mesmerized by the beauty of the cosmic panorama he beheld as he sat in a rather unusually shaped seat next to Lynextius. Peat really wanted to ask Lynextius about the trilling battle he'd witnessed on the estate but he got the impression that this quite, stern warrior was far from being disposed to extolling his triumphs in battle.

Instead Peat asked about a matter of greater personal concern to him, "So do you think many of the other candidates will have made it out ok?" Looking straight ahead Lynextius responds in word, but his body remains unresponsive,

"I'm not sure? We cannot risk sending a transmission from this ship... we'll know when we reach Ros Crae. Till then, we can only hope."

Peat sat back in the seat and with a somber expression upon his face he stared into outer space.

Meanwhile on the planet of Piallatar, in a

secluded apartment in the royal palace of Lord
Defas, a tall muscular humanoid creature,
Commander Kysol entered. He too had a dark
covering, similar to that of Lynextius', although it
was colored a dark red, and the V-shaped mark on
the his face was emerald green.
Kysol spoke to a Lord Defas, "Sire, all but one of
the Koinonia's candidates have been destroyed."
"Who survived," Lord Defas asked in a sinisterly
unsettling voice.

"A Peter Black my Lord, of your son's age! It
appears he escaped the planet with the aid of an
Xtaron," Kysol answers.

"We must prepare for the Trials... Earth is a
weakness for Koinonia. Bring me my son." Defas
orders.
With a graceful bow Kylos acknowledges Defas'
instructions, "Yes my Lord," before he exits.

While these ominous happenings unfolded on
Piallatar, across the other side of this galaxy
Lynextius and Peat arrived in Ros Crae. As the
craft approached the Planet's capital and prepares
for landing, Peat is struck with awe to see the
vastness of the City, the boundary of which could
only be seen from a phenomenal height. The city of
Ros Crae was structured around the lands
topography, in particular four massive lakes which
served as an unofficial means of dividing the City
into quadrants. The city followed a very orderly
manner; districts were typically dedicated to a

particular purpose or area of commerce, so for instance there were entire districts dedicated to trade while others would cater for entertainment and leisure. The transport system was so efficient and quick that the question of distance when it came to inner-city travel was largely of no practical consequence. If the city's layout was somewhat segregated, this was not the case for the monstrous residential complexes interspersed throughout the city. These residential towers were like cities themselves, comprising of numerous levels on which one could find any manner of things; residencies, public parks, giant natatoriums, outlets, archives, arenas, etc... At the center of the city was a circular zone called Concentricis, it was heavily militarized at its perimeter but inside, it was the essence of tranquility. The most exquisite dark red colored marble-type material made up the pathways; plant and water features were common and stood in contrast against the metropolitan buildings. However, the entire zone had two main focal points, firstly, a marvelous building which consisted of a large dome-shaped construction with two large cylindrical superstructures spiraling out of it into the sky. This spectacular edifice was effectively the nerve center for not just the entire city but to a large extent the whole planet. In this monumental structure; all major legislative and administrative duties for the city were carried out, the planet's Council had its chambers there and

148

perhaps most significantly this was where the Koinonia assembly had their headquarters. The only structure in Concentricis which exceeded the aforementioned in grandeur was that of the Patriarch's Palace, a truly majestic residence which also served as the base for the Xtaron Communion and home of the Xtaron Paladins who were the leaders of the Xtaron Communion.

After Lynextius had landed on the Southern side of Concentricis, himself and Peat were shuttled to the Palace. Peat was overwhelmed by the futuristic nature of everything, there were non-human creatures at the landing pad ready to greet the two travelers, and their appearance defied anything Peat had ever seen in science-fiction comics. Everywhere there were technological wonders that stunned Peat, but to everyone else these seemed to be just conventional features, part of daily life. Peat was also struck by the scale of everything, he'd seen pictures of big cities before and even a few sky scrapers but what he was witnessing in Ros Crae dwarfed his notions of a city. Lynextius remained absorbed in thought during the trip from the landing base to the Palace but Peat, on the other hand, was in an excited state of awe and found his maiden journey on an airborne inner-city shuttling pod trilling. As the pod approached its destination Peat could not take his eyes off the Palace and the countless arrays of gleaming lights which contoured the colossal complex. As they reached the first check point to the Palace Lynextius raised his head, coming out the trance like state he was in.

After clearing it Lynextius turned to Peat, "The Patriarch will be anxious to meet with you, I'll see you to the elevator," he said.

They were stopped, very close to the actual Palace, for a second time and again a guard dressed in the most ceremonial of outfits took one look at Lynextius and waved the pod through.

Just before they landed Peat, rubbing the back of his head and feeling a little awkward said, "Aaa I just wanted to say thanks, I mean for everything. This is all just so unreal... "

Lynextius responds with a slight tilt of the head and then the pod touches down.

As the two disembark and make their way from the hanger Peat is met with an entourage, one of the group steps forward, "Greetings Peter Black, I am Councilor Fizer. It does me well to see you safely arrived. It's a great privilege to finally meet a native of the mysterious planet Earth, there's been so much speculation, finding your planet was perhaps the greatest discovery since the Tar Limatu."

The implications of what the Councilor has just said sink in as Peat inquired with noticeable concern, "Am I the only one from Earth here...?"

A little taken aback by the question the political savvy Fizer responds as he put his hand on Peat's shoulder and leads him to the elevators, "...As of yet, but of course we live in hope. But now you've a very important meeting with the Patriarch! Also, I was curious about this Planet Earth..."

Fizer walks Peat towards the elevator followed by the rest of the entourage as the two speak some more. Lynextius accompanies them staying close to Peat until they reach the lift and then, unknown to Peat, he inconspicuously slips away.

Fizer looks to see that Lynextius has left and leans close to Peat, "Now remember Peter if you ever have any difficulties you can visit me, I know all too well what it is like to be separated from family and friends, those who you love."

With that the large metal door of the elevator opens with a wave and Peat walks in by himself. Before he can even ask, 'What floor?' the entourage have disappeared and the doors shut automatically. The conveyer starts with a jerk and suddenly Peat is left wondering what to expect. He tries to remember back to the message Donamis had sent but the moment he began to think back, he found his thoughts drawn to Tom, Claire and Jim. Questions abound, as they did while he was in the craft with Lynextius; Is Claire alright? Is Tom going to understand all this, or even believe Jim? Is the Apoleia still looking for me on Earth? and so on... Peat knew if he allowed himself to drift too far down this path he'd find nothing but despair, nearing the top floor and looking out through the glass casing at the back of the elevator far across the city Peat resolved to keep focused on the things in his control, he knew he would crack up if he permitted himself to delve into his fears and doubts and of these there was no shortage.

As he gazed out across the city's skyline Peat's mental undertakings were interrupted by a "dong," somewhat similar to that of a church bell.

Looking around, the door waved open once again to reveal the most impressive vista; a long regal corridor with a royal blue carpet and gilded framed portraits forming a type of honor guard up along this perfectly symmetrical entranceway to a door which had the most striking coat of arms imprinted on it, the seal consisted of the richest colors depicting a galaxy enclosed in the most intricately interwoven circular pattern and above this symbol a banner line with the strangest symbols were faded into the background, as if a watermark. Peat presumed that this seal must be that of Tryloss or the Patriarch, or perhaps it served as both. Making his way towards the door Peat found it interesting to note how the ostentatiousness of the portraitures seemed to intensify as he proceeded up the corridor with far grander regal apparel on the figures depicted, and more and more meretricious jewelry adorning their persons.

It was with some surprise then, that just as Peat got close to the door it whisked opened and a robust, plain robed man appeared, "Come in Peter," he said with a smile.

Peat entered and was amazed to see the vastness of the room in which he now stood, the impressiveness of its size was only surpassed by the eclectic mix of art, machines, decorations, weapons and much more. In a way it reminded him of Jim's house in that one would be likely to find almost anything in it.

"It's so good to finally meet you." Donamis said as he stepped back and took a good look at Peat.

"Thank you Sir, amm you're the Patr---?"

"Yes I am but you can call me Donamis," he said as he walked away towards the back of the room, "...I cannot imagine how difficult this has been for you; this tragic loss coming on the day you are forced to flee your home planet, leaving everything you've ever known..., that's not easy! All Koinonia mourn this tragedy!"

Sighing profoundly Donamis continues,

"...Unfortunately Earth still finds itself in a grave position, those who perpetrated this vicious crime would seek to exploit you planet's perceived weakness for their own malevolent ends. But the light of hope always shines and here you stand amidst the darkness of this day, a testament to that, Earth's own Representative."

Standing in the center of this massive room Peat feels his heart beginning to palpitate forcefully and his knees weaken. The overwhelming sense of deference which had muted the many questions Peat wanted to ask the Patriarch dissolved when he heard the title 'Earth's Representative' being

applied to him. Taking a moment Peat responds in a tone of disbelief, " 'Earth's Representative,' but what about the others, I mean... I can't..."
Donamis looks somberly at Peat and moves close to him, he puts his right hand on Peat's shoulder and speaks steadily to him, "Peter, I thought Lynextius had told you; I'm truly sorry but all the other candidates were killed..., you are the only survivor!"
For the first time the life-and-death nature of this whole undertaking hits Peat as he shrinks away from Donamis and stares at the ground trying to reconcile himself to what he has just been told.
"The truth is we share in the responsibility for their deaths; it appears one of my most trusted analysts, an Xtaron himself, leaked the whereabouts of our candidates before taking his own life," Donamis explains. Peat can only remain silent as his thinks on how fortunate he and his loved ones were, while Donamis continues, "Peter, I want you to know I would have spared Earth any involvement if I thought it possible but my hand was forced."
Feeling frustrated and still looking at the ground Peat asks, "But why me?"
"When the Council and I decided on choosing a Representative from Earth we knew exactly what type of person was needed to complete the Trials. Traditionally the Creaton Trials were designed to test both the strength and cunning of only the best Pillatarian warriors. The Creatons themselves are a fierce warrior race notoriously averse to outsiders,

they would sooner annihilation than submission to any external power and therefore in return for hosting such trials the neighboring planet of Pillatar agreed to respect the independence of Creaton. Travelling to Creaton to test the best of the Pillatarian warriors became a cherished event for our foes, in fact this tradition was so important to them that the Koinonia delegation which negotiated the peace treaty were obliged to concede the incorporating of such trials as a means of settling quarrels of disputed territories. Rightly or wrongly, it was agreed that Creatons would host the trials to resolve territorial disputes between the two planetary coalitions of Koinonia and Apoleia. The Treaty had firmly established delineated boundaries to limit Apoleia's sphere of influence and so it was never envisaged that a legitimate territorial dispute could arise under the terms of the Accord, as it stood. Then Earth, an extra-galactic planet was discovered, and the weakness of our position under the treaty soon became apparent. As far as Tryloss is concerned Earth, like all planets has complete autonomy, free to determine its own course. However, as I explained in my message, Apoleia do not share Koinonia's philosophy on interplanetary relations. I personally selected a contingent of seventy one Xtarons to individually travel to Earth, they spent nearly a year secretly searching and observing potential candidates until finally all returned to Tryloss with one name each.

They chose only those who had the required character and who lived apart from their respective societies, those who existed on the margins if you like; you see it has been a long and painful lesson for Tryloss that first contact with other planets is often fraught with fear and aggression, we learned the hard way that discretion is best practice at first. ...You know, your particular case was a curious one; you were initially deemed too young by the Council, however, the Xtaron who had first identified you as a potential candidate appealed directly to me and trusting his judgment as I do, I was able to secure a majority vote for your inclusion."

Peat breaks his silence, "Wait, you said you need a warrior for the trials, I'm not a warrior, I don't even... I, I --,"

Donamis speaks, "Yes, traditionally the Creaton Trials *were* designed to test brute strength and one's skills with a sword but the Pillatarian delegation which partook in the treaty negotiations were obsessed with the power of the Sumboi and insisted the Xtaron ritual be integrated into the Trails under the terms of the Accord. And so, with the consent of the Creatons themselves, a new set of Trials came into being."

Hearing this Peat looks up at Donamis wide eyed and feeling a little indignant he loses grip of the decorum he'd sought to maintain around the personage of the Patriarch, and asks bluntly, "Do

156

you mean you expect me to let one of those creatures, those Sumboi, into my head, risk my life in these trials... I'm not the person you want!" Looking at Peter anew Donamis nods his head in understanding, "Peter you're right, this is truly too much to ask, a tremendous burden has been placed on your shoulders. It is unfair! There is no compulsion on you..., we have already selected other possible representatives who are willing to represent Earth in the trials, I simply wanted to give you the first choice. ...Against my better judgment the Council and the Koinonia Assembly have decided to hold the official signing of the declaration tomorrow, which means there are twelve hours before a final decision is needed one way or another..." Moving closer to Peat, Donamis looks with paternal concern on the young adult, "...Peter, the choice is yours and yours alone, many of my most seasoned warriors would not take on this challenge so know that you are under no pressure, there are others who can be called upon."
In an attempt to reaffirm Dumanis' consoling words in his own mind Peat says, "Yes of course, I mean you must have loads of others better suited for this than me..., I mean look at Lynextius, He's incredible ... I just think the fate of Earth belongs in better hands. I mean I appreciate all the effort everyone took in getting me here but..., well you know."
"Of course. Now..., we can select a Representative for Earth tomorrow but you must be hungry after

157

your long journey," Donamis leads Peat out of the room and back down the corridor towards the elevator. Donamis makes light chat as they strolls down the corridor and points at the framed portraits jesting, "A serious looking bunch eh, my predecessors. We must never have had an artist with a sense of humor in Tryloss!" Peat smiles at the Patriarch's self-deprecating dynastic jape but inside he felt a deep sense of guilt and disappointment. He kept asking himself 'Why me?' 'Why was I picked?' Donamis had given a descriptive answer to these questions but Peat wanted more, he wanted to know why someone selected him personally and petitioned the Patriarch for his inclusion as a candidate when the Council had already decided against it. It was clear to Peat that the person he needed to talk to was the Xtaron who had chosen him. As he reached the elevator it became evident that Donamis was not going to be accompanying him any further, "Now I have had food left for you in your chambers, to get there simply go right once you leave the elevator on the ground floor, at the end of the corridor you'll find your room marked, 749-X1. I will see you---" Peat interjects, "I'm sorry to interrupt your Sir but I was wondering; who was the Xtaron in charge of my case, the one you mentioned before?" Rather artfully the perceptive Patriarch replies, as if he were ignorant of that which played on the mind of his young guest, "Ah yes, your Xtaron was actually Lynextius. I believe you'll find him ruminating in Loutous Halls. It's very close to your own quarters, so once you get to your room just turn right and continue on straight I'll have someone meet you to show the way from there."

However, just as the shrewd Patriarch guides the young Peat, on the other side of the galaxy, on an impressive open air walkway in the heart of Pillatar's epicenter, the antithesis was unfolding. Lord Defas looks out across the city of Naratalese, capital of Pillatar, and from behind him a young slender figure appears, it's Oratron, Defas' only son. He is wearing the most striking dark purple robe which contours perfectly to his body. Oratron is as handsome as he is well dressed, with wavy blond hair, a thin face with high cheek bones and deep red lips. His eyes however, are dead and his face shows no real sign of emotion.
"Father," the he says with a soft sober voice as he approaches Defas whose back remains turned.
"It is time," Defas responds prophetically.
Oratron looks out over his father's left shoulder and with ambition and longing in his voice he speaks, "At last father, we shall be exiles no longer… We shall finally restore our royal lineage."
"Earth is merely the beginning," Defas says raising his head slightly. Then turning towards his son Defas holds out a small fluid filled tube in which a purple colored Sumboi swims. Oratron looks obsessively at the Sumboi, an eerie smile across his

face, while Dafas looks at his son with twisted paternal pride saying, "Soon, soon my son!"

Peat has made his way down to the ground level, it is late and there's no sign of anyone around. Having followed the Patriarch's directions and passing his own quarters Peat finds himself in front of a large entrance, but unlike the other doors which seem to be metal this door seemed to consist of a type of semi-transparent glue which blurred the things on the far side. Peat had been very cautious since arriving, aware that he knew nothing about the world he was on and he had therefore resisted his natural desire to fidget with unfamiliar devices and gadgets but since talking to the Patriarch he'd become less apprehensive. Poking a pen from his pants pocket he poked the non-viscous gel-like substance but despite some obvious elasticity it seemed impenetrable. Having tested to see if there would be any corrosive effect on the pen Peat cautiously tapped his hand against the barrier until eventually he was using both his hands to push as hard as he could against the gel. He found that with a sufficient application of force there was a considerable spring off the substance, enough to cause a rebound effect, and giving into in his vivacious inclinations, which Claire was also so adept at tapping into, he leaned into the field forcefully and sprung back out. This frolicsomeness escalated quickly and after checking to make sure there was no one around Peat decided to give the
160

elasticity of this semi rigid impediment a thorough test. Moving back down the corridor Peat turned and with a cheeky smile on his face he sprinted full pace at the partition but just as he took position to hurl himself against the wall the field suddenly disappeared and despite his best attempts to stop himself he went stumbling backwards across the threshold. Crashing to the ground Peat opened his eyes as he lay dazed on the floor, feeling a slight pain coming from his lower back. Then he heard a clapping noise, he rolled over to see a hazy figure approaching him.

He couldn't make out who or what was approaching him as he was still somewhat disorientated after the tumble but then he heard a voice, "Hah, you Earth boys sure know how to make an entrance, let me help you up."

And taking his hand Peat got to his feet, in doing so he caught a proper look at his helper; the strangest looking little creature with long black beaded hair flowing from his head, bright red skin and a single row of horns running like a mohawk along his head and travelling down the back of his neck disappearing under the plain robe he wore.

Peter jerked back in shock saying, "Jesus..."

The colloquially ignorant creature in a concerned voice raised his hands; "Wow, are you okay Jesus; that was a pretty bad tumble."

"I'm Bellza, I was told to meet you here?"

Peat smiles broadly and Bellza smiles back while the latter says to himself, "The Earth boy ain't to bright!"

Peat, overhearing this derogatory remark snaps out of his bewilderment and indignantly responds, "Hay, I understand you! I'm Peat, Peat Black." Moving closer to Peat and tapping him on the leg Bellza addresses him as if they were old friends, sighing he says, " Awa Peat, it's been a tough day for you, that treacherous bastard! Did you know any of the other candidates?"

The two stroll further down the corridor as Peat responds, "Aaa no..., no I didn't."

"Yah, all the guys are pretty torn up about it..."

"What guys?" Peat asks curiously.

"The Xtarons' of course, they were the protectors assigned to the candidates. Each candidate had their own Xtaron, kinda like their own guardian... very sad! I actually know a few of the Xtarons who had a candidate, yah... in fact I even saw the profile of a few of the candidates and let me tell you some of the females were, well you know, but ah... of course, it was terrible what happened to them, Apoleia bastards!"

Trying to keep his characteristically flippant manner in check while chatting to Peat, Bellza continues, "...So, word has it that the declaration is happening tomorrow, big news around here you know. How are you feeling about it? ...Soon you'll be joining the ranks of the Xtarons, wow... of course

Creaton is no walk in the park there's..." Bellza
continues talking, going off on numerous tangents as
Peat, totally perplexed, looks down at this
diminutive chatter box and remembers that his
objective was to find Lynextius as quickly as
possible.

"Amm, sorry to interrupt, but I was wondering; do
you know where I could find Lynextius?"

"Ah yah, that's right you're Lynextius' candidate.
Well there's only one place he could be now and that
in the meditation hall, come on I'll show you where it
is."

Leading Peat down a maze of corridors which all
looked the same to him, they eventually come to
another large gel-like screen at which point Bellza
raising his hand says, "There you go Peat, through
there you should find him. It can be a bit confusing
in there so just make sure you take the last
entrance, or is it the second last..., no no; it's
definitely the last entrance on your right. I wish I
could take you straight to him but...well... I was
kinda banned from the place..., they said I wasn't
'aptly disposed,' whatever the hell that means, eh."
Peat moves towards the barriers and touching it
with his hand, he encounters the same problem as
before. Turning to Bellza the absent-minded red-
skinned lilliputian was tapping his head, "There's
something I was meant to...amm...that's it!" and
trotting over to Peat he says, "Give me your wrist
for a second."

Peat, a little nervous, but trustingly nonetheless, kneels down and extends out his right arm. Bellza takes hold of his arm and using his other hand he produces the strangest looking syringe-like device and injects a blue dye into Peat.

Peat instinctively tries to draw back his outstretched arm but Bellza is deceptively strong and has the procedure done in a flash, "There, I knew I was forgetting something," Bellza said releasing Peat's arm.

"What was that stuff?"

"It's kinda like a passport to nearly anywhere in the Palace, but it won't get you into the lady's quarters, trust me on that I've tried!" Bellza says with a cheeky grin running across his face.

As he turns and walks away he yells out, "See you around kid," before disappearing back down the corridor.

Getting to his feet Peat looks at the field once again before glancing down at his arm and then walking towards the partition, he gets about one foot from the shield and it simple vanishes, Peat proceeds through to the other side. The entrance opens into a type of foyer and a selection of hall ways branch off from this antechamber. Above each separate hallway there's symbols, not understanding their meaning Peat shrugs his shoulders and follows Bellza's directions, moving down along the last hallway on his right away from the main entrance the light grows dimmer, Peat

164

expects that motion sensors would activate the lights but this is not the case as things become pitch dark. Not deterred, Peat slowly continues on, treading softly, and using his hands to feel for upcoming obstacles. After about four minutes of blind wandering in the pitch black, Peat feels a large cold object blocking any further advancement. As he runs his hand up and down what he presumed to be a door he hoped to hit a release switch of some kind, then remembering that a number of entrances in the Palace had operational panels beside the doors he maneuvers himself over to the corner of the aphotic hallway and taps his hand around the area where he expects to find a control panel, if indeed there was one there to be found. After a number of strokes Peat finally got lucky and a bright yellow light came from the area he was patting, a few seconds later the xanthous panel deluminated and a small blue light appeared near the roof of the hallway just above the center of the door. Peat took a few steps backwards staring at the light which suddenly gave off a bright flash, temporally blinded for a split second Peat looked up and around to see multiple blue lazars oscillating up and down his person from all angles. When they'd finished the door waved opened to reveal a plane white pathway which led to a black chair. The route was narrow, enclosed by tall walls which were of a violet coloration. Peat suddenly felt rather uneasy but he was determined to find Lynextius and so walked towards the chair. Halfway up the narrow path Peat looked around and could see nothing behind him, there was only darkness; it was as if the lane was disappearing behind him once he'd passed over it. Peat then turned around fully and stood still to consider this anomaly, when he glanced back around he noticed that the chair was now further away and the light around him was fading into darkness. A sense of fear welled up inside him and he made a frantic dash towards the chair but the darkness seemed to keep pace. Peat reached the chair and gripped it firmly as the room achromatized to a state of acherontic darkness. Peat's uneasiness grew and feeling a strong desire for security Peat sat into the chair just as the last tiny glare of light died in front of him. Peat sat silently in the chair looking around unsure of what to expect next in this fantasia. He then heard three pronounced knocks coming from a distance behind him although turning on his seat he saw nothing, but again the ternary raps came and Peat thought that it must be someone trying to gain access.

He shouted, "Hello. Hello..., I'm in here!" but no reply came.

Still Peat believed someone was knocking, and the thought that he could find a way out of this disturbing phantasm spurred him to cautiously get up and move through the darkness towards the triplex knocking which was continually increasing in

166

frequency and volume the closer he got to the source. The sound became so loud that Peat expected to find a way out at any moment as he carefully shuffled towards the beckoning sound. But all of a sudden it just stopped, Peat took a few steps forward feeling the air with his hands anticipating some sort of wall or boundary, but nothing, then he called out again, "Hello, Hello Lynextius?"

Swinging around in a circle Peat became increasingly agitated, he could see nothing nor find his way out, "Hello!" he shouted again but as before there was no reply.

Peat then decided to continue to walk forward until he reached the wall, then skirting around the room's edge he would eventually find the door through which he'd entered, but just as he began to walk onwards he noticed a white dot of light in the corner of his eye which ever so gradually seemed to be growing in size and brightness, then as if approaching at great speed the light grew and grew both in dimension and luminance until Peat, blinded by its radiance, raised his arm to cover his eyes and flinched in fear of being struck by an oncoming object. When he opened his eyes and lowered his arm, he found himself facing an old wooden door. He looked around inspecting his surroundings and realized he was back in Jim's barn yet something was very different, everything was covered in dust and it appeared that the place had long been in a

state of disuse. He opened out the barn door, the hinges of which squeaked from lack of oil, and walked slowly out into the yard. Peat was struck by the disheveled appearance of the estate, grass was growing up through the tarred laneway, the lawn had become grassland and the gate to the garden had vegetation sprouting through its cavities. Peat knew this was a hallucination of some sort yet it answered a deep longing of his, namely, to be home, and as such he felt a certain pseudo-contentment. He walked up towards Jim's house, a little worried that this dream world would end with him hitting the wall of whatever place he was really in, however, after he'd made his way up onto the veranda and opened the door Peat was intrigued with the prospect of what he might find inside. Entering the house Peat was surprised to find everything orderly and clean, there was also a soft sung melody to be heard coming from down the hallway, wondering towards the beautiful feminine voice Peat peeked into the kitchen to see a middle aged woman washing dishes in the sink, nowhere was there any sign of books or papers, it was almost like a different kitchen to what the young dreamer remembered. 'Perhaps Jim no longer lives here!' was the thought that came to the forefront of Peat's mind.
He then tried to speak to the lady, although he knew she was merely a hologram of some description, "Hello, aaa Hello...." but the lady carried on as if Peat were not there.

168

Peat decided to go upstairs to see if Jim was there. As he reached the top of the stairs he had something of a metaphysical epiphany, how could an external source spontaneously manifest such a personally detailed reality, this must be in his own head, a dream or something. This 'epiphany' may seem self-evident but such a realization while still in a subliminal state was rather curious; 'Perhaps it had something to do with the scanning lazars?' Peat thought to himself as he pushed opened Jim's sanctuary door. Peat entered the room to see a surprisingly plain and, compared to what he'd expected to find, banal room.

A bed, wardrobe in the corner and a dresser beside it. Near the window Peat saw the back head of someone sitting in an old rocking chair and without hesitation he called out, "Father.., Jim it's me!" but there was no answer.

He moved around beside the chair to get a look at the person's face, and there in the chair as if catatonic sat Jim, looking out the window at nothing in particular. Peat attempted to get his attention but Jim seemed to be in an almost vegetative state, a feeling of sorrow suddenly welled up in Peat as he looked upon this once larger than life figure.

Less than a minute later the door to Jim's room swung open and in came the lady from the kitchen carrying a platter full of pills and a tall glass of water, "It's time for your medication Father," she called out in a voice Peat found full of patronizing matriarchalism.

Stepping back he looked on in pity at the feebleness of his idol as the lady tended to him. Feeling rather upset Peat dashed from the room but upon crossing the threshold he found himself in a new setting; it was Peat's old house, the back room to be more precise. The last sight Peat had of the cabin was of it destroyed but he could see no sign of any damage in this dream-world. He made his way with familiarity through the house and came to his father's room, out of habit he knocked on the door, then recalling that this was a dream he simply opened the door and entered. There was no one there but Peat was surprised by the messiness of the room; Tom was always very neat around the house and kept on top of all domestic chores. As he proceeded through the house it became evident that practically the entire house was filthy; dirty cutlery was to be found left haphazardly around the place, empty whisky bottles lay on the floor and atop tables, papers were scattered on the ground and there was a stench of stale air caused by a lack of proper ventilation. Moving through the kitchen towards his bedroom Peat heard a faint sobbing emanating from his room, approaching his bedroom door which was slightly ajar he slowly pushed it open. His room is exactly as he remembered it and unlike the other rooms in the house it had be kept unsoiled. As he gave another push, the door opened

170

fully and he saw his father kneeling at the side of the bed stooped over onto the mattress his forehead pressing down on the duvet crying while clutching in his hands what appeared to be a framed picture of his son.

Peat found this too much to take and forgetting the false existence which was being simulated around him, Peat rushed over crying, "Dad", but when he tried to embrace him his arms passed through the apparition as if it were a matterless ghost.

Peat's initial shock lasted all but a split second and was replaced by anger and frustration at the deceptiveness of this self-made delusion. Backing away from his weeping father Peat said aloud to himself, "I'm stopping this!"

He turned and bursted out of the room, out of the house, and down the road running as fast as he could while repeating to himself the mantra: "I have to wake up! I have to wake up! I have to wake up…", he continues to run down the road until the surroundings begin to look strange to him, and pausing to take stock he realizes he has no idea where he is. It's a rural setting in the countryside, about twenty yards up the road from him Peat sees a very high wall at the entrance there are two large limestone pillars between which there's an imposing black cast-iron gate with a cross forming at its apex. Peat makes his way wearyingly to the gate; light is beginning to fail and the sky is now clouded overhead adding to the rather dull and dreary ambience. Evidently unable to escape this nightmare, Peat counsels himself, 'Perhaps I need to see it through.' He ambles up a steep pathway through an eerie cemetery. Close to the back of the graveyard, at the right hand corner Peat saw a tall slender female figure wearing an all-black dress, her head covered with a black funeral hat. Peat felt nervous and although part of him knew what he would find he still approached the lady with trepidation. As he got closer he could hear that the woman was crying as she stood over a plot but her back was to Peat so he couldn't identify who the person was. Peat stopped about twenty yards from the lady and looked all around the churchyard, things had become very dark and murky indeed. The unidentified woman then ceased her sobbing and crouching down, she placed a flower on top of the grave before striding away. Peat moved out onto the grass in an attempt to catch a glimpse of her face but it was concealed behind a dark lace face-veil. As the woman vanished down a side pathway towards the entrance, Peat's attentions turned to the grave at which she had mourned. As he had expected the tomb stone was that of 'Claire Smith.' Indeed Peat had presumed the lady standing at the grave was Stephanie.

By this point Peat had to remind himself, "This is not real, I know Claire's ok!"

Taking a second look at the grave Peat notices a rusted object, hunkering down he takes up the

172

corroded thing in his hand, it was the musical box he'd made for Claire, the winding key was gone but, at least externally, it looked intact even if the worst for wear. Peat smiled and placed the musical box back on the grave. He began to feel slightly better in himself and believed that he would now wake up, but the darkness continued to fall, dusk had set in with unnatural rapidity. Peat wanted to make his way towards the gate but despite jogging back down the lane he could not find it.

"I just need to get to the gate," Peat said to himself in the belief that that would end this mental torment, but despite running to and fro around the cemetery Peat couldn't find his way out. A coldness now began to accompany the increasing darkness. Upon feeling the chill Peat became very disturbed and wanted nothing more than to leave this place but he could not find a way out! Peat then got a quondam smell, vaguely familiar to him but he couldn't place it. He began to get the sense that something latent was lurking in the recesses of his mind, his feeling of panic grew. He now heard three more knocks, and frightened he ran away in the opposite direction eventually reaching the boundary wall of the cemetery and a tall narrow gate. This was not the gate by which Peat had entered through, however, at this stage, the young unsettled man was simply content to get out of the cemetery any way he could. Passing through the gate Peat found himself in a slender bower. At the top of this secluded leafy area was a lit candle and for some reason Peat felt a deep draw to it. As he approached Peat began to feel even colder and that strangely familiar smell grew stronger filling the air and triggering a strong mix of emotions in him. Sweat began to appear on his forehead and his throat dried up, although part of Peat wanted to turn around and go back he felt compelled to continue up the dark arbor towards the light. As he got close he could see the candle was resting on a grave but it was too dark to see the name on the tombstone and so reaching down Peat raised up the candle to reveal the name, 'Megan Black.'

Peat's lips dilated ever so slightly as he murmured the word "Mum," and his eyes began to tear up as the most harrowing feeling cut through him. Placing his hand on the top of the tombstone for support, and feeling himself about to breakdown Peat heard a woman let the most excruciating of screams from behind him but before he could turn to see the source of this harrowing cry everything disappeared and all Peat could hear was a concerned voice calling him, "Peter, Peter wake up!"

Peat opened his eyes to see a blurred figure stooping over him and felt a hand on his shoulder, "Dad?" Peat asked as his visual acuity began to return.

He raised his head, "Lynextius!" Peat says in a rather confused state before arching his reclining body up off the strangest looking of chairs.

174

Peat looks around to find himself and Lynextius alone in a large empty hall. He's sitting in the most peculiar reclining chair which has a pink pigmented semi-solid substance supporting his body.

"What's going on?" Peat asks.

Helping Peat out of the chair Lynextius explains, "You entered the introversion chamber, designed to help Xtarons plunge deep into their minds."

"It all seemed so real and vivid...I could actually smell the grass and feel the breeze on my face."

"Yes, this chair acts as a powerful stimulant for subliminal activity; it is just one of the many new technologies the discovery of the Tar Limatu opened up to us," Lynextius expands.

"The ship with the little creatures, right?" Peat seeks to confirm.

In a mildly sarcastic tone Lynextius responds, "Yes, the 'little creatures.' ...Peter, why did you enter the Loutous Halls?"

"Actually, I was looking for you. Amm... I was kinda hoping you might be able to...amm well the Declaration of a Representative is happening early tomorrow and I don't think I can do this, and aaa... well you were my Xtaron and aamm--"

Straightening himself and commencing to walk towards a large semi-circular door Lynextius says, "Peter, come with me I want to show you something."

As they left the room they entered the most elegant hallway with marvelous designs and decorations on the walls but at this point Peat's only concern was on listening intently to Lynextius who now began to answer the questions which had originally prompted Peat's venturing into the Loutous Halls.

Lynextius continues, "...As I am sure Lord Donamis had informed you, I like many in the Xtaron communion, was commissioned to travel to Earth secretly and locate a suitable candidate who might one day act as Representatives for the planet. My search was long and difficult, I had to remain undetected and yet gather the most detailed of intelligence which would lead me to potential candidates. It took me almost a year but eventually I found you! There were many considerations to be taken into account but I, like the rest, knew the most important thing was to find someone in whom there was no bile or malice, you see the Trials will require that Earth's Representative become an Xtaron, an honor which few are suitably disposed to take on. Since the first Xtaron, Greeto Ron, it has become painfully obvious to most in Koinonia that joining oneself with a Sumboi takes a heavy toll on the mind. The lust for power and glory which lay dormant in Greeto's heart overtook him as an Xtaron. Tragic lessons have thought us that only beings graced with a suitable depth of character can be entrusted with this great responsibility and honor, even at that though; it is a constant effort to humble oneself. We therefore could not simply

176

choose from among the greatest warriors on Earth, as important as combat skills will be there is something far more essential, we had to seek out the lowly and humble. The truth is we can never fully know the impact a Sumboi will have on its symbiont either in body or mind but that it is profound and continuous, is without question. In secret I observed your life; one of fellowship, discipline, selflessness and peace. Despite your age I recommended you for the Trials because I believed you to be the most suitable."

When Lynextius paused for a moment, Peat looked around and found himself in the most magnificent of settings; a beautiful water fountain was to be found in the center of this giant atrium, a most impressive spiraling column rose all the way up to a huge glass skylight which captured the star filled sky.

On the lower parts of the slanted column Peat noticed a number of statues and inquired, "Who are those statues of?" pointing at them.

"They are all the deceased Paladins, leaders of the Xtaron Communion, it is here that they are remembered and honored in a very special way; daily their images remind us of the call to selfless service and care of all peoples."

Looking up in awe Peat asks, "Wow... is this what you wanted to show me?"

"No, follow me," Lynextius said while moving to the nearby elevator. When they reached level eight Lynextius led Peat to the entrance of a large amphitheater partitioned by a set of glass panels, through the glass Peat was able to see the happenings inside. A ceremony of some sort appeared to be in progress. The first thing the young onlooker noticed was the darkness of the room lit mainly by the candles being held by a relatively small number of the hundreds assembled, many of whom were dressed in some sort of ceremonial garb, much like the one Lynextius wore, but all had their hoods drawn. The second thing Peat was struck by was the large projection of what looked like the Earth which floated high above the room's omphalos. When Peat saw the model of his home planet he took particular interest and pressing up against the glass he observed that those with candles were slowly processing down to the center and once someone reached the base of the dais they would proceed up it one by one, placing their candle in what appeared from afar to be some sort of holder above a type of machine. When the congregants withdrew their hands the machine would generate a type of charged sphere. The candle holder then automatically withdrew and the sphere, suspending the candle upright, drifted upwards towards the model of Earth which appeared to rotate on its own axis as if to meet the sphere at a particular point. Once the sphere reached a given point on the globe all the candle bearers below would raise their lights to the air before, to Peat's astonishment, the sphere would simply implode leaving no sight of anything. Yet with each candle that vanished the light omitted from the projection grew stronger.

Peat watched this solemn spectacle for a time before asking Lynextius, "What's going on?" Lynextius had kept his distance but now walking up beside Peat and looking in through the glass he answers, "Here we are marking the tragic loss of all the candidates who died today. Each Xtaron who was responsible for the care for a candidate carries a candle signifying the life of the fallen. Each light will rise to the particular area on Earth where the candidate lived before being symbolically extinguished."

Walking away from the glass back towards the elevator with Peat accompanying him Lynextius continues, "...Peter, Koinonia is far from perfect but there is no utopia to be had in this universe, not in our galaxy or your own..., but in Koinonia at least there is a system of planets which strive towards an ideal; a situation of inter-planetary peace and co-operation, working towards a shared society where life is respected, where even the most vulnerable are cherished. As Xtarons we take a vow to uphold these ideals in communion with Tryloss and koinonia, as best we can. At present Apoleia poses a very great threat to the peace and stability of the entire galaxy, already Lord Defas uses lies, hatred and fear to manipulate other planets into doing his bidding just as his father thought him. To those who would follow Defas, the Sumboi are instruments of power and control not an aid in service of peace. Earth is not privileged in this regard, while on your planet I found those who would use the Sumboi for their own selfish ends. As with all planets, there exists a struggle between good and evil, between life and death... In you I found someone who cherished the good, someone who could serve Earth as it comes to terms with the new epoch which is soon to be trust upon it. After the Trials, no matter what the outcome, the embargo on travel to earth will eventually be lifted and the peoples of your world will have to face a new reality, they will need people like you. So no matter what you decide tomorrow at the Declaration, you have an important role to play in Earth's future." Summoning over a soldier stationed at one of the multiple entrances to the amphitheater Lynextius looks at Peat as the elevator door opens and says, "You should take some time for quiet reflection and rest, there is also food in your chambers. They will call early tomorrow for your final answer but remember the choice is yours and yours alone."

Lynextius turns to the waiting soldier saying, "Please show Candidate Black where room 749-X1 is."

To which the sentry replied, "Yes Sir."

As the elevator door shuts Lynextius remains on level eight looking in at the somber commemoration. A very tall man, Po-Kal, of equal

180

height and wearing a white colored robe stands alongside Lynextius and as if pretending not to notice one another, they converse:

"What of young Black?" asks Po-Kal.

"He is capable, no doubt, but as yet he does not believe in himself."

"Lynextius, the betrayal ruined everything; no one could cope with so much in just a matter of hours. There are others who could represent Earth," Po-Kal insists.

Turning his head towards Po-Kal Lynexous changes the subject, "What of the leak and Nataan's death?"

"It's still unclear, he died by an Xtaron blade but we cannot know if it was his own, all the evidence suggests he betrayed us but I just find it too hard to believe he would do such a thing."

"And his Sumboi?" Lynextius inquires.

"Dead. The Patriarch and the Council are satisfied that Nataan was the culprit and that he acted alone."

Clearly deep in thought Lynextius warns, "We may have a traitor among us but for now I must focus on the Trials. I've stationed Omatage outside Peter's chambers."

"Yes I agree, Earth is too valuable to be lost, I'll lead the investigation while you attend to the Trails. Something tells me Defas is beginning to move his pawns into position, I fear it may not be long now."

Staring at the globe hovering above the room's center Lynextius gently nods his head in agreement.

- Chapter Eight -

The night proved to be a restless one for Peat as he
mulled over all that had happened to him and took
stock of what it all meant; the terrifying
experience in the introversion chamber, the
encouragement of Lynextius and Donamis, the
constant worry as to the welfare of Claire, Tom and
Jim and the fate of Earth, the fear of being killed
in the Trials should he assent, and so on... In the
early hours of the morning Peat had reached
breaking point so lowering himself onto the floor he
employed the meditative techniques he'd learned
from Master Miyamoto and within an hour he was in
a deep sleep. Peat was woken to the sound of three
firm knocks and for the briefest of moments it
entered his head that he was in another nightmare
but opening his eyes he found himself lying on the
bed in his chambers.

Opening the door Lynextius greeted him and
entered before stating; "They'll soon be here!" to
which Peat responded,

"I've made up my mind I---".

Lynextius interrupts, "Peter I'm here to support
you, whatever you choose, but it is the Patriarch
and the Council who should first hear of your
decision."

There was then a rattle at the door, "Peter Black," an authoritative sounding voice called out.

"I will go with you," Lynextius said as he signaled Peat to open the door.

Once done Peat was faced with a large stubby man dressed in the most grandiose military-like clothing and accompanied by a large military escort, "Candidate Black, I am Emissary Verdex of the Patriarchal House. Your presence is requested before Lord Donamis and the Council."

Peat looks around at Lynextius who gives a slight nod, and he leaves with the august cortege. Peat is led out onto a hangar and directed to a small craft, soon he is travelling with a massive delegation of dignitaries many of whom seem to be staring at him and chattering among themselves. On either side of him there is a number of armed soldiers and outside the vessel, a sizeable consort of aircraft. Looking out the window Peat sees they are drawing close to the other magnificent building he had seen yesterday when entering the city with Lynextius. Soon they had landed on top of the eastern tower and once disembarked, Peat was whisked away to a decorative room at the top of which was a large crescent shaped table with a gallery section running along the side. The Patriarch was seated in the middle flanked by eight councilors on both his right and his left, the gallery was full of dignitaries and delegates from the various planets that made up Koinonia.

Peat was shown to a central point in front of the table by Emissary Verdex who then spoke, "My Lord and Councilors, I present Candidate Black."
Peat was a little thrown by the formal dress Donamis now wore and felt rather intimidated by his surroundings.
Donamis raised his hand as if to signal for silence, "Welcome all, and a special welcome to Peter Black on this historic occasion. Along with Candidate Black we still mourn the loss of so many of Earth's sons and daughters, the perpetrators of these heinous crimes will be found and brought to justice. That said, we are honored to be able to greet the first of Earth's people to our Planet. I am confident that our two Planets can learn much from each other and work to create close bonds. ...As to the matter at hand; Peter I'm sure I speak for the whole council when I offer my deep apologies for the internal betrayal of one of our own which resulted in the deaths of so many of your compatriots..."
Donamis looks at the Councilors before continuing, "...Peter spoke with me yesterday evening and informed me that because he was forced to leave Earth, through no fault of his own, he was therefore unable to complete his training and has so selflessly chosen to cede his nomination as Representative of-- "
Donamis stops speaking midsentence as he sees Peat callowly raise his hand. Recognizing he has

something he wants to say Donamis smiles and abridges his speech by saying, "...It appears Peter would like to address the Council, Peter..." and sitting down he gestures to Peat to speak.

"Aaaa... I'm sorry to interrupt you Lord Donamis, aaa... well I was convinced from the moment I left Earth there was no way I could be Earth's Representative... I had intended to hide behind all the other candidates but then I learnt I was the only one left! This terrified me!

But the more I thought about what's at stake, the other candidates who lost their lives... well, I've decided to be Earth's Representative at the Trials!"

There is a lot of murmuring among the Councilors but the Patriarch simply sits back in his chair and silently looks on at Peat with a sense of admiration before glancing across at the corner of the room next to the gallery of dignitaries where Lynextius stands inconspicuously. After a few seconds have elapsed Donamis stands up and in a very dignified manner raises his hand for silence.

A hush descends as the Patriarch speaks formally, "Very well... Peter Black, on behalf of the sovereign planet of Tryloss, and with the support of the inter-planetary union of Koinonia, we hereby pledge our sponsorship to you as the Representative of Earth for the Trials as set out under the terms of the bilateral Hiltex Treaty."

An ornate table is brought out into the middle of the room and both the Patriarch and Peat meet

186

around it. On the table is a large scroll covered in symbols, then a person in regal attire, whom Peat presumed to be the Master of Ceremonies announces the arrival of the delegation from Apoleia, the main doors swing open and a large group of delegates enter superciliously, dressed in distinguished garbs. They proceed directly to the table at which Peat and the Patriarch are standing and stop about a yard short. The Patriarch signs the parchment and hands the quill to his attendant who passes it to Peat who in turn places his signature next to that of Donamis'. The Master of Ceremonies then rolls up the scroll and binds it using a gold ring before handing it to the Patriarch. Defas' chief emissary then moves forward expecting to receive the scroll from the Patriarch's hand but instead Donamis passes it to Peat saying, "Let Earth's own Representative present the declaration."

The emissary melodramatically recoils when Peat moves forward to hand him the scroll and he signals for one of his subordinates to take it from Peat's hand after which he proclaims, "We accept this declaration of *Tryloss' Representative!*" and with that Apoleia's delegation leaves.

The room is clamoring with chat from the council table and the gallery but for Peat the affront to him was not as disturbing as the first hand confirmation of Donamis and Lynextius' warnings about Apoleia's imperious intent for Earth. Peats musings on the incident were interrupted by a loud horn and looking around Peat realized that the Councilors and the Patriarch were now standing at their seats as were the gallery members and everyone seemed to be looking squarely at him. Quietness fell on the room before the Council's spokesperson Councilor Omarex, a low sized man with a husky voice, spoke, "Peter Black, it has pleased this Council to sponsor you as Earth's Representative in the Trials. In preparing for these tests you will have our full support."

Donamis then speaks up, "Perhaps Satrap Lynextius could continue to counsel Peter in preparation for the Trials..."

Lynextius moves out from the gallery area and putting his hand on Peat's shoulder says, "If it pleases the Council and Earth's Representative, I would willingly offer my services."

Looking around at the council members and consulting with the Patriarch, Omarex issues the Councils blessing, "It so please the Council, what say Earth's Representative?"

Peat, feeling somewhat disconcerted by the bureaucracy of the proceedings fails to apprehend that a response is being sought, Lynextius gives him a little pat on the shoulder which is enough to enlighten Peat and he responds, thankfully saying, "Yes, yes I am, that would be great."

"Very well, Representative Black in two weeks you will be transported to the planet of Creaton where you and another will compete in the Trials to decide Earth's allegiance. Till then you may remain a guest of the Xtaron communion, if you wish." Omarex declares.

It was not long before Peat and Lynextius were excused by the Council and making their way towards their transport. Peat felt somewhat strange and conspicuous upon leaving the Council chambers; it was as if his new title of Earth's Representative conferred a prestige over which he had little control. Lynextius remained typically silent and when the two were alone on the ship heading back to the Palace, it suddenly dawned on Peat that he'd never really found out what the Trials actually consisted of. His preoccupation with other questions and feelings had seen him conjugate multiple presuppositions but in truth he knew nothing of what might actually occur during the Trials. At first he felt angry at himself for having failed to get a clear answer but then his focus turned to Lynextius who surely, Peat reasoned, should have informed him as to what the Trials actually entailed.

Feeling rather annoyed at the prolonged silence Peat spoke to Lynextius bluntly, "It just dawned on me, I actually don't know what the Trials involve!" But Lynextius remained silent and simply looked out the window as if he had not heard Peat.

Peat held his tongue for another few minutes but his frustration grew and eventually he blurted out exactly what he was thinking, "Look I need to know what's going to happen at the Trials, you're meant to counsel me but I still don't even know what I'm going to be facing in two weeks!"

Looking at Peat Lynextius replied in a conciliatory manner, "You have shown extraordinary trust Peter... do not mistake this for naiveté. The truth is... we do not fully know ourselves! The Creaton Trials were traditionally designed to test the elite of Pillatarian warriors in all matters relating to combat. The Apoleia delegation which pushed for the Trials to be included under the Hiltex Treaty did so presuming an advantage in it. However, Creaton culture had already changed by that stage in one very important respect. It has been deeply influenced by romantically embellished legends surrounding a small number of rogue Xtarons who deserted Greeto in search of adventure and fortune, any trials which would include the Xtaron ritual would not be set in the conventional manner. Everything about these trials will be designed to test what the Creaton's consider the most admirable features of an Xtaron; fearlessness, toughness and cunning. The terms of the treaty do not offer much information, the main stipulation states that the Representative must be one who has never been joined with a Sumboi, that the Representative may only complete the Trials as an Xtaron and that both Koininia and Apoleia will provide the Sumboi, the placement of which is a matter for the Creatons. We can infer certain things, for instance, if the Representatives prove themselves... the Creatons will surely not pass up the opportunity to stage a spectacle which would involve two Xtarons facing one another in combat. Trust me, the best way to prepare you for these trials is to start you on the journey of becoming a true Xtaron, building on your prior training in two weeks you can far exceed the Creaton's shallow notions of what it takes to be a 'great Xtaron.' "

Feeling a little embarrassed at his lack of trust and totally disarmed by the depth of forethought Lynextius has shown, Peat stammers, "Ooo I see, aaa... that's, that's good."

Looking back out the window Lynextius then says, as if it were an afterthought, "Lord Defas will not hurry his declaration, it will be late next week before we learn against whom you will compete." Peat looks at Lynextius with concern and desires to ask him if he knows of any likely candidates for Apoleia but wanting to show deference he keeps silent.

As Peat commenced his training, on Creaton sinister happenings were unfolding. On the barren wastelands of Creaton, at the mouth of a cavern in the most desolate of places a ship touched down on the parched land.   Commander Kysol emerges from the craft and makes his way deep into the cavern using a small stone-like object to light his way. As Kysol makes his way further down this winding path a hoarse voice comes from a cavity just yards ahead of him, "Commander Kysol, is that you?" it inquired.

"Are you alone?" Kysol asked.

A large purpled skinned muscular anthropomorphic creature came forward with long coarse hair stemming from his head. "Ahh... I see the rumors are true, our people now have two Xtarons," the well informed and avaricious Lexpoltry responded.

"Do you know why I've asked you here?"

"The Trials, of course," Lexpoltry posits.

"Koinonia's Representative must not be allowed to reach the Cauldron," Kysol stressed.

"The Cauldron...?" Lexpoltry replies as if this piece of information were a surprise to him.

"We both know that the Trials can only end there!"

"What you are proposing is treachery; I could lose my head for merely talking to you," Lexpoltry says suggestively.

Taking something from the utility belt around his waist, Kysol holds up a small object against a light in his other hand as Lexpoltry moves closer to inspect it. Lexpoltry's eyes are fixated on a little fluid filled tube in Kysol's hand in which a Sumboi swims.

"Do what I ask you and it's yours!"

Lexpoltry looks directly at Kysol with voracious eyes saying, "Speak Lord your servant is listening!"

It is just over a week into Peat's training and the intensity is overwhelming. Every minute of Peat's day is accounted for, from sleeping to meal brakes, and the physical exercises are only matched in zeal by the numerous lengthy intelligence classes on the planet of Creaton, all of which from part of his daily schedule. In a way however Peat is grateful for having a jammed program as it means he doesn't have time to over-think and worry rather he remains focused on the Trials which are fast approaching. That said, Peat always drags himself out of bed a half hour early and takes that time to remember and pray for his family back home; Tom, Claire and Jim. Indeed it was Peat's love of those back on Earth that had driven him to take on this challenge and so safeguard his planet's future. Peat often found himself alone in his room in the early hours…, lost in thought as he gazed at the photo Claire had taken and so obviously treasured.

It has been ten days into his training and Peat is sitting in the canteen alone, it's late at night and Lynextius has arranged for nocturnal training outside. It has been a long if interesting day of lessons on the ecology, and peoples of Creaton, and Peat is actually relishing the opportunity to get out in the fresh air even if Lynextius has most likely planned a grueling list of activities. As Peat sits quietly eating his specially prepared high-protein meal he hears a clatter coming from the Kitchen which given the lateness of the hour, spikes his curiosity. Getting up he moves towards the kitchen door which operates by way of a motion sensor, once in range the door oscillates open and he enters to see a huge smorgasbord of food on top of the preparation counter clear on the other side of the kitchen. Peat moves around by the sorting bench to get a better view of the pantry where he presumes the late night gormandizer is, but without warning a loud shout, "Got ya!", comes from the utensil shelf above Peat's head and before he knows what's happening someone is on his back and there's an arm around his neck. Having been immersed in self-defense and combat training for the last number of months Peat instinctively swivels his body and using his considerable natural strength propels the ambusher across the room. As Peat cautiously moves around the counters to the other side of the room he hears a moan coming from the floor and looking around a large workbench he sees Bellza lying on the floor covered in all manner of food stuff after having being hurled into the platter. Appreciating he'd made a mistake and that Bellza was merely being his coltish self, Peat hurried over to him to check if he was hurt, "God I'm so sorry Bellza, are you ok?"

Rubbing his head and sitting up, "Oouuee, whatever Lynextius is teaching you it's definitely working." Peat helps him to his feet saying, "I didn't realize that---"

Interrupting Bellza says, "Ahh don't worry about it we Hellions are made of strong stuff...,"

There's a sudden pause as Bellza looks at the ground, his characteristic jovialness is gone and he

194

immediately qualifies the remark he has just made by mournfully adding, "We'll..., at least we use to be."

Peat knows he's missing something but doesn't feel it appropriate to pry into Bellza's obvious lament. Once Bellza realizes he's become melancholy he perks himself up and in a light-hearted manner asks as he moves towards the pantry door, "Well, anyway kid... has Lynextius turned you into some sort of fighting machine yet or what?"

Following Bellza into the Pantry, "Amm..., to be honest a lot of it is about how to survive in the Creaton wilderness and learning about the different creatures and peoples that live on the planet."

As he voraciously devours little disc shaped pieces of what looked like meat patties Bellza comments, "It's gonna be weird for him going back to Creaton, eh, in fact... if it wasn't for the Trials I don't think they'd let him in. But you're lucky to have him here, it's almost like having a man on the inside!"

"Who...?" Peat asks.

Looking up from the tray of food that he is in the process of ingesting Bellza responds, "What?"

"Who are you talking about?"

Opening his eyes wide in disbelief, "Really, you don't know."

Then taking a plate piled with food the small glutton makes his way out into the canteen followed closely by a curious Peat.

Sitting down at a table, although Bellza had to fetch a taller stool to reach a sufficient height, the little red creature elaborated, "Ok so you might know, Lynextius is in charge of Oleald; that's a large island south west of Tryloss but he's not even from this planet originally. Lynextius actually comes from Creaton!"

Surprised, Peat utters, "What!"

"Ya... Apparently he was like one of the greatest Creaton Generals they ever had but then when the legend of Greeto Ron, that was Donamis' uncle, reached his home planet he left in search of this great warrior hoping to join up with him and learn from him... but, and this is what I've heard, when he found the young prince he was horrified by his brutality and shocked that such a person could have such power. He joined one of Tryloss' immigrant legions and quickly worked his way up the ranks and eventually he lead his own battalion in Tryloss' Civil War, and can you believe it, they made him a General, the first non-native ever to hold that position in the Tryloss' Army. Well I don't know much about the history but apparently the civil war wasn't going that well and so Teea Ron, that's Donamis' father, made three of his best Generals Xtarons, and well... Lynextius was one of them! They went on to win the war... yah, Lynextius is a legend all over the Galaxy."

Taking a moment to absorb what he has just been told Peat speaks to Bellza who is meanwhile stuffing his mouth with food, "Wait, how could Lynextius be around for that long?"

Never one to be overly concerned with table etiquette Bellza, his mouth half full of food, explains, "Creaton's live long anyway... but the Sumboi seems to extend their lives a lot... I'm telling you Peat I've seen the strangest shit happen to different species when they've attached to a Sumboi, ha maybe you'll grow another arm or something, hehe!"

Peat smiles worryingly before Bellza adds, "Aaa... I'm only messing with ya, well listen I better go before someone catches me in here, technically I'm not allowed in here outside of official meal times, but I mean if they gave bigger portions they'd be no need for these night raids, am I right, eh!"

Walking towards the exit with Bellza, Peat has much more on his mind that he wants to discuss, "Bellza, why does Lynextius always have his Xtaron suit generated, I mean I see other Xtarons and they only generate their suit for training."

Bellza looks up ambiguously at Peat, "Look I'm not sure I am the one to be talking to you about this, maybe you should----"

"Ahh please Bellza you're the only one I get to chat with about this stuff, no one else talks to me about it... and I can't ask Lynextius he's, amm... well you know; kinda serious!"

Feeling benignant towards the young novitiate Bellza yields, "Ooo fine, but don't tell anyone I told you

197

this. Well a few of the Royal Medical staff told me
that the only thing keeping Lynextius alive is his
Sumboi, I mean let's be fair he's ancient even by
Creaton standards so... the suit must act kinda like a
life support. I don't suppose he could even
relinquish it now, not at this stage."
" 'Relinquish' what do you mean?" Peat asks
inquisitively.
"Now that I presumed you knew. Do they tell you
anything in all those classes you attend... An Xtaron
can choose to pass on their Sumboi, of course when
an Xtaron dies they have no choice it just happens
automatically but---"
A noise can be heard from outside the canteen's
main entrance, "...If they catch me in here I'm in for
it, see you later Peat!" And with that Bellza quickly
dashes out the side exit.
Peat looked over to the main doors to see Ritrak,
the palace guard charged with his personal
protection, standing there.
"It's time to go Sir", the dutiful soldier says.
Peat nods gently and making his way across the mess
hall and leaves with his military attaché to
recommence his training. But in his mind Peat
continues to ponder on all of what Bellza had told
him.

          It was late one night, only two days out from
the Trials and although Peat was meant to be fast
asleep after a long day mixed between practical
training earlier in the morning and then the

continuation of a comprehensive treatment of
Creaton hoplology which ran late into the night, but
unknown to Lynextius, and mostly everyone else, the
young Earthling had managed to convince his
nocturnal guardian, Xtaron Omatage, to bring him to
the Xtaron training circuit. Peat had become
enthralled with watching the incredible sight of
Xtarons training and so Omatage had agreed to
bring him to the empty viewing gallery atop the
circuit.

""You really should be resting," Omatage counseled.
"Yah I know, but Councilor Fizer definitely said that
two of the most skillful of Xtarons on the planet
would be training here tonight, I just had to see
them."

   "Yah, two of Fizer's own personal paladins no
doubt!" Omatage said sarcastically without even
thinking.

 "What do you mean?" Peat inquired, a little agitated
by Omatage's perceived negativity.

   "Ah nothing... it's just..., well lately he always
seems to be around the Academy befriending the
neophytes, especially the most distinguished of
them" Omatage vents.

  "What's wrong with that?" Peat wonders, genuinely
ignorant of the troubled relations Tryloss' Council
and the Xtaron Communion have had for years.
Omatage picks up on the young foreigner's political
innocence and decides against adding to his already
numerous concerns.

"Nothing... you're right he's probably just being friendly. You know me... always suspecting the worst!"

Peat reflects on this for a moment until Omatage points down at the circuit entrance and, as if excited at the opportunity to move the conversation along, he blurts out, "Oh look, here they come now." And so Peat and Omatage settled in to observe, what Fizer had promised the young Representative would be, a didactic exhibition. Meantime Lynextius, Po-Kal, Fizer and a host of other interested parties had convened an *ad hoc* meeting with the Patriarch in his private offices. The atmosphere was troubled and many of the attendees seemed uneasy.

The layout of the room meant that everyone was facing in towards the Patriarch's desk, Councilor Fizer stood up and bowing ever so slightly to the Patriarch he spoke, "We've received official confirmation as to the identity of Apoleia's Representative, Lord Defas' own son, Oratron who is of equal age to Representative Black."

Anxiously looking at the Patriarch, Omarex interjected with some alarm, "This changes everything, we cannot expect that Peter Black would ever be ready to face such a challenge."

"We must have faith in Earth's Representative, perhaps we could hear from Xtaron Lynextius on the progress of Peter's preparation....," the Patriarch states.

200

Lynextius stands up and after acknowledging the Patriarch he addresses the gathering, "My Lord, Councilors and colleagues, Peter is capable of completing the Trials, we must avoid the temptation of presuming too much, we cannot know exactly what these tests will consist of but that they will be arduous on both body and mind is certain. Many great warriors have been lost to the Creaton Trials but we must keep faith and hope in Earth's Representative. I have not seen such raw abilities in a neophyte before; his aptitude is matched by an unquenchable willingness to advance, Peter Black will serve his planet well in the Trials and beyond." The meeting continues long into the night.

The fateful day arrives and for the first time Peat awakes without the momentary confusions as to where he is. In fact, as he dresses in prescribed traditional Creaton clothing that Lynextius had left out for him, Peat is struck by a feeling of ease that has filled him on this momentous day.

Peat is due in the Great Hall for a ceremony but after spending too long praying for his loved ones and thinking about Claire he's running late, and so leaving his quarters he hurries down the hallway towards the stage entrance at the back of the great hall when, out of the blue, he hears a call from behind him; "Kid, Peat hold on!"

Turing around he sees Bellza jogging up to him, panting heavily, "Wow kid, you've..., you've gotten

fast, phew..." Regaining his breath he continues,
"...Ok so I know you're in a hurry but I didn't get a
chance to say goodbye and... well you know...,"
Peat smiles and in a calm but affectionate voice
says, "Thanks Bellza, you're a good friend."
Stirred Bellza looks away from Peat, "Ahaa shit...,
don't get soft on me now!
Next time I'll see you you'll be an Xtaron and oo,
wait a minute... I knew there was something else,
amm ahh yes here they are! "
Bellza holds up what looks to Peat like two tiny black
marbles except for a small blue cross-sectional
strip which had two tiny snags protruding from its
surface about one inch apart at the nearest points.
Wanting to be gracious Peat put out his hand to
accept them saying, "Thanks" and inspecting them
for a few seconds he inquires, "What are they?"
"Awwe Peat today is your lucky day, these were left
to me years ago by an Xtaron whose great-
grandfather was Patriarch Feelexus' Chief
Researcher on the Tar Limatu and I want you to
have them."

"Awaa thanks Bellza, aaa what do they do?"
Raising his head slightly and adopting a perplexed
expression Bellza admits, "To be honest I don't
really know! Mill Yak, that's my old friend, well he
died suddenly just as I started my training as a
neophyte and he left these for me along with a note
saying, amm, what was it again... 'To my good friend
Bellza, Around evil...,' no that wasn't it... '*Amidst.*'

202

yes, 'Amidst evil, when the veil of...,' aaa *prudence,* ...when the veil of prudence, not the sword, is required grip one per hand and and...' aaa well I've forgotten the rest but I'm sure you'll figure it out, I mean the truth is I'm never going to be an Xtaron now..., well you know it's all politics and that, but I want you to have these whatever the hell they are, they were meant for an Xtaron and aaa, well anyway they might be of some help in the Trials I thought."

"I really appreciate it Bellza, amm Representatives aren't allowed to bring anything to the Trials with us but maybe you could mind these til--"

In a hushed voice Bellza seeks to persuade Peat, "Don't worry Peat not even the best scanners can pick up the crazy stuff that comes off the Tar Limatu, they'll never know you have them!"
Smiling at Bellza's cunning, "I really appreciate it Bellza but---"

Not allowing Peat to finish Bellza continues to try to and coax Peat, "ahh come on Peat..., you just know those sneaky Apoleia bastards are going to break the rules every chance they get!"

"Maybe so, but all the more reason to do what's good and just!"
Putting out his hand to take back the gift for safekeeping, "Awwee you're a good one Peat, there's no doubting that, you'll make a great Xtaron. I'll keep them for you till you return then."
Peat hands back the spheres to Bellza and just as he turns to proceed up the hallway towards the

stage Bellza opens out his arms and moving towards Peat as if to hug him, he says, "Come on down here." Peat kneels down and embraces Bellza who, with accustomed competence, slips the two black spherical objects into one of the many slits on Peats inner garment before saying, "Well that's enough of that, now you better get to the Great Hall for the send-off!"

Peat smiled and dashed down the hallway. Bellza stands there looking at Peat disappearing up the hallway and simply shakes his head with a bemused expression plastered on his face and fondly says to himself, "Good luck kid!"

When Peat finally reaches the backstage he is met by a very disgruntled Master of Ceremonies who, while tossing an opulent robe around the young man's shoulders chastises him for his tardiness and then rapidly bloviates through the ceremonial protocol: "Okay so when I give you the signal walk out beside the lectern, bow to the Patriarch, we're not talking kowtowing; less is more, then take the scepter in your right hand placing your left hand on your right chest before bowing to the Councilors, then raise the rod in the air towards the crown pause and allow for adulation from the assembly then, and only then, move to the vacant seat on the Patriarch's right hand but make sure you only sit down if the Patriarch is already seated. When the speeches are finished you can move with the procession down the center aisle and out the main door of the Great Hall but make sure you stay behind the Patriarch at all times, and remember dignity, confidence and so on! Ok have got that?" Peat had followed practically nothing of the instructions and had long since tuned the Master of Ceremonies out, so that during his condensing monologue most of what Peat heard was a background babbling, while his eyes peered out around the stage looking to locate Lynextius. But, recognizing the cue to respond from the haughty MC, Peat nodded his head and moving to the left wing where he could look out at the row of dignitaries on the stage, he marveled at the diversity of the creatures which were present, most of whom shared some semblance to humans but others were of a completely different physical makeup, which fascinated Peat so much that he could not help but stare.

Peat was startled by a tap on his shoulder which was followed by the instructions, "Go, go quickly." Peat staggered out onto the stage as Councilor Omarex, who stood at the lectern, drew the attention of the crowd to Peat's presence, loud acclamations ensued and overwhelmed by the reception Peat found himself frozen as he looked out over this enormous auditorium. Omarex went to Peat and securing the bedazzled lad's attention handed him a most decorative of scepters with the image of Earth on one end and a seal on the other. Peat looked at the rod intently and wondered what the seal stood for but Omarex gestured for him to acknowledge the crowd and so, with some hesitation and a strong feeling of embarrassment, Peat raised the scepter wavering it slowly in the air to the adulation of the masses. Then Peat gladly took his seat beside the Patriarch who smiled at him as if sharing a private joke in this most public of events and after three more speakers had delivered rousing speeches on; Tryloss' prosperity, the security and peace of Koinonia and finally the mysterious planet of Earth, Peat got up and join the cavalcade as it made its way through the jubilees gathering. Peat could see some familiar faces but there was no sign of Lynextius as he was ushered towards the hanger, from where he will depart for Tryloss, his fears begin to grow that his mentor may not be accompanying him on the journey to Creaton as had been planned. From the moment Peat had left the Great Hall a multitude of well-wishers and delegates began approaching him and the opportunity to inquire as to where Lynextius was never presented itself. Before he knew it Peat was standing in the royal hanger bay meeting Captain Conateeve who explained the flight schedule to him. Peat continues to feign interest in what was being said to him but he was preoccupied with locating Lynextius, but the moment the Captain had finished speaking he was led up to the ship's main entrance by an overbearing official. Then the craft doors shut and for the first time since he'd

206

left his room earlier that morning he found himself alone with nothing but his thoughts. Peat was walking around inspecting some of the compartments when he felt the craft lift off the ground and remembering a bit of what the Captain had warned he made his way to a passenger suite and strapped himself into a seat. Taking off proved rather bumpy but after fifteen minutes Peat felt comfortable enough to explore the rest of the ship. He left the suite and made his way along the craft's long deck checking each compartment as he went. Nearing the back of the ship Peat saw two of the Patriarch's own Cerberus Guards, they made up Donamis' own personal legion comprising renowned warriors who swore allegiance directly to the Patriarch himself. Peat was aware of their fearsome reputation and approached cautiously, announcing his presence with a "Hi," he got no reply. Getting closer he saw that the duo were guarding another entrance and Peat's inquisitiveness was peeked as he approached, and although he felt somewhat intimidated by these burly elite armed guards he nonetheless mustered his confidence to approach them.

And in the hope that his conferred status as Earth's Representative might count for something he inquired, "Amm... can I, a go in there?"

With that the two soldiers stood to attention and then one of them responded, "Sir, you are so authorized to enter."

Peat looked at both of them once more and nodded his head slightly as he walked through the passageway with three layers of metal doors sweeping open one after another. Inside, the compartment was almost completely dark except for the center of the room where a bright, lazar generated, shield protected and encased a transparent vessel in which a Sumboi swam around. Peat recognized the creature from his studies in the Xtaron archives but it was the first time he'd actually seen one in real life. Peat presumed that this Sumboi was the one intended for him as part of the Trials, yet despite all the preparation and theoretical knowledge that Peat had assimilated, it still felt surreal for him to look with his own eyes upon this separate biological entity intended to join in the most complete of unions with himself, body and mind.

As he approached the shield for a closer look at this Sumboi he felt a certain exhilaration before a voice came from across the room saying, "Careful...!" Peat was startled and froze at first, then he moved to one side of the shield to get a better look at the figure which was emerged from one of the room's many penumbra alcoves. Seeing that it was Lynextius Peat smiled and slightly nodded his head out of respect.

Lynextius responded in kind before moving closer to the tube and continuing, "...this shield would dissolve flesh and bone in a fraction of a second, better if

I..." and with that he reached his hand down to a control pad beside the protective beam and entered in the security key while also calling it out aloud so that Peat could know it.

Lynextius took a step back as Peat moved in closer to the vessel before looking at his mentor to get the 'all clear,' which he did, before taking the small container in his hand and holding it up to his face peering in at this wondrous creature.

While inspecting the creature Peat confides in Lynextius, "I'm nervous!"

In his typically judicious and forthright manner Lynextius responds, "Of course you are, that is normal."

Lowering the vessel and looking at Lynextius Peat feels the sting of despair entering his heart, "...I mean I'm really nervous, what if I die; all the warring clans of Aloss, the fierce creatures, the sea monsters, the prince of Piallatar, everything you thought me about...how can I do this..., how could I ever have possibly thought I could do this?"

Peat places the vessel back on the pedestal before moving over to a utility trunk on the ground and sitting down on it, he sighs deeply and looks up at Lynextius, speaking candidly he says, "What am I going to do?"

Lynextius slowly goes about reactivating the shield and while still looking towards the vessel he offers advice, "Peter, there's nothing wrong in feeling fear, the dangers of the Trials are both real and substantial. I have thought you everything you need to get through these tests and I know you are capable, but only you can decide if you're ready." Lynextius pauses for a minute and wanders around the room slowly, "...You know, I was once a member of Creaton society and for years I saw many of the greatest warriors perish in the Trials, but they did so not because they were wanting in strength or bravery but rather because their hearts were full of arrogance and pride...", moving towards Peat and kneeling down in front of him Lynextius goes on, "..Peter, look at me. You are capable of meeting any challenge, Trials and beyond, that is why I chose you. But without steadfast self-belief you will surely be lost!"

Rising to his feet Lynextius turns and leaves the room while Peat, contemplating, remains seated on the utilities locker staring up at the Sumboi.

- Chapter Nine -

After a good deal of time has elapsed Peat still remained in the secured room while Lynextius stood in a dark plain compartment close to the front of the craft meditating. As still as a statue Creaton's native son stood pensively, then a warning beacon sounded in preparation for entry into the Creaton's atmosphere. Lynextius took a seat beside a transparent panel through which he peered out upon his home planet and then feeling somewhat nostalgic he produced a small disk from under his right shoulder pad and tossed it to the ground on the center of the floor. He activated the device using the controller on his forearm which saw a voiceless reel of holographic visuals light up the room. Then, as if Lynextius had somehow downloaded copies of his memories to this device, there appeared an initial depiction of two small young Creatons; Lynextius and, presumably his brother, playing games and performing chores. Numerous clips passed showing the structured daily life of these two siblings. Their youth seemed typical and happy but then, with greater frequency as they got older, the scenes hinted at the harsh and cold nature of Creaton life. More serious scenarios replaced the carefreeness of their childhood as their father

became ever more prominent in the reels. A number
of similarly themed projections followed which
captured the growing sibling rivalry. In the most
regal of attire the father trained both brothers in
the way of Creaton combat, both seemed to excel
but it was Lynextius in particular who received
highest praise. For instance, Lynextius was shown
being presented by his father with the most ornate
of daggers, clearly an heirloom. Tellingly, the
younger brother could increasingly be seen fading
into the background looking equally less and less
content. What then followed from this disk shaped
device was a series of representations of Lynextius
establishing himself a high ranking and respected
member in the bellicose Creaton society. The final
clip showed a great open top stadium built upon a
rugged mountain. The grandstands were full with
the most ornery of spectators, who looked on in
twisted excitement at the many dead bodies that
lay on the ground in a deep pit at the kernel of this
crucible. Only four living Creatons remained among
a scattering of corpses which suggested a most
brutal melee was taking place. Although this clip
was projected mute, the image of the bloodthirsty
spectators in the stands and the intent observation
of the dignitaries in the mezzanine, spoke volumes
about the nature of this contest; this was surely
Creaton's ultimate battle royal. As the holograms
zoomed in closer on the last four battling warriors
it was clear that all were masked except for a young

Lynextius. The quadruplet were divided two on two at separate ends of the pit, the skill and agility of competitors was awe-inspiring, while the slayed remains, scattered all around, were potent reminders of the brutal nature of this whole affair. Lynextius fought with a ferocity which, when contrasted against the calm and composed manner he was now known for, was frightening. After a short period of time Lynextius' superiority as a warrior began to show over that of his opponent and with a threefold sequence of baleful blows which were delivered with lethal precision he dispatched his opponent. Then with an elongated shield in one hand and a sword in the other he approached a blue circle in the center of the pit and stood on its edge watching the two other combatants dual in their penultimate struggle. One of the warriors gained the upper hand and knocking his foe to the ground made as if to deal the final blow raising his sword but, lying on the ground, his adversary produced a small dagger and with deadly accuracy hurled it. Then just as the larger of the two combatants crashed to the ground with the dagger lodged firmly in his neck the other Creaton got to his feet and with sword in hand he approached Lynextius, stopping at the opposite side of the blue circle. Both turned to the dignitaries and reverently bowed before facing each other, weapons in hand. As Lynextius approached with malicious intent his counterpart removed his mask, it was his younger brother! Lynextius' face dropped as did his sword, stunned and horrified by the fact that his own brother stood before him as his challenger. The younger sibling had an emotionless, steely expression and with his sword he gestured Lynextius to pick up his weapon but the elder's shock and horror soon changed to a pitying disillusionment. It was if a veil had been lifted from over the eyes of Lynextius' soul as he looked around at the lifeless bodies, the blood stained ground, the sanguinary faces of those in the stands and finally, peering into his own brother's hate filled eyes he saw the mirrored reflection of jealousy, blind ambition and hatefulness which had shackled him for so many years. Lynextius turned and walked away, while being pelted with stones from the angry crowds. As the younger brother looked on at the actions of the elder a burst of rage over took him and he charged at his kin from behind raising his sword and just as he committed to delivering the decisive blow Lynextius, as if having sensed impending blindside, tumbled to the ground and rolled to the remains of a nearby warrior. Picking up the long metal spear he defended himself against a flurry of frenzied blows. But soon Lynextius was on the offensive, he began to gain the upper hand with some impressive footwork and in a moment of frustration the younger, more inexperienced, made a wild swing for Lynextius' torso but anticipating this Lynextius leaned back before using his long weapon to upend his brother to the ground. Loosing grip of his weapon the second-born's defeat was all but certain as Lynextius stood over him with the spear pointing at his throat. Then drawing back his weapon Lynextius offered his hand to his sibling, but the younger felt humiliated and this fraternal gesture only enraged him more, he spat at Lynextius. Lynextius dropped the spear on the ground near his brother and made for the exit in a somber manner, it was clear that the crowd were ecstatic cheering on Lynextius. As the disgraced younger brother realized the elder had effectively won the contest and the acclaim of the crowd, he picked up the spear and launched it at Lynextius. The crowd's collective gasp presumably alerted Lynextius because he turned just as the spear was about to perforate his head and almost instinctively he leaned backwards, the spear grazed his chest while Lynextius rolled to the ground and with lighting reflex took hold of the jewel encrusted dagger he had been gifted by his father and flung it at his assailant. The dagger plunged into the left eye of his brother, as the younger fell to his knees, arms outstretched and palms turned upwards, he raised his left hand and wrenched out the aureate weapon. Tossing the dagger to the ground the defeated warrior clenched his fists while raising his head to the sky offering a roar of perdition. A grief-stricken Lynextius looks on before turning his face to the ground and dejectedly walking towards the exit as the crowd cheered and praised him. With that the holographic exhibition is over and another alarm sounds, notifying all to prepare for landing. The craft along with a convoy of battle cruisers came down in a massive secure compound on the edge of Creaton's capital city Qa Talo. When the flag ship's door opened it was Lynextius who was the first to disembark and a few moments later Peat proceeded out without a hint of apprehension, confidently striding down the walkway carrying the Sumboi vessel in his arm and flanked by the two Cerberus Guards. Peat sees Lynextius speaking to another Creaton but as he approaches the pair Lynextius walks away towards a complex of buildings.

Peter moves to meet Lynextius but is intercepted by the other Creaton who introduces himself, "Greetings Representative Black, I am Prefect of the Trials, Polexiamas Atar, I trust you had a pleasant flight."

Peat gives a slight nod and smile before reservedly saying, "Yes."

"Good, your transportation is ready to take you to the starting point; Representative Oratron already waits at his designated point."

Then noticing the vessel tucked under Peat's arm Polexiamas continues in a somewhat pretentious tone, "...Aaa I see you've brought a Sumboi as requested, how wonderful. However, there has been a slight change in plans... This Sumboi is no

216

longer needed but fret not, the Xtaron ritual will still comprise an important part of the Trials."

One of the Cerberus Guards immediately moves forward and Peat hands him the vessel before the two legionaries make their way back to the ship. Polexiamas beckons two Creaton guards and instructs them, "Show Representative Black to his transport!" then turning to address Peat he says, "I hope to meet you at your designated commencement point but an urgent matter requires my immediate attention, please excuse me for now."

With a slight bow both parties go their own way, Peat found the appearance of Creatons very interesting and their skin color in particular was a marvel to him. He'd seen images of them during his research in the Palace and knew a great deal about their civilization but he was still fascinated to see them with his own eyes, their purplish skin was a particular sight to behold. Peat wondered how Lynextius would compare in appearance, especially given his advanced years. More seriously however; Peat puzzled over where Lynextius had gone and what he'd talked to Polexiamas about. Peat was brought away from the city of Qa Talo and travelling in a speedy chalice-shaped machine which based on appearance would seem far more suited to parades than traversing rough terrain. Peat was mesmerized by the scenic landscape which changed dramatically from dry land to lush green forestry over a matter of miles. After about fifty minutes of rapid travel Peat reached the terminus a quo where three Creatons waited for him. Peat was surprised that there were only two guards and a delegate there to meet him, he had expected, even if he didn't desire, a huge crowd for what was built as a most crucial affair.

As Peat stepped down from his transport a Creaton delegate rushed over to him, "Representative Black, you're most welcome, I'm Ly Amas, Prefect Polexiamas sends his apologies to both you and Representative Oratron but some last minute modifications to the Trials required his personal attention. As we speak on the other side of this ridge your competitor is being briefed on the Trials so let us commence; each Representative is required to travel along the Polmorian Way to the Cauldron which lies on top of Mount Crewux, the use of any life form or machine for transport is not permitted, be warned, violation of this rule carries heavy penalties up to and including death. Along the way you will have to find three objects, each one is valuable in itself and an essential part of the proclamation ritual but they will also serve in leading you to your Sumboi. However, you must only approach the Cauldron with all three objects and then only once the Xtaron ritual has been complete. Should you reach the Cauldron's pit, be aware that only one Representative can stand undisputed in the Doombeg Circle, as long as two stand in the circle either way!"

218

Taking from his pocket a small silver cylindrical object Ly Amas shows it to Peat, "...You will need to find three of these and remember they are necessary to make the proclamation so don't lose them."

Suddenly a siren sounds from somewhere on the cliff-face, and anxiously Ly Amas crouches down fumbling to open a case on the ground beside him. "...Aaah here we are," he says as he pulls out a jet injector and a small rectangular case about the size of Peat's palm.

Unnerved Peat asks, "What are they?"

Ly Amas places the two objects on the ground and then reaches in for a larger black device with two handles protruding from its sides and then replies, "Well actually, this comes first, I need to scan you to make sure you're not carrying any prohibited items."

Ly Amas thoroughly runs the scanner all over Peat's body from head to foot and then putting the device back in the case he reaches for the gun on the ground.

"Now, this injects tiny hyper sensitive pressure spheres which also omit a coded positioning signal, both Representatives are required to be fitted with a number of these spheres, they are placed in the base of your feet so that your movements and position can be observed at all times but only Prefect Polexiamas has access to the monitoring system."

Peat takes off his boots and hosiery allowing Ly Amas to shoot multiple monitoring devices along the base of his feet, "They won't interfere with your movement in any way," the official assures Peat. Ly Amas then places the gun back in the case and picks up the small rectangular container off the ground before saying with a sigh, "Lastly then, these are digital lenses you place over the surface of your eyes, they allow Polexiamas to see everything you look at."

Ly Amas places the lenses over the surface of Peat's eyes adding, "You must not interfere with any of the monitoring devices, the spheres and lenses are very durable and resistant to the elements so they will last..., and should you make it to the point of merging with the Sumboi they will be naturally expelled from your body."

Then for a second time the siren sounds and Ly Amas hurries Peat to a stone column at the base of the mountainous valley, saying "There isn't much time, now remember Representative Black, this is a race..., retrieve the objects as quickly as possible, find the Sumboi and get to the Cauldron to make your proclamation. Ensure you do not, intentionally or otherwise use any life form beyond yourself, or any machine as a means of transport, remember you are being monitored closely and the penalties for breaching this rule are severe.

Ly Amas then handed Peat a large gadget taken from the case on the ground, "This tracker will lead you to the first cylinder."

Then for a final time the horn sounds and without hesitation Ly Amas says loudly, "You may begin Sir," before turning and walking briskly away from Peat towards his shuttle.

Peat looks around for a moment before appreciating that just like that the race for Earth had begun! The shuttle disappears into the distance and Peat stands alone beside the column running over in his head all Ly Amas has told him. Now mostly everything the young Earthling had been told made perfect sense to him; Peat had being given comprehensive albeit general lessons on the planet of Creaton and so what Ly Amas had said registered with him. Composing himself Peat looked at the tracker which was a traditional Creaton homing device, the workings of which he'd been shown the first week of his training. As he turned on the gadget and jogged into the valley, the screen on the device showed a map with a marker identifying Peat's first destination. Peat was very familiar theoretically with the Polmorian Way, indeed the moment Ly Amas had mentioned it he'd felt a type of studious elation similar to the sense of excitement he would feel when he given particular attention to a specific topic in the hope that it would appear on one of Jim's terminal test, and it did. However, no sooner had such an insouciant sentiment arose than Peat dismissed it by refocusing on his primary objective; namely, getting to the first rarity as quickly and safely as possible. From Peat's detailed studies of the Polmorian Way, he was aware of a whole plethora of things he hoped to avoid and had already started to visualize possible encounters he may face and plot out the best way of handling them. Yet in the back of his mind lingered the unsettling realization that he knew nothing about Prince Oratron or the path he was taking to the Cauldron, 'what if their paths should overlap?', 'What if the young Prince should gain the lead and claim Earth for Apoleia?' ...these were among the most unsettling of thoughts which arose for Peat, yet he sought to neutralize their sting by reflecting upon Lynextius' words of encouragement. Peat was now following a trail winding up a cliff face and racing around a sharp bend he noticed some small Jillnooms scurrying down the path by his feet, he had identified these hairy little creatures straight away by their distinctive forked tails. He was concerned though that they may be fleeing a larger predator and so Peat pressed in against a cavity in the escarpment. Concealing himself for about a minute he was about to re-emerge when he heard a pattering descending at pace down the path. From his position he could only catch a glance, a partial sighting of a furry creature, about the height of a large dog, speeding down the slope, presumably after its meal. From

Peat's ecology lessons he knew of three furry animals of similar height which lived in this region and fed on Jillnooms, all of them were best avoided. Before continuing up the path Peat took out the only weapon he was permitted to carry, a traditional Creaton firearm which shot tiny glass-like pellets that, upon impact, shattered causing a chemically induced rapid oxidation reaction resulting in a violent explosion. Peat's training at the Palace in operating weaponry was perhaps the most difficult part of Lynextius' entire program, when Peat became aware of the advanced and destructive nature of many of the weapons in Tryloss' arsenal he knew exactly why Earth's fate was in such jeopardy. Creaton weapons were relatively primitive in comparison to what was to be found in Tryloss' and other more advanced planets in the Galaxy. After tucking his weapon in under his belt Peat hurried up the pathway conscious that every time he stopped he was possibly allowing his opponent to gain on him. A heavy mist began to set in as he went higher up the mountain and a cool breeze began to blow. Peat was keeping a steady pace when he realized that Ly Amas had never said the cylinder had to remain in the same place; it had never dawned on him that the inanimate objects he sought could easily be moved by someone or something. Peat felt annoyed at not having thought of this earlier and he quickly rechecked his vade mecum. He was relieved to see the destination had not changed and that he was still on course, but from now on he would periodically check the homing device to make sure he was still going the right way. After nearly an hour tracking up the inclining slope the fog had become so dense that Peat had to resort to carefully placing one hand against the cliff face when moving forward and stop completely when checking the homing device, luckily for him the map on the screen gave an illuminated red flash otherwise it would have been unreadable in the fog. Evermore frustrated by the slow pace of his progress Peat eventually reached the designated destination at which point the screen simply went blank before a green flash of light went off after which the machine simply shut down as if powerless. Peat shook the machine at first but it was totally unresponsive and checking it for a switch of some kind proved equally fruitless. The fact that the machine had seemingly shut down did not worry Peat much because according to the homing device the cylinder was close by. Still effectively blinded in a thick fog Peat crouched to the ground and moved his hand around but he could feel nothing of any consequence... Standing up Peat took a few steps forward before putting out his hand to lean against the cliff only to fall to the ground. Presuming the path must have reached a sharp bend Peat felt around and discovered he'd actually stumbled into the entrance of what he presumed most likely to be a cave. Peat was wary of entering but felt

224

compelled to inspect this entire area thoroughly to find that which he sought. Before stepping into the dark passage Peat took out the only other item, along with the loaded gun and reserve clip of ammo, that he was permitted to bring on the Trials, a set of three Creaton shockers which when activated travelled independently along a route for up to a mile unimpeded while omitting a forceful shock wave impacting on anything in the immediate vicinity. Although Peat knew that the wave would most likely not be anywhere near strong enough to undermine the structural stability of the passage the shocker might well trigger any booby traps. Peat took out one of the shockers and setting its direction tossed it into the dark passage and hearing a slight rattle from the passage way walls Peat knew the device was working and he proceed to follow the vibrations as he walked further and further into the tunnel while keeping a sizeable distance between himself and the hovering shocker. Peat began to fear that he was wasting time when the homing device emitted another green flash, he felt such relief and was now convinced that this meant he was getting closer. Yet Peat still kept a cautious distance from the shocker which navigated a number of yards ahead. Peat's wariness was also evidenced by the fact that he unconsciously kept his right hand on the butt of the weapon he toted. As Peat began to fear that he was going too deep into this pitch black adit he noticed, in the not too far distance, a glow lighting a bend in the passage. Peat glimpsed as the shocker disappeared around the bend carrying on with its program, as he drew closer to the bend a combination of the most unusual noises were to be heard coming from around the turn. Peat peeked around the corner to see a long narrow cul-de-sac brightly lit by numerous flambeaux which lined either side of the walls. What Peat found disturbing, however, was the many spears and blades which littered the ground. Looking to the end of the impasse Peat noticed what appeared to be a metal stand encircled with a low burning ring of fire, 'this must be where the first object is!' Peat thought to himself, as he guardedly proceeded down the path keeping vigilant out of fear that some other booby trap may not have been triggered by the shocker. Looking at the pedestal Peat saw the first of the silver cylinders standing erect in a small slot on the circular upper surface. Peat took the object out of the stand and suddenly the circle of fire died out. As he examined the piece he was startled to see the top circular slab of the stand rotating in a clock wise motion. While he was observing this disturbing anomaly he heard a loud jarring sound coming from back around the bend as if something heavy were being hoisted upwards. Once the gyrating stand had ceased turning, so too did the grating sound, but Peat felt that as a result of these happenings somehow his exit was not going to be as easy as his entrance. The first Shocker

226

was still pressing against the wall behind the stand and could not be reprogrammed to go in the other direction and so Peat released a second shocker which proceed back up the passage, nearly extinguishing the flambeaux with its shock waves as it passed. Peat pressed against the wall and took one of the torches from its holder as he followed. He then drew his weapon with his other hand. Peter could see small amounts of rubble trickle off the edge of the walls each time the shocker gave off a shock wave. As the hovering device vanished around the corner Peat once more saw the small trickle of pebbles down the wall following another wave. Peat moved up closer to the bend and was about to take the turn when he heard the most ghastly snapping sound, as if a predator had just pounced on its pray. At this stage he stopped and gently creped backwards four yards from the bend before pausing. Worried by the sound he'd heard, Peat froze and listened... but heard nothing. Placing his gun underneath his left arm Peat placed his right hand on the wall to feel for the vibrations off another tremor but he felt nothing! Peat took a slow step backwards and then he began to smell the foulest of odors; it was, as if a carcass were rotting. Listening intently Peat heard heavy breathing and a light growling sound. Trapped, Peat backed away from the turn trying to think amidst the panic that had set in..., at that point Peat mentally admonished himself, determined to regain his equanimity at once. 'Get a grip, think; the decaying smell - carcasses to feed an animal or maybe more than one. It would have to be comfortable in cool, damp settings and move well in small surroundings like this hollow...', Peat's mind worked thus, with brilliant fluidity.

He could think of seven animals that would fit this general profile but the more he thought about the setting and the orchestrated nature of these tests he felt convinced that it was an Allkcris; a savage predator with razor sharp teeth and claws whose natural habitat was mountains, possessing phenomenal speed and agility, this animal's attacks were almost impossible to stop. Peat knew that he would be only lucky to hit the Allkcris with the one or two shots he'd be able to get off, and of course that all depended on there being only one of them! All these considerations were mulled over in Peat's head in a matter of seconds as he quietly backed away from the turn. Then, less than fifteen seconds after hearing that chilling snarl Peat sprang into action. He quickly doused the flaming torches on the upper-half of the narrow stretch using his outer garment before picking up two spears from the ground. Then using the edge of his belt buckle he cut his arm slightly and let droplets of his blood fall over his slightly scorched garment before using his belt to make a cross out of the two spears. He then used two large rocks to keep the cross-apparatus upright before placing the blood stained cloak over it and quietly pressed the homing device down onto the tip of the spear to act as an improvised head. Standing next to the scarecrow-like decoy, Peat looked up the passage but could still see no sign of any oncoming danger. Then taking out his reserve ammunition clip he cautiously filled the strips on his outer garment with the fragile explosives, after all the capsules had been loaded on the garment Peat collected all the flaming torches which hung on the walls behind the mannequin and used them to made a crescent shaped line of fire around it. He had no sooner laid down the last flambeau than a frightening roar was heard emitting from the top of the burrow followed by another one.

"Dear God they are two of them!" Peat said to himself as he glanced up at two pairs of emerald eyes shining in the darkness.

Peat gently stood up and backed off, slowly moving away from the decoy but it was no good, the Allkcris' visual acuity was excellent and as the beastly pair stalkingly drew closer it was clear that their sights were set not on the dummy but on Peat. Gradually Peat moved towards a thick metal pedestal which lay at least ten yards away, the leading Allkcris then became partial visible due to the light coming from the torches burning on the ground and for the first time Peat got confirmation that he had guessed correctly. Knowing immediately that he had only one chance Peat turned sharply and sprinted for the metal stand while the beasts darted after him. Just before he reached the stand Peat lunged forward into the air while rotating his body backwards and raising his right hand he shot three hopeful rounds in the direction of the explosive filled garment before skirting over the surface of the stand and hitting the back wall, dropping in the gap behind. Before Peat had hit the ground the first two rounds had passed beyond the target, however, the third shot made direct contact with the intended target hitting one of the suspended capsules and setting off a chain of almost instantaneous explosions just as the leading Allkcris passed over the mannequin. Peat pressed up against the base of the stand covering his head with his arms and drawing his knees up against his chest. A perturbing silence followed the explosion and subsequent clattering of stone, Peat soon relaxed his muscles and opened his eyes slightly but a cloud of grit obscured everything and made it hard to take a breath without coughing. Getting to his feet Peat realized how lucky he'd been, the west side of the cave's wall had collapsed in, partially covering the exit, on the surface of the stand were scratch marks and the paw of the pacesetting Allkcris, the rest of which lay under seven foot of rubble. Peat's heart was still racing but his mind had begun to settle as the adrenalin-shock waned, he moved slowly towards a narrow gap by the eastern wall of the cave. Making his way over the

230

unstable rocks, which had spilled over from the cave-in, Peat saw some of the remains of the other Allkcris beneath the debris. Eventually he reached the bend and checking to make sure he was still in procession of the cylinder he made a relatively easy exit, passing the Allkcris' foul smelling cell on his way out.

Peat was relieved to get outside and took a deep breath of fresh air, the fog had lifted revealing the most splendid of views out over the dale across to a spectacular folded mountain range which extended onwards as far as Peat could see. It was not long though before Peat's sense of urgency returned and he quickly took out his newly acquired device which Ly Amas had said would show the way to the next object. Peat twisted a circular groove at the bottom and a dark red light shun onto his garment, turning the device upright Peat saw the light was actually a holographic chart showing him where the next object could be found. As before Peat would check the location of the second item periodically as he journeyed towards its location. Reminding himself what was at stake in this race Peat set off jogging up the mountain, the path become more and more hazardous the further he climbed but his sense of urgency remained steadfast and the young competitor kept up a brisk pace. Peter was extremely fit but the altitude and steep climb was beginning to take its toll; he found it increasingly harder to catch his breath and the pain in his legs was worsening. In the back of his mind there was also concern at the thought of suffering an injury while traversing this difficult terrain, even a small impairment might well rule out any real chance of winning the Trials, Peat feared. Moving through a pass close to the very peak of the mountain Peat reached the opposite side after about a fifteen minute jog before plopping down on a small boulder to catch his breath, his face red and hair wet from sweat. Resting Peat checked his map once more before looking out towards the point of his next destination, he felt a certain comfort in being able to name the various areas through which he was travelling and indeed so comprehensive was his knowledge of the Polmorian Way that he was able to catalogue the creatures that inhabited the various areas he would have to pass through on his way towards the second key. As he gazed out over the scenic landscape Peat's mind turned to his family, he wondered how his father and Jim were coping and most of all he worried for Claire. As Peat reflected on some of his cherished memories he felt a resolve to press on, in a way the brief respite had served to rejuvenate him in both body and mind. Rising to his feet and moving on Peat was delighted to be now descending. He worked his way down along a worn track-way, down the mountain's steep incline. There was a sudden shriek from up in the sky which caught Peat's attention, he didn't recognize the large creature which soared high above him but he watched intently as it passed overhead and flew away into the distance. Peat then pressed on hard for another thirty minutes before reaching an intersection, two paths, a major and minor one, trailed off in different directions. The charted map showed only the one main path leading down to the mountain base after which one could loop around to the forest of Kaz Olp which was where Peat needed to get to. However, from the steep angle Peat now occupied, it seemed, as he looked down towards his destination, that the byway was substantially more direct than the other apparent circumbendibus.

Considering the matter for a moment Peat decided on following the route outlined in the map but as he veered down the chosen path he heard a familiar sound coming from the east, "It's water," Peat said to himself.

To investigate would require him to travel down the byway for a bit but he knew that it would be advisable to take on water whenever the opportunity arose, and so he decided to explore the source of what sounded like gushing water, he resolved though to backtrack and follow his intended route. He did not have to go far down the divergent trail before finding confirmation; it was a free flowing stream of fresh water and cupping his hand Peat drank. Peat was just about to head back to the main pathway when he took a second look down at the Kaz Olp forest which appeared so close from where he stood relative to the other looping route..., after some rationalizing along the lines of; 'Darkness will soon be falling and the shelter of the forest will be vital!' and 'The time I could save might prove crucial!' Peat finally decided to take the ostensive shortcut. Peat trekked for nearly two hours as quickly as he could in the direction of the forest regularly checking the map just to make sure the sought after item had not been moved. By the time Peat had come close to the base of the mountain the belief that he'd made the right decision about choosing the more direct path was unquestioned in his mind 'After all,' he thought to himself, '...the object of the Trials is to get to the Cauldron as quickly as possible, how we do that is pretty much up to us once we obey the rules!' Peat was close to the bottom now and felt a huge sense of relief as twilight had begun to fall, the thought of being stuck on the open mountain face after nightfall was a chilling prospect for him. As Peat drew closer to the foot of the mountain he noticed a sheet of orange flowering across a dense row of rocks and boulders which led into the most scenic grassy meadow, across from which, lay the edge of the forest. Reaching the great scattering of large rocks and boulders Peat's attention became fixated on the countless vines of a dark-orange colored flowering plant that crept like ivy across the entire base of the mountain as far as his eyes could see.

Indeed, Peat found himself becoming severely worried as he moved in for a closer look at this plant, "Ah no," Peat bemoaned loudly as he stood peering at a clump of the plant's flowers sitting on a nearby rock.

Peat's fears had been realized, the entire passage to the meadow in this particular area of the mountain's base was practically impassable on foot due to the encompassing presence of Creaton's deadliest carnivorous plant, the Crypousa. Peat had spent many hours watching archival footage in the Palace on the subject of Creaton's ecology but he had seen no Creaton life-form which came close to comparing the Crypousa for lethal efficiency. Thin and ultra-sensitive vines branched out over vast areas acting as trigger pads for the copious flowering stems which sprout throughout the length of the plant and spat numerous toxic darts when triggered. Once the toxins enter the prey's bloodstream it becomes fully paralyzed in a very short time. The vines would then release a powerfully coercive acidic substance through tiny pores gradually dissolving the paralyzed organism while another set of orifices reabsorbed the mixture with the Crypousa benefiting from the nutritionally rich medley. Peat could not get too close for fear of standing on one of the many vines which littered the ground but from a safe distance he inspected along the mountain's base as far as he could go, seeking a passage across to the meadow

but he could find none. At that stage Peat knew
he'd made a serious blunder; there was no time to
backtrack and night fall was fast approaching.
Taking a few moments to survey his surroundings
once more and thinking about the problem at hand in
his typically level-headed and enterprising manner
Peat formulated a plan to make it safely to the
other side. Walking past a tall narrow tree growing
out from the bedrock Peat purposefully proceeded
about halfway up a large crag which extended out
over the Crypousa covered terrain below, and
prostrating himself on the rock he produced his
firearm and carefully took aim at the slanting tree
below before shooting one round at its base causing
it to topple forward towards the side of the
protruding rock on which he lay. In fact, the trunk
of the tree came so close to hitting the side of the
crag that the upper branches whipped against the
rock itself as the tree fell to the ground. Peat
looked on with interest as the pressure of the
fallen tree on the vines beneath caused a barrage
of darts to be fired in almost every direction in the
area below. After a few minutes had passed Peat
was convinced that all the darts, triggered by the
fallen tree, had been fired and so he walked back
down the rugged rock and carefully advanced out
along the tree's trunk which led close to the area
under the crag. Now Peat reached what he
considered to be the most dangerous part of his
plan, carefully moving along a large branch which led
236

in under the rock, Peat got closer and closer to the nook at the crag's base and, as he had learned in his botany lessons, there was no plant life to be found on the ground in this light deprived spot. Nervously Peat jumped from the branch to the ground pressing up against the edge of the load-bearing wall, cautious not to step out any further than was necessary to get a solid footing.

Raising his arm he then rubbed his hand along the crag's under-surface till he stopped at a point and excitingly blurted out "Yes."

Bringing the other hand up also Peat stretched his body upwards and pressed his hands into a deep crevice in the crag's underside. Having felt around in the cranny for a time Peat lowered his hands and removed his last ammunition clip from his gun and with extreme cautiousness he took out all the glass-like capsules and placed them resting on an ever so slight ledge which had formed up inside the deep crack within the crag itself, one at a time. When he'd finished placing the explosives he very carefully hopped back on the branch and showing great balance moved to the trunk of the tree rather quickly. When Peat reached the base of the tree he turned and crouched down taking out his last Creaton shocker and programming it he releases it, gradually it hovers towards the nook at the base of the crag. Rising up, Peat turns and sprints up the mountain and climbing up on top of a large rock he watches from a safe distance as the shocker floats out of sight under the large protruding rock. The shocker reaches close to the edge of the nook's wall systematically emitting powerful shock waves in quick succession as it advances, one of the small explosive projectiles is shook off its stony groove and falling to the ground cracking and causing an explosion which in turn detonates the remaining capsules still sitting in the crevice. Peat looks on in anticipation, first came a large duding sound followed closely by the propelling of the jutting rock out away from the mountain down onto the ground below. Then a large cloud of dust and silt rose into the air. Peat waited till the plume of debris had settled before venturing down to the edge of the rock face that remained, hoping that the mass of rock which now lay between him and the meadow would be suitably placed to act as a bridge over the Crypousa. Peering down Peat saw that the blast had indeed driven the fractured rock sufficiently close to the meadow's edge. However, it was evident that the force of the explosion had if anything pushed the fragmented rock too far! Peat went down to the ledge and closely appraised the gap between the edge of the detached rock and where he stood while trying to figure out if he could possibly make it across.   While he always had a natural talent for gaging distances by sight he remained uncertain if he was capable of actually making this jump. Peat knew the more he thought about it the less confident he would feel and again calling to mind what was at stake he walked calmly back towards the mountain a few yards before turning and sprinting towards the edge. Propelling himself off the rock face, Peat fluttered through the air flailing his arms and legs over the Crypousa below, he went tumbling onto the back surface of the rock with less than a meter to spare. Peter lay on his back full of adrenaline and breathing heavily, taking a few moments to compose himself he got to his feet and looked back over the obstacle he had just cleared, with a real sense of accomplishment before turning his attention to the far more manageable task of jumping to the grassy meadow. 'One good run and jump should do it,' Peat thought as he poised himself at the back edge of the rock before once more sprinting towards the ledge and using his powerful legs to propel himself out over the remaining vines and onto the grassy meadow. Peat felt delight as he got to his feet and firmly believed that he had now established a substantial time advantage over his opponent in this race. But unknown to him as he took his first step towards the forest boundary Peat had just stepped on the tip of a single roaming vine that had grown a considerable distance out away from the plant's array. With that, a Crypousa flower at the edge of the meadow spat a scattering of darts in all directions. Peat meanwhile was looking at his tracking map to ensure that the item was still in the same location, when he felt a sting on the back of his ankle, then putting the holographic generating device back into his pocket he kneeled down and pulled out the dart, it was only when he inspected the stinger that he realized what it was. Getting to his feet Peat ran towards the forest but after a few yards he felt his right leg become numb and after limping for a few further yards he collapsed onto the ground. Peat began to find it hard to breath and had already loss feeling in many parts of his body before he passed out on the meadow's bed. Hours later a faint chirping sound is heard by a semi-conscious Peat, gradually he opens his eyes to see a clear blue sky above him, he slept through the night. Despite strong muscle tension in his legs Peat manages to get to his feet, disoriented and light headed he looked around as he recalled what had happened to him. In a haphazard manner Peat made his way to the forest and entering it he wandered around as if seeking something, then wide-eyed he stops before making a dash towards a large blue flowering bush and plucking large amounts of berries from its branches he began to consume them voraciously. After the plant was practically fruitless Peat lay out flat on the forest floor beside the shrub and fell fast asleep. Peat awoke feeling rested and stretching out his arms and legs he got to his feet. The serene feeling he had was short lived as the realization that he'd lost considerable time in the race suddenly dawned on him, flinching he quickly reached into his pocket for the cylindrical device. Looking at the map briefly, Peat quickly ran in the direction of his next target having frustrated at how much time he'd lost due to the Crypousa's toxins, while also feeling grateful for having found Hayrawl Berries which he knew to have antitoxin properties.

It was not long before Peat had crossed through the forest and reached his prescribed destination; a small clearing on the other side of the woods. Peat approached cautiously and hid behind a large tree as he peeked out across a large glade, to his surprise everything seemed staged, there was a thick layer of sand covering the ground instead of grass and in the center a stake stood upright, 'that must be it!' thought Peat. The blatantly contrived setting both convinced him that the object was somewhere in the glade while also triggering warning bells in his head; clearly this was some type of trap but 'how to get the cylinder?,' this was the question. But before Peat could even begin to formulate a plan on how best to venture out into the clearing he caught sight of something small lying on the sand, moving closer for a better look he saw a small dead animal speared with an arrow. Then moving even closer again, he noticed that in fact there were multiple skewered animals lying scattered across the sandy periphery along with the numerous arrow ends sticking up out of the sand. Looking at this unnerving scene and thinking back on the booby traps in the cave, Peat could only imagine what manner of pitfalls might await him in approaching the pole. However, time was of the essence and he'd already more than lost the gains made earlier from taking the 'short-cut' down the mountain after getting darted. Therefore Peat decided to quickly peruse the perimeter before determining how he was going to go about entering the clearing. Half way around Peat caught sight of a motionless figure tied to a nearby tree, it looked similar to a Creaton but was much smaller. Peat picked up a stick from the forest floor and approached apprehensively from behind. Pressing against the opposite side of the large tree to which the captive was tied Peat wrestled with whether or not to see if this creature was alive or dead.... After a short spell of contemplation Peat decided to carefully go around and inspect the fettered stranger, just as he came into sight of the prisoner the captive gave a loud moan. And as Peat looked on at the pitiful sight of the mysterious prisoner he felt a deep sense of empathy for this malnourished and bleeding figure. "Hello, hello..." Peat called at him, but no response came from the obviously afflicted stranger who seemed barely conscious.

Peat felt a moral compulsion to try and free him and so he used the sharp stick in his hand and began thrusting the pointed end against the ropes but the Representative was not without internal conflict in doing this, he was suspicious of this poor distressed soul and his proximity to the place where the cylinder just happened to be, it all seemed unsettlingly contrived to him. Peat managed to cut through two ropes and then lifted the miserable creature up and out of the remaining restrictions which bound him to the tree's trunk. Liberated the stranger remained largely unresponsive, seeing that his lips were dry Peat dashed into the forest and fetched some eatable berries carrying them in the front of his garment which he'd pulled up forming a make-shift pouch. Returning, Peat squeezed handfuls of berries and allowed the drops to trickle down into the stranger's mouth. The sickly humanoid drank what drizzled in, then after a while Peat laid him flat on the ground and tended to his wounds as best he could. Following this Peat went and gathered more food including some bugs and insects that he knew to have high protein content, by the time he got back it was evident that his succoring had paid off as the patient had regained consciousness and was standing up inspecting his dressed wounds.

Peat called out to the raggedy clad native, "Hi..., I'm Peat," as he approached him.

At first the greeting startled the recuperating local but when he saw that Peat was carrying food and so obviously the one who had helped him, his fear was replaced by deferential gratitude as he spoke, "O fortune, bright you shine once more...Thank you Sir for taking pity on me in my wretched state."

Peat plopped the food on the ground and wiping his garment with his hand, he smiled and quickly glanced across the clearing at the pole before saying, "Please…, eat!"

Both sat down around this foraged smorgasbord of berries and insects, the malnourished stranger was clearly famished and with a, "Thank you Sir, such graciousness," he began to eat.

Peat was curious about who it was that was sitting opposite him and also more than a little suspicious about his intentions.

Shrewd as ever Peat wasted little time commencing his informal inquiry, "So, what's your name?"

Demonstratively the stranger stops eating and looks on Peat with appreciative eyes, " '*My name…*' O Sir, well… I suppose it's Timijus …, yes Sir, Timijus it is! Amm… I'm a local farmer Sir, I, I live not far from here."

To say Peat was unconvinced by Timijus' response would be an understatement but he remained nonchalant and eating some berries he followed up with another question, "…How did you end up here, bound?"

In a far freer and more convincing manner Timijus answered, "O Sir.. It was terrible…, I was collecting berries two days ago in the forest when I saw a group of Creaton soldiers approaching, so in fear for my life I hid up this tree. But the soldiers didn't pass by Sir, they stopped in the clearing and began all manner of depraved doings. They worked

244

for hours but I kept quiet and eventually all the
soldiers left… or at least I thought they'd all gone!
I got down from the tree but just then two sentries
spotted me, they tied me to this tree and began
pelting me with stones then one of them placed a
sack on the ground in front of me and, and oh Sir…
out came a Cokilsa! Well Sir I was terrified of
course, I mean no one wants to die like that! Then
providence proved kind; at that very moment a call
came summoning the soldiers away, they departed
leaving me to suffer a horrendous death but I
managed to free one of my legs and just as the
little brute pounced to inject his venom into me I
stamped down with my foot and crushed its head
with my heal. I was so relieved Sir, but I could not
free myself so here I remained until you liberated
me, Sir I'm so grateful."

Peat found himself warming to Timijus' affable
manner but he was still unsure as to the truth of
what he was being told and so in an off-the-cuff
way Peat astutely responded, "That's awful, I mean
what you went through it's, it's…, well I'm just…, I'm
glad you're ok!" Hay, do'yah know; I always wanted
to see a Cokilsa, amm…," Peat looks innocently to the
base of the tree where Timijus was bound, coaxing
an explanation for the absence of the creature's
remains.

Picking up on Peat's subtle cue Timijus dutifully
stood up and moving towards some nearby growth he
said, "It should still be here Sir I flung it over into

these shrubs...I didn't want the smell attracting any animals, Oh here it is!"

Peat stood beside him and looked down at the decomposing Cokilsa, its head crushed exactly as Tehimajas had said.

Tehimajas backs away, "O Sir I can barely look at it... uah, the mere thought of it!"

Satisfied that Tehimajas is not a threat to him Peat turns his attention back on getting the cylinder, he had used up a considerable amount of time tending to Timijus and collecting berries so he decided to take his chance and venture out into the clearing.

"I just have to get something..." Peat says as he moves past Timijus and walks towards the clearing.

"Sir, Sir, don't go out there...It's not safe!" Tehimajas shouts dramatically as he moves in front of Peat.

"What do you mean?" Peat asks.

"Sir I saw everything they did when I was up the tree. O Sir, they have all manner of traps out there, it's not safe to go into the clearing."

Peat pointed to the pole in the center of the glade responding resolutely, "I have to get to that pole and quickly, did you see where exactly they put the traps?"

"They're everywhere under the sand; all manner of horrible things Sir, no one could... O wait Sir... there might be a way...."

Getting rather excited Timijus elaborates, "....You see they tested everything together... well I mean...

I saw them all go off at the same time; there must be some sort of trigger?"

Peat is pleasantly surprised at Timijus' insightful deduction and queries him further, "Did you get any hint of where this trigger might be?"

Thinking hard for a moment Timijus begins to recount aloud what he saw just prior to the test, "I was looking down at an officer who was standing in the center of the clearing next to the pole, he shouted something, I didn't hear what it was but all the other soldiers ran into the forest.

Then the officer singled something with his hand and ran into the forest like the others, the traps all went off after that Sir!"

"Can you show me roughly where the officer signaled to?" Peat asks tentatively.

"O yes Sir, I think so, follow me."

With that Timijus hurried off around the clearing's boundary. Peat followed, surprised at how energetic Timijus was given the stricken state he had found him in. In no time they'd reached the area where Timijus estimated the officer had signaled to, the two meandered around for a minute inspecting the area before Peat paused and asked, "Timijus, can you remember if the officer was looking up when he signaled, did it appear that he was signaling to someone on a height, up a tree perhaps…?"

Timijus thought hard and then enthusiastically replied, "Yes, you know Sir I think he was looking upwards."

Peat then instructed, "Let's check the trees for any unusual marks or holes along the trunk..."

The duo spread out and began examining the trees around them, after about five minutes Peat had moved further down along the clearings edge and came across a particularly large dark leafed tree which had a two paralleled sets of small vertical holes running up along the trunk of the tree on one side. Placing his finger in against the edge of the holes Peat could feel the tread marks and surmised they had been drilled to attach some type of scaling apparatus. Peat called for Timijus and after showing him the holes he states, "This might be it, I just need to get up there."

Peat fetched two pointed sticks and brakes off the points to about the length of his hand and then with a boost from Timijus he begins to scale the tree. The task proves very difficult and Peat thought about how he could really use Claire's help, eventually he reached the lowest of the tree's boughs and at that point the small sets of holes ceased. Peat was glad to be able to get a stable footing on the large branches but he could find no sign of anything. Peat suspected that they took with them whatever they had used to trigger the booby traps but he still felt it best to climb up to the top just to make sure. From that point, ascending proved relatively easy, higher and higher Peat climbed this towering tree, Timijus called up, "Are you ok Sir?"

Peat shouted back down, "Yah, but nothing yet!" and then continued his ascent.

Reaching close to the tree's crown Peat was elated to see a tiny metal sheet attached to an offshoot roughly nine foot above his head. Scaling further up he discovered that indeed he'd found what he was looking for. The metal sheet was actually a sonic transmitter with a circular recess in its center, above the indentation an initiatory sphere floated independently.

Peat had an introductory knowledge of this device and taking the sphere in his hand he called down to Timijus, "Timijus, I'm going to set off the traps, get back and cover your ears."

An "Okay!" came from below before Peat forcefully pressed the ball into the transmitter's dip.

What followed was the emitting of a piercing high-pitched sound, Peat plugged his ears but he could still hardly stand the head-racking sound. Then two things happened simultaneously, the sound stopped and a deadly sequence of occurrences began to unfold in the glade. Peat looked down from on high as a small but very thick wall rose up enclosing the entire clearing then in a matter of seconds hundreds of spears, arrows and other projectiles came shooting out from hundreds of small meurtrières scattered along the inside of the barrier. As the final arrows shot across the clearing darting into the sand at various points, a number of mines exploded tossing up clumps of sand

and gravel. Finally, another bombardment of projectiles came spewing from the wall after which there was a fearful silence, Peat could hear nothing, not even the constant ambient noise of the forest creatures. Peat climbed down from the tree to see Timijus standing near the clearing's boundary looking out over the wall.

Peat stood beside him and was disturbed to see the horrified expression on Timijus' face, "Are you ok?" Peat asked.

Timijus nodded and turned his head towards Peat softly saying, "Yah, yah I'm ok Sir, I just can't believe it."

Peat stared across at the pole which still remained upright and untouched. Peat broke off a large piece of bark from a nearby tree and carrying it, as if a shield, he carefully hopped over the wall and proceeded out across this no man's land. Getting closer Peat prayed and hoped that the cylinder was, as he expected it to be, in or around the pole. The stake was a simple wooden stake at the top of which there was a familiar seal, that of the Patriarch of Tryloss. Peat could see no sign of the cylinder and so he activated his map and once again it showed the object to be somewhere nearby. Putting the activated map back in his pocket Peat pulled up the pole and inspected the post-hole but found nothing. Then a thought occurred to him, he leaned down and examined the pointed based of the pole, wiping off the soil and gravel he noticed that the last three inches of the post running to the vertex was actually metal. Fidgeting for a moment Peat found that he could untwist the metal fitting and sure enough inside the hollowed out container was the sought after cylinder. Peat twisted the dial at the bottom of the device to see where his final clue was to be found, the map showed the third and final device to be in the Minnonite city of Ra-Lif. Peat knew a great deal about the tumultuous history of the Minnonite people and the hostile relations they had with the Creatons. The Minnonites, once rivals to the Creatons for domination of the planet but suffered a decisive defeat in a major battle which took place at the base of Mount Crewux. Having conquered nearly all Minnonite's territories the Creatons, in return for their enemy's unconditional surrender, allowed the Minnonites to keep control of their smallest city, Ra-Lif along with an area of land around it. This became the sovereign principality of the Minnonite's Royal family. Briskly, Peat made his way across the clearing towards Timijus.

"Well done Sir," Timijus said.

Peat smiles and says, "You saved my life, thanks!" Embarrassed Timijus responds, "O no Sir, you saved mine and found the trigger... nothing less than brilliant."

Now it might strike one as strange that Timijus had not asked his liberator one question about his purpose, after all, it was now more than apparent that the traps were all meant for him. Indeed the same notion had occurred to Peat briefly but, in Timijus he discerned a person with heavily conditioned fatalistic and servile traits which would all but preclude him asking such questions. This actually made being around Timijus very easy because Peat thought it prudent to keep his mission to himself.

Peat looks at Timijus saying, "I think we're even, anyway I have to get to Ra-Lif so I---"

"Ahh Sir I'm actually heading that way myself, maybe we could travel together! Aaa... I actually know the shortest way to the city, O Sir I'll take you there, it's the least I can do after all the kindness you've shown me?"

Expecting that Timijus would seriously slow him down, Peat explains, "I appreciate the offer Timijus I really do but you've already done more than enough and well, amm, I must get there as soon as possible, I'll probably be running most the way... and you need your rest!"

Seemingly unwilling to take no for an answer Timijus begins to trot away from the wall in the direction of the city saying, "O I'm fine Sir...come on and I'll have us in Ra-Lif by supper."

Peat sighs but seems content that Timijus is trustworthy and although he'd prefer to be travelling alone he reluctantly agrees saying, "Ok so, lead on!"

Timijus begins to jog onwards calling back to Peat, "Follow me Sir."

Peat is just about to hop the wall when he notices an unmarked halberd lying on the ground, he picks it up and jumping over the enclosure he makes chase after his new guide, weapon in hand. As they dash through the forest Peat felt somewhat confounded as he struggled to keep up with Timijus, in fact it was obvious to him that his alacritous guide was actually checking himself so as not to get too far ahead.

It was not long before they had reached the forest's edge and then, as if having just remembered something, Timijus stopped and turning to Peat, he made a request, "Aaa Sir, I still need to collect a few berries, but I lost my basket and..., aamm it's very bold of me to ask Sir but might I borrow some clothing... I wouldn't ask but it's important."

Peat was a little taken aback by this sudden and strange request but yet not wanting to refuse him, tares off both of his sleeves and hands them to Timijus saying, "Here you are."

Timijus looks surprised, "Oh I didn't mean so much Sir, I'll aaa... make this up to you Sir, thank you." Then without another word he quickly disappeared back into the forest and only then Peat heard him shout, "I won't be long Sir."

Five minutes later Timijus returns with two bulging make-shift sacks flung over his shoulder, "Sir, I'm sorry for the delay, we can make the time up..., no problem," he says as he jogs out of the woods leaving Peat sitting on a tree stump caught in the middle of checking his map.

"Oh good," Peat responds fumbling the device back into his pocket, having been startled by Timijus' unexpected emergence from the dense growth.

Peat could not get over the obsequious manner of Timijus, it was rather endearing but also a bit sad. As Peat ran out of the forest across the open rocky fields struggling to keep up with his speedy companion his mind was also racing, among the many questions that passed through his head one in particular was arresting; 'What did Polexiamas Ata mean by changes to the Xtaron ritual?' As Peat mulled things over in his head he noticed that Timijus had gained a good distance on him and so he quickened his pace just as the frontrunner passed around a large tor.

Peat was just approaching the rocky outcrop when he heard a loud and aggressively commanding shout, "Hey you!"

Peat was slowing down when Timijus came dashing around the corner and bashing into him he fell back onto the ground.

As Peat helped him to his feet he inquired "What's wrong?"

And in a rushed state of heightened agitation Timijus explained, "Minnonite tugs, there coming..."

Realizing that he was dressed in highly provocative Creaton attire he clasped his shirt and replied, "If they see me wearing this...!"

Quickly Timijus led him to a grass covered gap at the base of the large, free-standing residual rock mass and just as Peat concealed himself two large and armed Minnonites ran around the corner, Peat wanted to call his friend to join him but just as he was about to beckon him he heard a rough voice firmly say, "How dare you run from us slave, come here."

Submissively Timijus approached the duo, his head lowered and eyes firmly fixed on his addresser's feet.

"What are these?" the smaller of the two asked before reaching out and grabbing both sacks from Timijus' hand.

In a timid voice an intimidated Timijus answers, "Berries Sir, for my Master's house."

The bag is smelt and then thrown to the ground before Timijus is asked, "Who owns you?"

Responding calmly Timijus says, "General Mex-Ol Sir."

Lunging forward and grabbing the back of Timijus' neck, pulling him towards himself the larger brigand orders, "Come here."

Then the ruffian takes out a slender device with smooth edges and in the shape of a circle, placing it against the nape of Timijus' neck a small beep is

heard before he withdraws the gadget and both of
the brutes look intently at the device's screen.
Then once Timijus' identity as General Mex-Ol's
slave has been established one of the boors produce
a common holographic pod and while activating it he
explains, "We're looking for a dangerous outsider.
They'll be a handsome reward for whoever helps us
find it dead or alive... enough to pay off your debt
slave, I should reckon!"
Timijus couldn't believe it when he saw a clear image
of Peat being projected before his eyes, "Well, have
you seen it?" the smaller lout asked impatiently.
Peat meanwhile could hear what was being said but
could see nothing; Timijus looked at his
interrogators and answered, "No Sir, but perhaps
this creature hides in the forbidden forest..."
Placing the holographic machine back in his pocket
the unmannerly couple grunt at Timijus and depart
hurriedly, the larger one brushing against the small
slave forcefully as he leaves, knocking him to the
ground while chuckling.
As Timijus gets up Peat crawls out from his hiding
place asking, "Are you ok Timijus?"
"I'm ok Sir but those Minnonites were looking for
you, Sir there seems to be a bounty on you! Those
marauders had your image and spoke of a reward...
Sir I'm beginning to think Ra-Lif might be best
avoided for your own safety."
Sighing and taking a moment to mule the implication
of this over in his head Peat calmly responds, "No, I

need to get into the city as quickly as possible, there's too much at stake!"

Looking at a confused and bewildered Timijus, Peat reveals something of his predicament, "aaa, the truth is Timijus, I'm searching for something very important, an object... you might have seen me with a little cylinder earlier," and taking out the device in his hand and showing it to his confidant before continuing, "well... this is what I'm looking for. I got this one when we were in the forest but there's another in the city. There meant for me but... aaa, they were hidden by the Creatons..."

Peat activates the map to show Timijus, "Here, you can see it shows almost exactly where it is..., I must retrieve it as quickly as possible. It's the last one!"

Staring at the device and then looking fondly at Peat Timijus says absorbingly, "Sir, I think I can help! Can I see the map again?" Once more Peat held the device vertical and once more it was readable.

"The red dot is--"

"Yes, that's where we'll find the object." Peat affirms.

Pointing to the tracking beacon Timijus discloses, "I know this place; this is the storage section inside the Royal Armory, sometimes I accompany my Master in there."

Peat had been curious as to why the ruffians had referred to Timijus as a "slave," and so, subtly picking up on his statement, Peat inquires, "Your *Master...?*"

Coming clean, as it were, Timijus responds, "Aaa yes Sir, well amm..., please forgive my deceit, you see I'm a slave to the Minnonite General Mex-Ol, I was a farmer that's true, many years ago now but I was unable to pay my debts and sold into slavery when I was just young. I didn't want you Sir to think less of me."

Peat had just placed the map-generating device back in his pocket and began consoling Timijus, "God no Timijus, you saved m-------", then suddenly a voice was heard,

"Hey slave, are you still there?"

Peat turned just as one of the Minnonite brigands returned, stepping lively around the corner of the rock, the big interloper froze as he noticed Peat. Staring at them both with an oafish expression for a split second he reached across his chest and produced a firing weapon and pointed it at the pair. Peat then, without hesitation, pushed Timijus to the ground and dived himself in the opposite direction just as a shot was fired. The round passed between them as Peat tumbled with purpose towards the gap he had been hiding in and almost in a single motion he reached through the long grass which concealed the cranny and taking hold of the halberd which lay on the ground inside, he flung it at his assailant with maximum force before prostrating himself on the ground. The second shot fired right over Peats

258

head just as he threw himself to the ground and impacted on the base of the tor.

Then Peat heard a slight groan followed by a large "thud," raising his head he looked up to see the Minnonite lying motionless on the grassy slope, the halberd wedge into his gut.

Timijus slowly moved towards the body while Peat rushed to the corner of the tor to check for the other bounty hunter but with no sign of him Peat rushed over to Timijus and looked down at the lifeless corpse.

"I've never killed anyone before."

Kneeling down, inspecting the remains, Timijus looked up at Peat's distressed face and in a consoling tone said, "He would have killed us both Sir, I've no doubt of that. You saved our lives."

Looking warmly at his newfound friend and smiling Peat responds, "I guess that definitely makes us even now."

Timijus smiles back before Peat takes charge of the situation and in an assertive manner he says, "Ok, so maybe I can make use of his cloak…"

Peat wrenches the spear from the dead Minnonite's torso and then removes his capote and chest holster. Peat also picks up the firearm lying on the ground beside the lifeless Minnonite.

Peat instructs Timijus to take hold of the deceased's legs while he grabs his underarms and lifting him up Peat jesters with his head towards the gap under the rock, advising, "I wish we could bury him but we need to hide the body quickly, his friend could come looking for him at anytime."

They rolled the body into the grass covered opening beneath the tor, Peat also places the blood stained halberd into the gap. Then Peter dawns the capote, which was evidently too big on him, but if anything this lengthily garment along with its hood, helped to conceal Peat's identity.

Peat also strapped the holster to his chest under the cloak and affixes the weapon to it, "Okay so how do I look?" he asked.

Timijus nodded his head, "You'll fit right in Sir."

Throwing back his hood Peat grinned and said," Timijus, please call me Peat... now how can I get into the armory's storage facility?"

"Well Sir, if you'd permit... I think I could retrieve your item for you."

Shocked Peat protests strongly at the idea, "Oh no Timijus, it's far too dangerous, I mean you saw the kind of traps the Creatons have laid to test me...No I'm afraid I have to do this alone, but thanks"

"To test you Sir?" Timijus puzzles.

Peat expands on what he has said a little, "I know it sounds crazy, but this whole thing is just one big sick game!"

"Oh I see Sir, I think I understand..."

"You do?" Peat responds.

"Oh yes Sir, I mean...that is; everyone knows the Creatons love holding savage tests and games to challenge elite warriors, they've being doing it for

260

hundreds of years... But Sir, the only way the Creaton's could have smuggled in such a device into the Royal Armory would be to conceal it in a lightly protected shipment of arms or ammunition being transported close to the border. The Polmorian Raiders love to ambush inter-city shipments bound for Ra-Lif and then sell the spoils to the Minnonites, high quality arms often end up being sold directly to the army and the equipment is stored in the Royal Armory. The Creatons must have known this... I don't think it could be booby trapped Sir."

"No, if you're right I guess it wouldn't be but---"
Continuing to try and persuade Peat, "Oh please Sir, my Master runs the Armory and I know everything about the building and how to get into the storage section... besides, it would be almost impossible for anyone unauthorized to get in, it's very well-guarded and any intruders would be shot on sight."
Peat lowers his head and with a frown he acquiesces saying, "Ok but I'm not sure about this!"
Excitingly Timijus smiles, "Thank you Sir, I won't let you down."
Looking up at the excited Timijus and worrying that his friend doesn't appreciate the seriousness of what he is proposing Peat sternly says, "You just need to take care of yourself, and if you don't get a chance then forget about it, ok?"

Timijus adopts a serious demeanor and nods assentingly after which Peat continues, "...Ok so, when will you be able to get in?"

"Well the General brings me along most days but it's too late for today...hum, it will probably be tomorrow night, I think."

"I just don't have that time Timijus, I'm in a race and there's no prize for second place! There must be some way I can get into that----"

"That's it!" Timijus shouts.

"What?"

"Well Sir, a few years back there was a security breach late one night and aaa...well any threat to the compound means the General has to be there and an inventory of the stock piles must be done by hand, it's a security protocol. But anyway, the General got me to do the inventory list the last time, I'm really quick at things like that! But if there was a security breach, like an explosion near the outer wall, well that would be enough; the General would have to go to the armory and he always brings me to help when there's a lot of administration to be done, he might even get me to do the inventory again which would give me lots of time to find the object!"

"Humm... that's a great idea Timijus ...I just don't know if I could intentionally set off a bomb."

"Oh but Sir, it would only need be a tiny one. If it only chipped the wall that would be enough to cause a security alert to be issued. Believe me Sir, everything about the Minnonite system is based on abuse, power and greed especially the Army. They would never help you in your quest, Sir this is the only way for you to get your device quickly. No one will be hurt Sir, I think I have a plan... I know from hearing the armory guards gossip that one of the night sentries on the outer eastern wall is constantly leaving his post unguarded..., if there was just a tiny explosion at the outer wall next to his security hut that would do it! But... I don't know anything about bombs aamm..."

"Leave that to me, do you know where we can buy explosives?"

"Sure, just about anything can be purchased in Moo-R Street."

"Okay let's go."

Having outlined their plan the pair made their way down the rolling slopes and along the glen which led to the City's outskirts. It was late evening by the time Peat and Timijus reached Moo-R Street, they strolled casually so as not to draw attention to themselves. Timijus had insisted he walk behind Peat as if he were his slave so as not to look conspicuous, and Peat, for his part, had drawn his hood deep over his face out of fear of being recognized. Peat's ordnance knowledge was ephemeral, Lynextius' program had insufficient time to go into detail but the young Representative's almost eidetic memory meant that he could readily draw on what information he had acquired in relation to explosives and as it turned out this would serve for his purposes. Peat had in mind exactly what to look for and after a number of unsuccessful attempts he eventually spotted a store which openly displayed the very items he sought. He entered while Timijus stood outside waiting.

"Good day Sir, how can I help you?" the storekeeper inquired.

Peat was taken aback at this creature's appearance; tall, very hairy with broad shoulders and a dark robe. Peat was determined however to keep up the appearance of being nonchalant and responded immediately, "I need; a simple Rastist Crystal, a pound of grey adhesive clay and a JAL-28 detonator."

"How will you be paying Sir?"

Peat reached in under his capote which made the shopkeeper visibly nervous, and unstrapping his holster Peat tossed the weapon on the counter saying, "I'll throw in the gun for free!"

The shopkeeper looked at the holster and weapon for a moment and then laughed heartedly and shuck his head saying, "Ahhaha... such a sense of humor." Then taking both holster and gun, placing them in a shelf at the back of the store, he called out to Peat, "I'll go get your order Sir."

It was not long before Peat walked out of the store; he looked at Timijus and gave a slight nod and grin before walking on towards the Royal Armory compound which they had passed on their way into the city. Peat and Timijus had worked out an elaborate system of coughs so that the latter could direct the former while all the time remaining behind him, in keeping with the socially submissive role a slave had in Minnonite society. By the time they'd reached the armory complex it was dusk, the pair took up an inconspicuous position in an alleyway just off the main street which looped around the back of the outer perimeter wall. Timijus was beginning to have second thoughts about the plan and shared his concerns with Peat who was assembling the bomb.

"Are you sure you want to do this Sir... I mean I'll be ok but if you're caught, the penalty is death, and I mean I'm not even sure if the gossip about that guard is true, and aaa--"

Peat seeks to reassure him, "Don't worry Timijus, I'll only move-in if the coast is clear and detonate the bomb when there's no one around..., no one will get hurt and at worst they'll be some minor structural damage, nothing major."

"I know Sir, I'm just worried about you, if they find you...!"

Touched by the genuine heartfelt concern of his friend Peat again seeks to assuage Timijus' apprehensions, "The moment the bomb goes off I'll follow the route we agreed and wait for you at the Western Arch like we planned, we can then slip out of the city while it's still dark."

Timijus thinks for a moment and then it registers with him..., "*We...?*" he queries.

"Aaa yah, that is I mean... if you want you can come with me, I know I can get you off this planet! You could have a new life, freedom!"

Timijus puts his hand on his head and walking aimlessly around in a circle, muses over the offer while speaking aloud to himself, "Wow, I mean can I really leave, I was born here it's my home. I can't leave, can I? But why not I suppose... my family are all dead... what's keeping me here?" Timijus stops and addresses Peat directly, "...I've paid my debts and then some, a chance at freedom, a new life, how can I say no!"

Excitedly Peat seeks to reaffirm this conviction in Timijus, asking him, "It's a yes then?"

"Yes Sir, I'm..., I'm in."

"Excellent, but you have to stop calling me Sir, it's Peat."

"Yes Si--, aa Peat."

Moving to the edge of the alleyway and peering across the street at a compact security station in which a soldier monitors the vicinity aided by numerous stationary monitoring machines fixed to the top of the outer wall.

Peat restates the plan one last time to Timijus, "Okay so Timijus, the change in guard will happen soon, and when it does I'll wait for the new guard to disappear from his post and then I'll place the explosive at the far side of the buttress next to the security hut, when I get back here I'll detonate it. By this stage you'll be at the General's house, make sure he knows you're back. When you've finished at the armory we'll meet at the Arch, remember, just act natural and if you can't find the device don't worry, I'm sure another opportunity will present itself. Oh here I nearly forgot..."

Peat reaches into his pocket and takes out the second cylinder he acquired, "...you can use this to check where the object is, just in cases it is moved between now and when you get in, oh yah and make sure you take care of both the devices, I need them all."

Taking the small cylinder in his hand Timijus fidgets with it for a moment before switching on the map. Peat continues, "Okay so that's everything amm... good luck!"

Turning the map off, Timijus grips it firmly in one hand and takes hold of the two sacks of berries in the other before looking admirably at Peat and saying, "I'll see you at the Arch Sir", he then hurries out of the alley and down the street towards the General's august residence.

Soon after Timijus has left, right on schedule the change of guards takes place, the replacement's uniform was noticeably disheveled and his whole comportment exuded ineptness. Peat remained vigilant for nearly four hours, in the shadows of the alley he watched and watched for the opportune moment until finally the guard emerged from his station and made his way across the street towards a nearby food store. Peat made sure he had gone inside before making his move; the security monitors on top of the wall kept tabs on the streets but because they were open to the public Peat was able to calmly stroll across the street from the alley cloaked and hooded towards the station without raising the alarm, everything was going okay but as he glanced up at the tip of the wall he could see an overhead monitor rotating in his direction, he knew someone would be watching but of course, as of yet he'd done nothing to warrant undue suspicion. Briskly Peat walked up along the pathway by the security station making as if he was going to pass on by like a normal pedestrian but instead he ducked inside. Peat was scrupulous about potentially injuring someone so he wanted to be absolutely sure that no one was in the hut. As he looked around the small station all he could see was monitors and storage containers, he then checked the only other room which smelt and looked as though it were some type of lavatory, thankfully that too was empty! He then slipped out a side window but just as his foot hit the ground outside Peat heard a loud siren sound, he then panicked and instead of going to the far side, Peat attached the explosive on the near side of the large buttress which lay right next to the security station. Running across the street Peat looked over his right shoulder just as the absentee guard emerged in a flustered state from

268

the store. He stood on the edge of the street visibly disturbed by the siren and then he looked across at Peat who was in the process of fleeing the scene. The guard dropped the goods he was carrying and drew his firearm taking aim for Peat. Once more Peat glanced over his shoulder as he drew closer to the alley, down which he hoped escape, and seeing the imminent danger posed by the guard he pressed down on the detonator. Almost immediately a massive bang was to be heard by anyone in the area and, although a good distance away, both Peat and the sentry were knocked to the ground by the blast's force. There was debris everywhere and the station had been almost completely blown away, there was also a huge cavity at the base of the outer wall.

Dust was floating everywhere as Peat rolled over on his back and sat up looking around in confusion, then realizing his error he threw his head back and tossed his eyes to heaven, saying, "Augh shit, he gave me the wrong crystal!"

Staggering at first Peat made it further down the street before disappearing down a dark lane way just as military vehicles and soldiers began to converge on the eastern wall.

Less than a minute had passed after the explosion when General Mex-Ol emerged from his chambers in full uniform. He instructed an attendant to fetch slave LT-7. All slaves were required to be registered with the state's municipal authority and then they were allocated a registration number. All their details were uploaded to a main data base and an information tag inserted into them at the base of their neck. When both the General, two of his advisers and Timijus exited the house there was a military escort waiting to bring them directly to the armory. Timijus' heart was racing but he made a conscious effort to conduct himself in his usual manner and not show even the slightest sign of suspect behavior. It took only a matter of minutes for the convoy to reach the site of the explosion, Timijus looked out the shuttle's window shocked at the extent of the damage and concerned for Peat's welfare.

According to Peat there was to be only a small hole in the buttress and no real damage to the security station. All Timijus could think about was if his friend was okay. He had listened intently to the General being briefed on the journey to the armory but heard nothing about anyone being caught or injured.

General Mex-Ol spent a few minutes talking to military personnel after which he returned to the shuttle and leaning in through the entrance he addressed his primary adviser, "Check the surveillance recordings and interview the monitoring team."

The General then drew his head back out of the vehicle, as if departing, but to Timijus profound relief he suddenly leaned in once more and issued

270

one final command, "Oh yes, and put LT-7 to work on that damn inventory list I want it updated before dawn."

"Yes Sir," the dutiful advisor responded.

Once inside Timijus was put to work immediately and although he was physically exhausted the mere thought of getting one over on the General was a source of excitement and motivation. The storage hall for the arms and ammunition was massive but of course at this time of the night the entire place was deserted except for Timijus. The tracking device indicated that the sought after item was somewhere in this grand facility but as to where exactly it was, Timijus could not be sure. Knowing that he'd have to complete the list before he'd be able to inspect the sealed crates, Timijus immediately set about getting the list done as quickly as possible. Each crate had a special seal which had to be scanned by a hand held device. If the seal was unbroken the existing inventory data would register anew with an updated list on the system, a tedious but relatively straight forward job. As he systematically went about his task Timijus thought about how he might locate the item, then it hit him, the item would most likely be in a crate that was only recently brought in. If this were the case it would narrow down the possibility to only a hand full of containers. Timijus pushed himself hard so that he could finish in time to find the item and make it out to the Arch before dawn;

he knew how important the cover of darkness was. Hours had passed by the time Timijus reached the final row at the back of the massive storage hall, it was here that all the newly acquired stock was kept. Timijus hurriedly finished scanning the remaining boxes, completing the list by hand in a record time. Having done so, Timijus was careful to register the updated list on the system fully before he turned his attention to the newest crate to have been added to the stock pile, having arrived just two days earlier. Breaking the seal Timijus began to remove and inspect the most peculiar looking of weapons; they appeared to be spears but instead of points they had some type of generating apparatus at their tips, one by one he carefully inspected the weapons until about half way through he noticed a slight peculiarity with one of them. At the bottom of the spear he was handling, there was a circular groove, all the others did not have this distinctive feature and Timijus grabbed a random spear from the box just to confirm this. He then attempted to twist what he thought might be a cap at the bottom of the shaft. To his delight it turned, he removed the lid and shuck the end of the spear towards the ground and out fell the gadget. Timijus looked behind him to make sure he was alone and then picking the device up he quickly re-screwed the cap onto the end of the spear and placed it back in the crate. The broken seal would not show up until the morning when the machines would do their daily inventory check and so all Timijus needed now was the General's pardon for the night, after which, he would be free to make his way to the Arch. Leaving the storage facility Timijus went directly to the General's offices and informed one of the two guards stationed outside that he'd completed the list.

The guard went into the General to inform him of this and after no more than a minute the tall bulky soldier returned with the message that Timijus had hoped to hear: "You're excused."

Timijus gave a deferential, "Thank you Sir" and with a nod of the head for good measure, he made his way out of the building briskly walking out of the complex's main entrance.

In fact, he felt so exhilarated that he struggled to resist the urge to run. Making his way out onto the street Timijus could still see the military lights from the cordoned off zone around by the east wall and at the end of the street a large crowd of onlookers had gathered. About halfway across the well-lit street Timijus did a volte-face and stopped to look one last time at the imposing gates to the Royal Armory, thinking to himself, 'I'm free,' savoring this new feeling of hope at the prospect of a future beyond the shackles of slavery.

Unpropitiously however, Timijus' momentary entrancement with the promise of a future would prove ill-fated with the curse of the present, for just as he stood leering at the magnificent building through the main gates one of the short onlookers at the back of the crowd who, frustrated at not being able to see the happenings by the eastern wall, turned around to notice a familiar figure standing in the middle of the street. The observer was the low sized Minnonite thug whose companion now lay dead beneath a tor on the sloping hills outside the city. Immediately this dubious character moved towards Timijus, he had come back to the city when his friend had failed to return to meet him after what was meant to be a quick re-interrogation of the slave. As Timijus darted off in the direction of the Arch this shady Minnonite secretly followed him, soon an overtaxed Timijus reached the free standing archway. Although there was light under the Arch this was a particularly dark and ignominious area of the city. Historically the Arch marked the beginning of an old, and now, largely unused trail which led beyond the Minnonite border close to the base of Mount Crewux. Indeed this is why the pair had chosen this particular point to rendezvous, Peat knew that he would most likely be heading in the direction of the Cauldron.

In a hushed shout Timijus called out, "Sir, Sir are you there Sir?"

There was the sound of footsteps approaching from the far end of the Arch and to Timijus' joy the light revealed the face of his friend. Timijus rushed to him holding in his hand the final piece of the jigsaw along with the other cylinder Peat had lent him.

The young earthling smiled and embraced his friend saying, "You've no idea how important this is to so many, I don't know how I'll ever repay you Timijus." Pulling back and looking at him fondly Peat continued, "...Are you ok? You look so tired, we can rest here for a bit."

Timijus shakes his head insisting, "No, no Sir I'm fine, we'd better go, once we cross the border we can stop to rest!"

Peat then says, "I found some scraps we can have, it's not much but it'll keep us going."

As the couple continued to speak under the lit arch, in shadows of a nearby doorway the Minnonite stalker looked on at the pair but his focus had turned from the slave to the creature he was speaking to.

Quickly the Minnonite produced a holographic pod which contained the image of the sough-after Representative, looking at this for verification the bounty hunter said to himself, "It's him!"

Excited the Minnonite put the holographic device away and activating a communications system on his wrist he whispered into it, "Sir, Sir I've found him. He's under the Western Arch at the city limits"

A creepy low toned voice replied, "Excellent, do nothing... wait till I arrive."

Looking over at Peat and Timijus the Minnonite saw that they are making to depart and taking a step out from the door's walkway he suggests, "Sir he is leaving, should I follow? ...perhaps I could finish him for you?"

Sternly the authoritative voice orders, "No, wait till I arrive, when I do you will be handsomely rewarded. I'll have little difficulty in tracking him now."

About fifteen minutes had elapsed since Peat and Timijus had departed, the fortune seeking Minnonite now stood under the Archway waiting and then heard the sound of a mono racer approaching from the city, it stopped not too far from the curved ruins.

"Hello, Sir are you there? Hello..." the Minnonite inquired as he ventured towards the pitched black space which surrounded this giant artifact, a testament to a once illustrious Minnonite past.

No reply was forthcoming as the Minnonite drew his weapon out of fear and tilted his head as a dark silhouette of a figure became discernible.

"Sir, is that you?" the advancing Minnonite asked once more before making a sudden gasp and glancing down at his stomach, the realization that he'd be skewered barely reached his consciousness when the life had slipped from him.

The lifeless body hit the ground with a thud and then walking into the light the masked slayer approached his victim plucking the spear from the corpse and looking around he reached up and removed his mask exposing the face of Lexpoltry. Lexpoltry looked with a steely stare out into the

276

dead of night through the Archway, and then walking back to his mono racer he took off through the Archway at great speed with murderous intent.

Peat had explained to Timijus the full story of what was at stake in the Trials under the archway and this seemed to have invigorated the former slave even further, Peat had wanted to set an easy pace to the border so as not to push his already over exerted friend, but as it transpired it was Timijus who set the demanding pace clearly having being spurred on by the magnitude of the mission he was now part of. Timijus was also driven by the sense that he was leaving a life of slavery behind him with every stride he took away from Ra-Lif. Peat had checked the final destination just before departing and indeed, as he'd expected it was en route to the Cauldron, in fact, the large intricate map showed only Mount Crewux but in incredible detail, an internal network of interconnecting passages was outlined which led up to the top of the mountain and in one of these channels a homing beacon marked the precise spot where Peat's Sumboi was to be found. Peat's mind had now turned to considering what the Xtaron ritual might consist of and why exactly was Pillatar's Sumboi not accepted..., in the back of his mind Peat strongly suspected the answer but the implications of his theory unsettled him too much so he chose not to think on it. The derelict pathway that the two companions now straggled ran along a glen, leading further into the countryside, until the duo reached a raging river which marked the border between Minnonite and Creaton territory. Timijus had reached the river bank first, and falling to the ground fatigued, he cautiously reached down and drew some water. Peat arrived just behind him, his face red and sweat dripping from his forehead, he was more than impressed at Timijus' resolve and crashing to the ground beside his friend he threw down the food he'd scavenged form the waste disposals in the alleyways behind the residences and stores in Ra-Lif.

Timijus asked, "How are we going to get across?" Peat lay flat out on the ground, "We'll figure something out, but first some food and rest."

By this stage of the day dawn had well set in as the two lay peacefully resting on the river bank eating their scraps and drinking from the fresh water source for about five minutes. All of a sudden Peat rose to his feet and stood staring back down the path towards a sharp dip in the trail. Timijus, a little disturbed by the somber face of Peat, asked, "What's wrong?"

"Can you hear that?" Peat said softly.

Timijus got to his feet and took up position beside Peat, listening carefully he said "Sounds like an engine."

Timijus had no sooner finished his utterance than Lexpoltry came cruising up over the acclivity in the glen at high speed hurtling towards the pair.

278

The natural reaction of both Peat and Timijus was to back towards the river, they both feared the worst and Timijus who stood beside his friend asked, "What should we do?"

Peat could think of only one obvious answer but before he could even draw breath to make his suggestion there was a loud crackling sound to be heard from the rampant approacher, almost simultaneously Peat felt a forceful and unexpected shove to his side before falling to the ground. Peat lay disconcerted on his side as he looked up at Timijus who had jostled him to the ground. Earth's Representative was aghast to see his friend stagger backwards towards the ledge of the bank, his blood drenched left hand was feebly pressing against a large wound in his upper chest, and just as Peat stretched out his hand and shouted "Timijus," the wounded exemplar turned his head slightly in acknowledgment and looking warmly on his chum he moved his lips one last time as if to say 'Peat' before falling backwards into the torrents. Peat dove in after his friend, cascading down the river he struggled to keep above the water as he was violently churned between the currents. Finding it increasingly difficult to struggle upwards for air Peat caught sight of an approaching bend and with all his remaining strength he made a burst for it, swimming against the forceful flow of the raging water. It proved successful as he crawled up the stony deposition on the edge of the river bank.

Struggling to get to his feet a soaked Peat looked around for his friend but there was no sign of him and so he wondered down along the bank of the flowing meander. Peat's main concern now was to find Timijus but he was still acutely aware that there was someone most likely hunting him and so he tried to remain vigilant and alert. After about a mile downstream the flow had subsided considerably and on a low-lying grassy verge next to the rive Peat came upon the lifeless body of his protector. Kneeling down Peat turned Timijus over onto his back and with sorrow in his heart stared down at the deceased. Peat sat on the verge for a while pontificating on the all too often cruel nature of fate and pondered the perennial questions of life in his head for a while. After a good deal of mournful contemplation Peat got to his feet and lifted Timijus' remains over his shoulder carrying them to the base of a tree close by. Then laying Timijus' corpse down gently under the tree Peat used his cloak to drag piles of small rocks over to the tree, after about eight trips to the river's edge Peat placed the cloak over his friend and buried him beneath a gently laid mound of rocks. After a solemn prayer Peat once more checked his tracking device and although not fully sure if he was going in the right direction he made his way up a steep incline through a lightly wooded area until he reached the top and looked out across Haldran's gap, a tree-less forest of large jagged rocks, boulders and deep furrows stretching close to the western base of Mount Crewux. Without delay Peat maneuvered down the steep esker and began to make his way across this toilsome pass. Peat had just passed his first stone protuberance, when that haunting crackling sound was once more heard by him, just as he turned his head to inspect it's origins, the shattering sound of stone came from behind him and throwing himself to the ground he rolled back against the rock for shelter. Moving to the opposite side and keeping low he peeked out up at the hill to seek a tall well build creature descending the serpentine ridge in pursuit. Although Peat brimmed with anger over the killing of Timijus and had strong desires of revenge stirring in his heart, the influence of figures like his father, Master Miyamoto and Lynextius enable him to quell these dark stirrings and prudently he took flight across Haldran's gap. Peat knew from his lessons that the western base of Mount Crewux was littered with numerous passages hewn out by the Creatons during the great battle they fought against the Minnonites in Haldran's Gap, if he could make it there it would be almost impossible for him to be tracked due to the countless intersecting tunnels which run up the mountain. And so Peat raced as fast as he could towards the mountain, however the trials and tribulations that he had already experienced, along with a lack of rest and proper nourishment had begun to take serious effect and despite a willingness of the spirit Peat found his body unable to keep pace. A dizziness set in as he pushed himself onwards and nearing the plane level tract of land which surrounded the base of the mountain Peat collapsed. Laying on his back, his eyes drooping shut, Peat heard the sound of his chaser approaching with steady strides. Peat got to his feet but realized that any attempted dash across the open plain in his current condition would be doomed so he careered over to a very low lying rock jutting out of the ground just a few degrees and falling to the dirt Peat squeezes in under the tight gap and passes out from exhaustion. A good deal of time passed before Peat regained consciousness, the gap in which he found himself wedged was so tight that he wondered how he'd managed to actually squirm in. Wiggling himself towards the opening Peat stops when he hears a grunt and oncoming stomps, he waited for a few seconds... the noise had stopped. He was just about to worm himself out from under the rock when he sees a set of boots appear before his eyes. Someone is standing directly above the rock facing towards the mountain, while Peat remains silent staring at the heels of, presumably, his hunter. Then Peat hears voices conversing.

"My Lord." Lexpoltry opens as he addresses his commander Kysol.

"Have you found him?"

"He is hiding somewhere in Haldran's Gap, but I have him trapped."

"You're sure he has not made it to the mountain yet!" Kysol inquires anxiously.

"No my Lord." Lexpoltry reassures.

"Very good, Prince Oratron should arrive soon. Make sure Peter Black does not make it to the mountain and the Sumboi is yours." Kysol promises.

"Yes Lord Kysol."

Understandably Peat cannot identify either of the voices nor does he know who this 'Lord Kysol' is but what he is now sure of is that this whole assailment, which has cost Timijus his life, was not part of the Trials but rather, a surreptitious plot by Apoleia. Peat waited till he heard his attacker move on then managing to extract himself from his hiding-place Peat ran a short distance from rock to rock until he reached the last of the rocky shelters between him and the mountain base, all that remained now was roughly two hundred meters of dry flat land. Peat did not dare try for the mountain; he was convinced that his assassin was just waiting for him to make a move. Peat was effectively pinned down, going back was not an option and the clock continued to tick, every passing second Peat spent trapped was an advantage to his opponent. Peat peeked out from behind his large stone cover towards one of the many tunnels at the base of the mountain. Frustrated at his lack of options Peat propped awkwardly against the edge of the large rock but felt a slight discomfort, something was pressing into his side just below his ribs. Standing upright Peat looked at the smooth surface he was leaning against and then patted his right side discovering, in one of the many slits to be found on his traditional Creaton garments, the two small spheres Bellza had slipped into his clothing. Peat smiled at Bellza's cunning and briefly reflected on how his little red-skinned friend was right about Apoleia's likely attempts to subvert the Trials. Then Peat thought hard on what Bellza had actually said about these items, he recalled that they'd being taken from the Tar Limatu, that treasure trove of technology, that their purpose was, according to Bellza, somehow to veil one from evil. Peat began to think that they may provide an answer to his current predicament. Remembering Bellza's incomplete instructions Peat held a sphere in each hand, but he was unsure as to what to do next... looking at them he noticed the two small knurls on each of the mysterious objects. Peat took a chance and gripping the devices firmly in his hands and using his thumbs and index fingers he attempted to pinch the two sets of tiny ridges together, to Peat's delight the miniscule protrusions both moved together. Just as the tiny grooves joined Peat's fists clamped shut, at first Peat thought he had dropped the small globules but when he opened out his hands he was shocked to see that the objects had liquefied. Peat tried to rub the gelatinous substance off his left hand using his right wrist but the dark blue semisolid simply began to expand and spread, moving up his arms at some pace. As it began to cover his body Peat's anxiety grew, panic was about to set in when he noticed, looking down at his hands, he could see only the barren ground below. Dumbfounded Peat gawked as gradually his exposed arms also began to disappear until it seemed all of his body was invisible. Peat rubbed his hands together and could still feel the gel-like covering of the substance, coming to terms with what had just happened Peat wondered how he could best use this to his advantage. Evaluating the situation Peat proceed to strip out of his clothes and then pulled down the fringe of his hair as he tried to establish if he was indeed totally invisible. It appeared that he was, and so routing through the buddle of clothes on the ground he picked out the three cylindrical devices and sighed while shaking his head. Peat wanted to make a dash for the mountain base there and then but he was still not completely convinced of his invisibility, he needed to be sure and therefore, completely naked, he quietly crept towards the central area of the rocky frontier. Peat knew his enemy would be lurking in the most strategically opportune place to pounce, and sure enough, after a few nerve racking minutes searching the maze-like area Peat caught sight of the large Creaton squatting in a deep hollow on top of a large stone crag looking out upon the open tract of land, simply waiting for his pray to make its move before he would strike. Peat had already planned his escape route if it turned out that in fact he could be seen but he was nonetheless hopeful of his complete invisibility. In one hand Peat clasped the three devices which, while covered by his grip, remained effectively invisible, in the other he took up a small stone and stood out from the rock around which he was peering and threw it at the base of the crag upon which his foe was perched. Lexpoltry turned around and leaned back over his extemporaneous lookout to check the cause of the sound but he could see nothing, Peat moved closer as the scoundrel was turned but he went unnoticed as Lexpoltry turned back around. Then Peat moved even closer and picked up a larger stone which he flung so forcefully at the base of the crag that the projectile split in two upon impact. This startled Lexpoltry and he leaped up out of his cubbyhole holding his fire arm and pointing it towards Peat. Totally exposed and vulnerable, Peat felt like running but kept his nerve and stood motionless, his eyes fixed on this Creaton. Lexpoltry took a glace over his shoulder towards the barren pass before hopping to the ground. Kneeling down the large Creaton picked up one half of the stone Peat had thrown and looked at it suspiciously. Lexpoltry's manner seemed to indicate that he suspected Peat was seeking to lure him, he advanced towards Peat with his firearm readied, swiveling his head around

286

as if expecting a trap. Peat was struck by the sheer size of the Creaton as he passed him by completely oblivious to the fact the person he sought was standing right in front of him. For Peat nothing now stood between him and the mountain but as he looked at this villain pass him by, the sense of fear and worry left him only to be replaced by a sudden surge of anger; anger at the brutal and needless killing of his friend, Timijus. Then, as if fate had conspired to test him, he spotted a long jagged stone lying by his foot. Blinded by rage Peat picked up the shank and softly walked up behind Lexpoltry. Internally a battle was raging, Peat was struggling to resist the temptation to drive the pointed fragment into the back of his foes skull but just as Peat lifted his arm he took a step back recoiling in horror at what he was about to do. Peat had lost control, and shaking, he gently laid down the stone on the ground before backing away discreetly towards the flat plain.

- Chapter Ten -

Peat moved slowly while crossing the stretch to
avoid making any noise, but once he reached the
tunnels at the base of the mountain he sprinted in
along one of the channels, filled with a deep sense
of relief. This positive feeling was short lived as
the light from outside faded forcing a cold and
unclad Representative to slow his pace to a walk.
Peat checked his map once more, illuminated as it
was, and after figuring out which tunnel he had
entered he worked out the various turns he would
have to make as he weaved his way up the steep
maze of cross cutting passages, it then dawned on
him that his tracking devices might well serve
collectively as an improvised torch. Peat checked
the first two devices he had acquired to see if they
still worked and although they no longer showed a
map they did omit a red light, so grouping the three
devices together Peat activated all of them, and
although the illumination was patchy with only an
immediate range reaching no more than four yards
it allowed Peat to quicken his pace considerably.
Although Peat knew that all the tunnels would
eventually lead out near the Cauldron, the map
having indicated so, there was still no way of

checking where exactly he was at any given point and therefore it was imperative that he follow the route he'd planned out in his head exactly. If Peat unintentionally took a wrong turn at one of the multiple intersecting tunnels he would not arrive at the precise point where his Sumboi was to be found, in which case he would have to travel all the way to where the passages converged so as to get his bearings. The track was both grueling and frustratingly complex; the winding tunnels became increasingly steep and because they overlapped so often Peat had to constantly check the map hoping that he was still following the pre-planned route. After hours of painful and tediously slow assent Peat was exhausted, his jogging has been reduced to a lackluster walk as he trudged upwards refusing himself a brake. The tunnels Peat was traversing were long since abandoned and the Craton's had forbade access to them, it was their desertion that made them an ideal spot in which to accommodate the Xtaron ritual. Checking the map once again Peat realized that he should soon reach the Sumboi, he hoped and prayed that he was still on the right course. Looking around Peat could see nothing out of the ordinary but if he had followed the right course then, according to the detailed schematic, the Sumboi should be close-by. Cold and tired, his feet blistered and cut, Peat shun the light on his body to check if he was still fully invisible and indeed he found that he was. Peat walked on cautiously, he wasn't expecting there to be any traps but he knew that he could not be sure. Suddenly the map detailing the internal network of passages vanished, replaced by a single linear light, just like that of the other devices. Peat stopped, at first he though the gismo was broken but it then struck him that perhaps, like the two others cylinders it may signify he had located the Sumboi. Peat shun the torch around in every direction and yet there was no sign of anything. Peat moved a little further up the tunnel a few yards when he glimpsed a reflection from his light as it had passed over a section of the wall close to the ground. Moving in to investigate Peat found a shiny little cube resting on a small ridge at the base of the wall. He examined it for a few moments before reaching in to pick it up but the second his finger touched the small box a powerful white light was omitted by the device. The light was so strong that Peat staggered backwards, temporally blinded, and tripping he fell back against the opposite wall dropping two of the three cylinders. Rubbing his eyes Peat lay on his back sore and dazed, it was then that he realized he'd dropped two of the devices and looking to his right, his eyesight still blurry, Peat saw the two red lights rising through the air as if levitating. Peat took another few blinks convinced that his eyes were tricking him, but then as the lights moved closer Peat's eyesight retuned and he noticed a tall hooded figure pointing the tip of a Creaton spear. At that instant Peat was convinced that somehow he had been followed by the assassin and that this was the end but then a familiar voce spoke, "Identify yourself, immediately."

Peat could hardly believe it, "Lynextius?" he asked in state of wonderment.

Withdrawing the spear Lynextius placed his spear against the wall and drew back his hood before extending out his hand to Peat, helping him to his feet.

"What are you doing here?" Peat inquired.

Lynextius didn't answer instead he reached down beside him and tossed a small sac in front of Peat's feet saying, "Put these on quickly, there is not much time."

Lynextius of course knew exactly where Peat was because the young novice was still holding one of the light emitting cylinders in his hand. As Peat pulled out the most exquisite clothing from the sac and began to dress himself he felt surprised and a little hurt that Lynextius had asked him nothing about all he'd been through, indeed he seemed not even to be interested in the fact that Peat stood before him invisible. Once dressed, Lynextius returned the two other cylinders to Peat. Then without a word Lynextius moved up the tunnel a few steps and kneeled down, his head lowered as if in prayer. Dressed, Peat approached Lynextius but did so discreetly, not wanting to disturb him.

The young adult was also careful not to shine the light directly on Lynextius who remained prayerfully poised, suddenly then he spoke ceremoniously to the young lad, "Peter Black, Representative of Earth, leaving family and friends you have responded selflessly to the call of Koinonia and acted courageously in the interests of Earth and its peoples. The responsibility and honor of joining the Xtaron communion is now open to you my young neophyte... serve in faith, hope and love."

Then lowering his head even further, Lynextius began to convulse violently. Disturbed, Peat shun the light directly on him and was agasp at what he witnessed unfold; a bulge began to form at the base of Lynextius' skull while at the same time the bulky life sustaining suit was receding from his body revealing a worn, antediluvian figure. Peat was stunned into silence as he watched Lynextius raise his left hand around to the base of his neck to receive the small creature which dropped into the palm of his hand. Lynextius was now on his knees breathing very heavily, he leaned over and placed the Sumboi on the ground in front of Peat before, straining to raise his head, he looked fervently at his protégé. Knowing what was expected of him Peat slowly, and with some trepidation, reached down towards the creature as it lay floundering on the ground and stretched out his hand to pick the Sumboi up. The moment Peat's fingers touched the creature it latched onto him, he held still, knowing at least in theory what the process entailed as the Sumboi made its way to the nape of his neck. Peat felt a sharp sting and then a strange sensation which ran up along into his head, it then felt as though a gently pressure was being applied to various areas of his brain. This lasted for a few seconds before darts of pain began to run up and down Peat's arms and legs, followed immediately by multiple spasms all over his body. The pain got worse and Peat let out broken cries of agony as he lay contorting on the ground, after a few minutes he lost consciousness.

Peat woke to Lynextius' voice and the feeling of a hand on his shoulder, "How do you feel?" Peat raised his head and looked around, he felt fully refreshed and energized and upon looking at the aged face of his guardian he recalled why this was so.

"I'm fine... aaa, are you ok, I mean I heard that, amm well that you needed the Sumboi to...aaa..." Lynextius got to his feet and grinned before engaging in some raillery, "Might I presume the agent responsible for you having invisibility spheres from the Tar Limatu is also your source for my medical history!"

"Aaa, well amm..." Peat mumbles.

Lynextius smiles and holds out his hand showing Peat the tiny monitoring items that Ly Amas had joined to him before admonishing his counselee, "You need to hurry Peter, this trail will continue uninterrupted for three miles until you come to a chamber, go the back right hand corner of it and you'll find the exit."

Peat, who has noticed that he's no longer invisible, gets to his feet and checks to make sure he has all three of the required devices and then asks, "What about you, aren't you coming?"

Becoming a little impatient Lynextius says sternly, "I'll follow, Peter you must not delay, get to the Cauldron, make your declaration for Earth before it's too late."

Then pointing up the passage Lynextius ordered loudly, "GO NOW."

Peat admired and deeply respected Lynextius' selfless dutifulness and with a heartfelt bow of the head and a profound "Thank you," Peat sprinted off up the passage without delay.

Peat had witnessed, and studied extensively, the general effects a Sumboi had on a being, but up to now, he could only have imagined what the experience would be like. From the moment Peat had set off up the trail he had got some sense of his enhanced facilities; every breath seemed at once deeper and more rejuvenating than he could ever remember and this despite his current subterranean location, he could also run noticeably faster and felt increased power in his legs, the longer he ran the more he marveled at the fact that he was neither tiring nor feeling any strain. Peat used the cylinders to illuminate his way but his reaction reflexes were so quick that he found being able to see only a few yards ahead of him at a time in no way prevented him from sprinting full pace. It took Peat just over ten minutes to run up the steep incline and reach the chamber, although his mind had not yet caught up to his new abilities and he found himself taking deep breaths while not actually being short of breath. As Peat inspected the dark cave with his torch, he made his way towards the back right corner of the chamber. He could now smell the air freshening as he approached a large bulge in the chamber wall. Standing in front of it Peat knew this bulge was actually one side of a large rock being used to plug the exit. Peat wasn't sure what to do, at first he sought to push the large boulder but it was far too heavy although the surge of strength he felt in attempting to do it was trilling. Then Peat decided on a different tact, moving to the side of the giant blockage, Peat raised his arm clenching his fist which automatically generated the legendary outer skin, then Peat delivered numerous blows to the giant rock in succession. After multiple strikes it became clear that although damage to the rock was being done, it would take far too long to work his way through this giant boulder. Peat thought for a moment, casting his mind back on what he learnt and witnessed in the Palace during his training, his mind settled on one of an Xtaron's abilities in particular. He stretched out his hand and concentrated... , gradually a flow of liquefied goo amassed in the palm of his hand forming the hilt of a sword and then developed outwards making a long double edged blade which was covered in a thin layer of the most majestic royal blue energy field. Once the weapon had solidified in his hand Peat proceeded to slash through the rock as though it were butter. Hewing out a tunnel through the giant boulder in a matter of minutes Peat's eyes squinted as he cut through to the brightness of the day and emerging from the tunnel he saw a large group of Creatons gawking at him in amazement. Peat found himself mentally able to control the suit and sword and so reabsorbed the weapons and then degenerated the covering before darting up the winding paths towards the summit. Crowds of Creatons seemed to be journeying to the Cauldron and as Peat weaved his way in through the stream of gaps among the large cavalcade of Creatons suddenly, bit by bit, there was a trickle of cheers and shouts..., until finally word of the approaching Representative, had filtered through the caravan, even faster than Peat could run, and the masses erupted into cheering. Many began pointing and gesturing at Peat but far from desiring adulation Peat thought of Timijus and this only increased his sense of revulsion towards the Trials as he continued racing up the mountain trail to the summit. Reaching the top Peat was blind to the impressive architectural feat that was this mountain-top crucible; instead he rushed towards a group of sentinels who stood guard at one end of the Cauldron. As Peat approached, the guards made a channel all the way to a large entrance at the west end of the Cauldron, over which was attached a panel with Tryloss' Crest imprinted on it. Seeing this sign Peat raced through the long passage, a dream-like sense fell over him as he passed through into the pit of the Cauldron and thousands of Creatons cheered and shouted from the stands. At the center of the pit there was a large raised platform which itself was surrounded by a wide reaching blue colored circular insert on the ground below. Earth's Representative walked cautiously towards the raised dais as an unsettling hush fell over the crowd. Peat kept moving towards the center while checking his surroundings for any sign of something untoward. Without even noticing, Peat passed over onto the blue colored threshold and the crowd's silence was broken with deafening cheers. As first, Peat feared his opponent had arrived but he observed that the circular insert on which he stood had turned a Persian green, immediately Peat recalled Ly Amas' reference to the Doombeg Circle. Peat felt a little more reassured that it would be relatively plain sailing from here on, and he walked in a dignified manner up onto the raised platform. Peat saw that there was two sets of holes either side of this dais along with two crests above each slot, one being that of the Patriarch and the other, Peat presumed, was that of the Pillatarian Lord

297

Defas. Peat also took note of a five foot plinth-like structure at the center of the platform, inspecting it Peat saw two sealed slots on its surface. He wasn't immediately sure what he should now do but he knew that the final step in the Trials did involve the cylinders and making the declaration, and so Peat took out the three treasured items. Looking at them he paused... he thought of how he would soon see Claire, Tom and Jim on returning home, his thoughts also turned to Timijus and the sacrifice he had made. Peat then crouched down and tested one of the larger slots under the Patriarchal crest to find that the cylindrical devices fitted perfectly into it.

"Thanks Timijus," Peat said aloud as he dropped each of the gadgets down the slot after which the aperture automatically sealed shut. Peat stood up waiting for something to happen and then hearing a rush of cheers from behind him, he turned to see what looked like a long narrow javelin rising up out from one of the holes in the plinth. Seeing the spear triggered a recollection from one of his classes on classical Creaton culture, in which he learnt that the traditional games and tests were often formally concluded with the victor thrusting a spear into the ground ceremoniously. Just as Peat grasped the spear he heard a loud collective gasp from the spectators and looking around towards the ˥stern entrance he was stunned to see a tall ˡer figure wearing the most striking regalia.

Peat knew that this must be the young Pillatarian Prince, the two stared at each other briefly before Oratron generated his suit and dashed towards the Doombeg circle while Peat pulled the spear from its holding and lunged towards the second opening beneath the Patriarchal crest. Just as the tip of the javelin was about to pass into its intended slot the opening seal shut. The spear tip scratched against the covering and Peat looked over at the young Prince who was standing, sword in hand, on the Doombeg circle which had once again turned blue. Then in a slow but steady pace Oratron menacingly advanced towards Peat. The young earthling jumped from the platform and backed away towards the far side of the circle knowing that as long as they both remained within, the slots would stay sealed and neither could make a declaration. Oratron did not even glance at the dais as he passed it, his sights were evidently set firmly on his opponent. Peat held his ground at the Circle's edge and readied himself for what promised to be an epic confrontation. But then Oratron stopped abruptly, his body language seemed to Peat to be one of surprise, there followed a massive cheer from the crowd. Peat glanced over his shoulder to catch sight of Lynextius who was armed with sword and shield. No sooner had Lynextius taken position beside Peat than another roar surged from the spectators as a tall aged Creaton with only one eye emerge from the eastern passage to the delight of the onlookers. Lynextius looked hard at this fellow Creaton as he, also armed with sword and shield, took up position beside Oratron. A loud horn was heard and the crowd went quite, Peat turned and looked at a small enclave which was situated in the middle tier half way between each end of the northern stand. A short fat Creaton moved to the ledge of the balcony and resting his left hand on the ornate baluster he used the right to appeal for silence. Then Peat saw a recognizable face step forward, it was the Prefect of the Trials Polexiamas Atar, "And so it has come to this, both Representatives have proven themselves worthy to stand in the Doombeg Circle but only one can declare for the planet Earth. Also today, we shall finally crown a victor to the only Creaton Games ever to go unfinished, which brother will emerge and earn the right to claim the ultimate prize; that of the fallen Representative's Sumboi? Die in peace, live with honor!"

Again the horn sounded and both Oratron and Kylos turned and faced their opponents. Yet Peat found himself staring at Lynextius in puzzlement, wondering if what the Prefect had said meant exactly what it seemed to mean, that is, that Lynextius and his counterpart were actually brothers. Peat then re-focused his attention and turned immediately to face the imminent threat
'ed by the advancing adversaries.

Lynextius looked at Peat with a seasoned intrepidity and calmly said, "Remember what you were thought, stay calm and focus... That spear will not suffice!" Looking at the javelin in his hand Peat explains, "Oh no.., I need this to make my declaration."

"Give it to me..." and taking the spear Lynextius affixes it to his back using a strap concealed under his cloak.

Then raising his hand Lynextius instructs Peat to, "Fan out."

Peat and Lynextius separate, walking slowly out around the perimeter of the circle as their opponents draw nearer.

Kylos stops close to Lynextius and facing him with a scowl across his face, he states, "You will not deny me a second time brother."

In a sagely manner Lynextius responds, "I fear my brother is long dead! And for the part I played in that, I am truly sorry."

Lunging forwards to deliver a blow the enraged younger sibling shouts "Coward."

Lynextius blocks the assault and so recommences an age old contest, while for Peat dialogue did not even enter into it as Oratron announced himself to his opponent with an onrushing flurry of sword strikes which Peat blocked with his Xtaron generated shield. This dual spectacle trilled the engrossed spectators who watched on as both the Creaton and Xtaron pair put on an epic display of combat skills; the agility, swordsmanship and sheer strength was

3

awe-inspiring, especially for a people who place a
supreme value on a person's warrior status. The
exchanges of blows and frantic footwork continued
at an incredible intensity for a good deal of time.
However, it soon became clear to the onlookers that
the two brothers, advanced in years as they were,
had become weary. Without the Sumboi both would
have died long ago and what natural reserves they
had built up while Xtarons were now all but depleted
as the strikes became less frequent and the two,
far less animated. For the two new Xtarons
however, no such limitations were felt as the
intensity only increased. Peat had trained hard
both on Earth and in the Palace but he was
astonished at how much the Sumboi had advanced
him physically; his reflexes, strength,
agility...everything had increased tremendously.
That said however, Peat found himself in trouble as
he was forced backwards towards the platform,
Oratron's years of training and practice were
becoming more and more evident as his blade came
ever closer to landing that fatal blow. Peat was no
doubt the fitter and more nimble which had served
him well in terms of defense but there was an
obvious disparity in ability when it came to
attacking. Peat eventually found himself backing up
the steps of the platform but missing one he fell on
his back, opportunistically Oratron seized upon his
ˀnent's mishap and delivered a powerful
ˀd strike of his sword which Peat just

managed to deflect as he scrambled to his feet.
Still slightly off balance Oratron swiveled around
and dealt a unmerciful double-handed sword blow
which impacted on Peat's shield with such force
that he was propelled backwards falling up the last
few steps and landing on the flat surface of the
dais. Oratron felt confident at that point that his
victory was all but certain; he slowly made his way
up the steps wanting to prolong Peat's sense of
inevitable death at the hands of a superior warrior
and, in the mind of the young Prince, a superior
being. For Lynextius the situation was far more
promising, although both had tired considerably, the
elder had gained the momentum and with an array
of beautifully sequenced blade work, Kylos now
found himself on the back-foot after an initial
raged-fuelled flurry. Kylos knew he was losing and
this only served to feed his bitterness and anger,
he then sought to counter with an ambitious trust
of his blade, but in a showing of expert adroitness
Lynextius pushed the oncoming blade upwards with
his shield while ducking in under his opponent's
guard to deliver a powerful blow to his adversary's
face with the hilt of his sword. Such was the force
of the impact that Kylos was driven head first
backwards crashing to the ground with a thud. The
crowd roared louder than ever, Kylos had lost grip
of both shield and sword which lay out of reach as
Lynextius stood over him, the tip of his sword
hovering over his brother's exposed throat.

"What are you waiting for... do it!" the hate filled Kylos screamed.

Lynextius' steely determination began to mellow as he looked down with pity at this tormented being which he once embraced as a brother. Then instinctively Lynextius looked across at Peat to see Oratron deliver a devastating butterfly kick which knocked Peat back against the plinth cracking it as the young earthling stumbled to the ground. Peat's energy levels had been severely taped as a result of the beating and he was no longer able to generate his shield. As he lay on his back exhausted by the ordeal Oratron sought to end the battle, and stepping on the hand in which Peat griped his sword he raised his own to deal the decisive blow. Now the moment Lynextius had seen Peat being kicked to the ground he had predicted what was about to happen and so throwing away his shield he stepping away from Kylos he took Peat's spear into his hand and hurled it through the air over the Doombeg Circle. Oratron had just commenced his downward lunge when the spear struck the right side of his upper-back and while not capable of piercing the Xtaron's suit the force at which the spear travelled was enough to cause Oratron to over-swing as Peat tilted his body to one side avoiding the descending blade. Without a flinch of hesitation Peat jerked his hand from under his adversary's foot before ·ısting his blade into the side of the young Prince ⁻ leaning over him. Oratron dropped his weapon and Peat looked on in amazement as the outer carapace faded away to reveal a handsome fragile looking young man, the pair stared at each other briefly before Peat gently drew back his blade. Everyone in the crowd was fixated on this scene as Oratron staggered backwards to the edge of the platform, and just as he fell back over the ledge and his lifeless body hit the ground below, the circle once again turned a Persian green which was met but rapturous cheers and acclamations from the crowd. Peat went over to the far edge of the platform where the spear had landed and taking it in hand approached the appropriate unsealed slot before driving it forcefully into the tailored opening. Unknown to Peat though, while Lynextius had gone about aiding his young apprentice, Kylos had seen an opportunity to expose his brother's vulnerability. Sneaking up behind Lynextius who watched as the spear flew through the air, Kylos produced a jewel encrusted dagger loaded with meaning for both these fraternal protagonists, and with one fell swoop plunged it into Lynesious's back. The elder drew a deep breath while looking on as Peat slewed his opponent, before collapsing to the ground. Amidst the roars of the crowed Peat saw the Prefect of the Games, Councilor Fizer and other dignitaries approaching him with an escort, it was only then that Peat turned in a state of joyous relief to check on his mentor. Seeing him lying motionless on the ground Peat rushed to his side.

Meanwhile Kylos had slinked over to the body of Oratron and taking out a small fluid filled tube he carefully placed the squirming Sumboi *in vetro* before abjectly making his way to the eastern passage of the pit, taunted by the crowd for the underhanded manner of his 'victory.' Peat ignored Kylos' devious doing regarding the fallen Prince's Sumboi as he dashed over to his comrade.

"Lynextius, Lynextius" Peat shouted as he kneeled down by his side.

Seeing that there was still life in his fallen mentor, Peat used his hand to raise Lynextius' head, "Quick...you can take it back! The Sumboi can save you!"

Lynextius shakes his head gently as he gasps for air, "No, my time has passed. Peter, Peter you long for home I know, but you must first finish your training as an Xtaron..., war is coming..., Peter... they will... they will need you, Koinonia will need you. Promise me!"

With a heavy heart and a tear rolling down his cheek Peat nods and softly answers, "I will." Breathing his last Lynextius' head droops beneath Peat's supporting arm as the young victor looks down upon his fallen hero.

It was to prove a difficult soul searching time for Peter back on Tryloss, he was hailed as a hero upon his return and decided to honor his promise to Lynextius, enrolling in the Xtaron as a neophyte. But he was constantly pained by a sense of yearning to be with his loved ones on Earth. And while he took comfort in the belief that one day soon he would be returning home... never could he have suspected it: but for Peter Black, the trials had just begun!

A Message to the Reader

Dear Reader,

I hope you enjoyed the first volume of the Peter Black series. I am currently working on my second book (expected: early March 2014) which will offer something completely new, but with just as much excitement.

Warm regards,

John A. Lupton

 www.facebook.com/JohnAnthonyLupton

 @luptonja

 www.johnalupton.com